She thought life was perfect now that her ex-boyfriend was back…until she saw what landed in her backyard.

Elizabeth "Lizzie" Lawrence thinks her junior year in school is complete when her ex-fling Trevor asks her out again. But oh, how wrong she is. She comes home from school to find Darrton, *Death* of The Four Horsemen, in her backyard. Darrton is arrogant, rude, self-centered, dangerously gorgeous, and out to kill. She takes care of him while he is healing from being damned to Earth, but that has consequences she can only imagine. Will their growing love for one another be enough to break the promise Lizzie makes to save Darrton's life, or will she be damned just the same?

I knew what he was, so why did I want him to stay?

I finally got off the bed and went to my closet. I pulled on a wife beater and a pair of sweats. Darrton had his fingers interlaced and resting on his knee when I came back out. "Something's wrong?"

He nodded.

I pushed my toe into the plush rug beside my bed. "Do I want to know?"

"Probably not."

"Well, I guess, tell me anyway."

"I found a trace of someone here. I sensed them again tonight at the game. They have all found each other. Now they're here to retrieve me." He twisted his ring. "This isn't the first time they have visited, but this time they haven't made themselves known. My brothers are checking on me."

I pointed down to his ring. "What is that? Can I see?" Grabbing his hand I tried to pull it off, but it wouldn't budge. "Have you gained weight?" I teased.

He rolled his eyes. "It's not meant to come off. It's forever there, engraved into me."

"Is that how you know they are here?"

He nodded. "Yes and no. I feel them when one of them is near. Also, the ring has been weighing down on me lately. It also has been scorching me. It's letting me know it's time. They connect with me through the ring. We can communicate mentally."

"Time to what?" He didn't answer. But I knew. *Kill. Destroy. Bring The Apocalypse.* "Have you seen them? How many? Which ones?"

Darrton reached over and patted my hand, "Don't you worry about it, okay?" he said, reassuring me. "I will make sure you and your family stay safe. You don't deserve what they will try to make me do to you."

I could see he was telling the truth this time. I didn't know how but I knew. He left and I wanted to grab after him. *Why, Lizzie? Why reach after...Death?*

KUDOS for *Damned*

Damned ~ Book 1 by Brittany Booker is a complicated, thrilling, and fascinating story about fallen angels, mortals, and the Four Horsemen of The Apocalypse...The story is definitely a page-turner. The plot is fast-paced, complicated, and has enough twists and turns to keep you reading right to the end. If you are looking for a good, solid story that will keep your interest from beginning to end, you can't go wrong with Damned ~ Book 1. – *Taylor, reviewer*

The book is well-written, and I agree it is a page-turner. And while I think it is a great book for adults or older YA, I certainly would not recommend it for younger teens. As exciting as the book was, I found the idea that angels would take it upon themselves to destroy the Earth and everyone on it just a bit dark and depressing. Still, I imagine it's a book you could easily read time and time again and find something new with each new reading. – *Regan, reviewer*

DAMNED

THE DAMNED SERIES ~ BOOK 1

Brittany Booker

A BLACK OPAL BOOKS PUBLICATION

DAMNED ~ THE DAMNED SERIES ~ BOOK 1
Copyright © 2013 by Brittany Booker
Cover Design by Hot Damn Designs
All cover art copyright © 2013
All Rights Reserved
Print ISBN: 978-1-626940-09-3

First Publication: APRIL 2013

Published by Black Opal Books **http://www.blackopalbooks.com**

DEDICATION

To Austin. Without your help,
this book would have never happened.
I love you.

Revelation 6:7

THE FOURTH SEAL

And when he had opened the fourth seal, I heard the voice of the fourth beast say, Come and see. And I looked and beheld a pale horse: and his name that sat on him was Death, and Hell followed with him. And power was given unto them over the fourth part of the earth, to kill with sword, and with hunger, and with death, and with the beasts of the earth.

CHAPTER 1

Lizzie

This is a serious matter, Tommy," my mother yelled.

Yes, yes it is, I thought as I leaned in closer to the mirror in my room, holding up a shirt to wear. *Someone breaking into our house is a serious matter.*

"I know it is, Jennifer. I said we would call the locksmith tomorrow," my dad said, using his calm voice to try and soothe my mother. From upstairs, I could practically see him rubbing her arms to calm her down.

I had awakened this morning to my mother yelling like a banshee. The house had been broken into and my emotional mother was not going to stop nagging until my dad did something about it. I would have been more worried about the situation myself if Trevor hadn't invited me to Aaron's party. Trevor and I'd had a short summer romance and then he showed up at school with Rachel. After him begging and pleading for me to go out with him again, I'd said yes.

Sighing, I tried to tune out Mom and Dad's conversation about the break-in. Nothing was taken by whoever broke in, but it still creeped the hell out of me. Throwing my shirt down, I picked up another one. *Useless!*

I heard a slight noise from my door and glanced over. "Get out."

"Yeah, right. You need my help." Samantha, my twelve-year-old sister marched into my room and rummaged around in my closet, throwing clothes everywhere. "I so lost ten dollars on a bet because of this. I just knew he would never ask you out again. Now, I'm not going to let you look stupid going to see him with your wanna' be rocker shoes and grungy T-shirt."

"I'm sorry did you not understand the meaning of get out?"

She sighed and turned to me, her dirty blonde hair swinging around her. "Here," she said, handing me an outfit and leaving the room.

I glanced down at the black strapless shirt, blue jeans jacket, skinny jeans, and boots. *Not too bad.*

I was in the middle of changing when my cell phone rang. "Hello?"

"Where the hades are you, comrade?" Millie, my best friend, shouted over the phone. I sighed. The only reason she called me "comrade" was because of the family tree project we had done the year before. Turns out my dad's side of the family was Russian.

"I'm getting ready, Millie. Calm down."

"Hottie Trevor is getting antsy over here," Millie yelled over the music. "Brett has to talk to him to keep him calm. He is nervous," she said, laughing into the phone. "You know that means Brett isn't paying any attention to me. My boyfriend is not paying attention to me. This should be a crime, Lizzie."

I smiled at the phone. "I'll be there in fifteen minutes, okay?"

"Ohmigod, total subject change: you know Lucas Johns?"

"Yeah, how could I not? He was suspected of raping that Holly girl last year. How would I not know him?"

"True. Anyway, he is missing. Like no one can find him. His mother is freaking out. Everyone is talking about it over here. Which reminds me, get ya ass over here! This is Cannon Beach, Oregon. When someone throws a party you come. It could be three years before something interesting happens ever again. You do not want to miss this, Lizzie."

"Okay, going to leave now."

"Yeah, yeah." She smacked her gum. "Get your cute ass over here!" she said and hung up.

I tossed my phone onto my bed and continued to get ready. Pulling my curled hair out from under my jacket I took a look at myself. I didn't look so bad. Then I heard another knock. "Leave me alone, Sam."

"It's not Sam," my dad said, opening the door, smiling.

"Oh, um, hey."

"You look nice, sweetie."

I narrowed my eyes and clicked my tongue. "Watcha' need?" He smiled. I knew he had an ulterior motive. His eyes were everywhere but on me, and he tended to run his fingers through his short brown hair one too many times when he was nervous.

"Well, you're going out tonight."

I stopped. *Oh no.* "Yeah, about that, well, I'm about to be late. Millie, Brett, and Trevor are already over there waiting for me."

"Well, wait a minute." He tugged on the collar of his shirt. "I want you to be careful, okay." I smiled, and my cheeks turned a little pink. He hesitated, smiled again. "I want you to know that you can call me no matter what the circumstances.

This is your first real party. If anything happens, just call me, okay?"

Oh God. "Okay, Dad."

"Don't forget your pepper spray."

God help me. "Okay. It's in my jacket pocket. But I have to go." I headed for the door and stopped while he walked down the stairs before me.

Mom was lying on the couch, her attention on the second season DVD of the *Vampire Diaries*.

"Bye, Mom." *So this is how Dad distracts her when he wants to change the subject.*

Her eyes never moved away from Damon's ridiculously hot body. "Have fun, oh, wait, and take Muffin out before you leave."

Ugh! There was no point in arguing with her. Her head was so far gone. I huffed and grabbed Muffin, our miniature Pomeranian, from the floor where he was curled up nicely.

"Hurry up, Muffin." I put him down and watched as he pranced around, smelling the small square of grass beside our one lonely shrub.

Keeping an eye on my watch, I eyed Muffin while he sniffed around our garage. Too bad we hadn't gotten the Pit Bull Dad wanted. We wouldn't have had to worry about an intruder.

"Hurry!" I walked toward him. He had started to growl. "Ugh, you little rat." I reached for him, but he growled and snarled, his teeth nipping at the shrub. "What is it, babe?" I looked toward the bush, all alone beside our garage. Then the bush moved. *Oh, snap.* I backed away.

Eyeing the open garage door, I sprinted for it. Digging around in the corner for one of Dad's golf clubs, I eased back around the corner. Muffin was still growling. Taking a deep breath, I faced the shrub.

"Okay, it's probably a raccoon." Taking the club, I swung it. I was just going to scare the little booger. In the midst of my swing, a shadow emerged, catching the club and snapping it into two pieces in front of me.

It took me two seconds, but I screamed at the top of my lungs. "Aaahhh!" The guy, robber, man, whoever, took another step toward me. It was at that moment, I noticed the black wings protruding from his back. That's when I fainted.

೧೫೧

I couldn't have been out more than two minutes. When I opened my eyes a fast forward of scenes flooded my head. *Please God tell me that was a dream.* I sat up quickly. I was still lying on the ground where I had fainted. I blinked a few times and then noticed him standing against the garage. I stood up quickly. I was going to try and make a run for it. As soon as I took a step, he moved toward me. He gracefully glided, and with his movements, everything else seemed to sway around him. I took another step back. But a slinky darkness curled and formed around his amazing body. It looked almost like a moving shadow. His eyes never left mine. He grabbed my throat.

"Don't hurt me!" I choked out. I began to cry, fumbling around in my pocket. I pulled out the bottle of pepper spray and, while swinging my legs and gasping for air, I sprayed him in the eyes.

"Ah! Damn you, worthless human." He rubbed his eyes and with only a swipe of his hands, they were fine. I got up from where I had fallen to the ground and tried to run, but he caught me around the waist and pinned me up against him.

"Please, just leave me alone," I sobbed and flailed with my feet trying to hit his legs.

"No. I need your help." His voice was rough and harsh. It sounded as if he was in pain.

I let my body go still while he gently released me.

"Are you ignorant? Would you dare try to fight me?"

I shook my head. "What? Am I ignorant? Are you demonic?"

He gripped my arm, his pupils growing larger. "How dare you call me a demon! I resided in Heaven with the Lord." My mouth was partly open in awe and confusion as I remembered the reason I fainted. *The wings. What the hell? Are those fake?*

Oh God! A religious man gone nutcase crazy!

"Okay, you're not a demon, I'm sorry! You're a—a…" I trailed off not really knowing how to respond such a bizarre statement.

"What are you?" I tried not to look at the wings but I couldn't help it…*oh God the wings.*

His eyes grew paler, the light blue contrasted with his flawless dark skin. "Well, I'm a Horseman, damned to Earth."

Like the Heaven? Horsemen, like The Apocalypse? I bit my lip, trying to hold in my nervous laughter, but it slipped.

"Angels normally come from Heaven and have white wings. And they don't try to kill people. What kind of thing would come from Heaven that had black wings?"

His eyes seemed to harden. A radiating heat seeped off of his body toward mine. "How dare you mock me, imbecile? I'm a Horseman not an angel. The Horsemen are not what you people really think. I was appointed a Horseman when I died. My brothers and I will lead The Apocalypse. We've each been given different titles."

I didn't know what to say, because as much as it seemed unreal to hear him, or see him standing in front of me, I was starting to believe he was something supernatural. "So you're saying you are a Horseman," I whispered, backing away from him. I was eyeing my car and tightening my hands around my car keys.

"Dare you run? Are you that full of stupidity?" He stepped forward. "Help me, and I will leave you be."

I swallowed hard. "What do you need?"

"Shelter."

I bit my lip while trying to make some sense out of all of this. My eyes traveled down his body and I noticed a deep bleeding gash on his side. I cringed. *How many different ways could helping him go wrong?* I motioned for him to follow me.

I was intrigued. His wings were such a deep, dark black that they gave midnight a run for its money. His face was calm yet menacing. His bare chest was chiseled and his long, black hair waved around his face. His abs curved down to a perfect V peeking out of his pants. But it wasn't just his utter beauty and enthralling pale blue eyes that struck me. It was what was folded around his back. I couldn't seem to stop looking at them. "Are those fake?" I mumbled to myself, taking a step back. I noticed again that his side was bleeding. It looked really gross and bad.

I blinked, twice. Watching this Horseman, or so he called himself, walk around my old tree-house in our back yard was not anything that I ever thought I would be doing. The tree-house had been built on the lowest limb of a large shady oak.

The man's beauty was unfolding in front of me as he walked around examining everything. "What is this?" he almost snarled.

I flinched. The black aura around him was frightening. It billowed out around his body and clung to his every move.

And I was too afraid to ask what it was. I pulled out a blanket from a wooden chest in the corner. "What's your name?"

"Darrton."

"I'm Lizzie. Well, my real name is Elizabeth."

His pale eyes darted to mine. For a moment he looked like he was in pain, then he blinked and it was gone. "Where can I find water?"

"I'll have to go inside—"

"Why? Isn't there a well?"

I raised an eyebrow. "Well, there is a water tower but no we don't have well water. We have city water."

His blank stare told me he had no idea what I was talking about. "I'll be right back." I hurried down the ladder and rushed toward the back door. I couldn't let my mom see me, or she would wonder first, why I wasn't off seeing the guy I had been crushing on forever, and second, why in the hell I was taking a pitcher of water out to our tree-house at this time a night. Since Mom was still drooling over Damon, and the rest of my family was locked in their rooms doing whatever they did in there, I made it back out without anyone noticing.

When I made it back up to the tree-house, Darrton was looking in a chest and didn't even bother to stop when I walked in. "What is this?" He pointed into the chest.

I walked over to where I could peer inside, standing as far away from him as possible. "It's an old TV."

He furrowed his brow. "Yes, but what is a TV?"

"You're kidding, right?"

"Does it look like I am teasing with you, girl?"

"Stop talking to me like I'm an idiot. Why don't you know what a TV is?"

"Well, stop acting like one. We didn't have that when I was here on earth."

I stomped my foot and his eyes darted down to my feet. "Do you want my help or not?" He stood still. I knew I wouldn't get an apology. "A TV is a machine which brings us pictures from places where people go and act out shows so that we can watch them." He didn't reply. His eyebrows furrowed in confusion. *Ugh.* I sighed. "Like plays only we can see them in our homes," I said.

He nodded. "I see."

Finally. I pointed toward the twin size bed in the corner. "That is where you can sleep. Here is your water." I handed it to him and he gulped it down in one swallow. "And there are some more old blankets under the bed there."

He didn't even look.

"Why are you here?" I whispered.

"Why are you here?" he asked.

I shifted my weight. "I live here!"

He was really pissing me off. I opened my mouth to say something else but just then my cell phone rang. I reached for it and Darrton snatched me up and held me against him.

"What is that? Get down!"

I ended up on the floor again. "What the hell!" I screamed. "It's just my cell phone."

"Your what?" He watched me wiggle on the floor as I dug around in my pocket.

"Hello?"

"What the fudge! Where the hades are you, comrade?" Millie screamed on the other end of the line, over the music from the party.

I sighed. "I'm kind of held up right now. You are never going to believe this!" I laughed. I heard Millie yelling as Darrton snatched my cell away from me. I had barely registered that he had taken it and in the same instant my phone was crumbled up in his hands.

"Dare you tell a soul and I will kill you myself!" My mouth hung open and I could feel the tears burning to break free. He glared at me. "Don't you dare weep over such a device."

I gritted my teeth and my tongue clicked nervously. Stumbling to my feet, I felt a tirade coming on. "You listen here. I am helping your ass out and you do this!" I pointed to the crumbled up phone on the floor! "I had a date tonight! With a boy! A boy I really like and you're ruining it for me!"

Darrton stared at me without an ounce of sympathy in his glare. His face was a mask, not one emotion showing. "I no longer need your attendance. You're making me ill. I want nothing more than for you to leave."

Hell no! "You're making me leave my own tree-house?"

"Yes, now leave, child, while I still have my patience."

I clenched my fists and my eyes meet his sharply. "You're an ass! I was going to help you with your wound but I'm not now."

He laughed without humor. "I don't need your help. I can tend to my injury alone. Would you like me to escort you out? Or will you leave voluntarily?"

"Why don't you just leave?" I yelled.

He cocked an eyebrow. "I have nowhere else to go. Now, are you going to leave?"

I stomped my foot, twisted around on my heel, and fled.

I mumbled to myself all the way down and into the house. *Stupid ass*! I just met the…whatever he was—two seconds ago and already I hated him. I glanced back up at the tree-house and saw that he watched me through the window.

ↀↀↀ

This had to be the most dreadful night I had ever had. I was already an hour late for the party so I didn't even bother. Trevor had probably already found another girl to dance with. Not to mention my *Android* was demolished. I slipped into a night shirt and pouted myself into bed. *There was a part of my brain telling me this was a dream.* There was no way anyone would have believed he was damned, one of the Four Horsemen, or anything even relating to that. *He could kill my family.* The thought of him being so close to us frightened me. But if I didn't help him, I felt there was a bigger chance of him hurting us.

Two hours later, after laying down and feeling sorry for myself, I heard a tap on my window. I sat up in my bed. *Oh no! Crazy religious guy is coming to kill me.* I slipped out of my bed and dug through my closet for my softball bat as another tap came. Sliding gently across the hardwood floor I peeked out the window. It was too dark to see anything. I raised the blind carefully. I heard someone fiddling around with the window. When it slid open, I raised my bat and said, "I didn't tell anyone."

"Lizzie," Trevor said from the tree outside my window. "Wait, it's me!"

I dropped the bat and stumbled back bumping into a chair. "Shit!"

Trevor laughed, pulled himself in, and reached over to help me up. There was light spilling in from the hallway. I wished it had been off, so he couldn't have seen me fall on my ass. While I was catching my breath, Trevor reached around in the dark where my bedside lamp was and turned it on. It hit me suddenly—he was in my room and I was only in a shirt! *Oh God! What have I done to deserve such punishment?*

Trevor glanced down to my legs and a smile spread across his face. "I'm sorry if I caught you at a bad time, but I wanted to come and see if you were all right."

I opened my mouth to say something but realized I didn't know what to say. I surely didn't want Darrton bursting in and killing us both. "I wasn't—"

Trevor stepped forward and his cologne seemed to wrap all the way around me. "It's okay. Millie told me you had an unexpected visitor."

Oh shit! How did she know that? "What…"

He laughed. "It's okay I have two sisters. I'm not grossed out by it like a lot of guys."

Visitor? Grossed out? I'm going to choke her in her sleep. I blushed, a violet red, and clicked my tongue. *Oh she is so getting it.* "Yeah well, I guess it's something I can't help." *Damn her. I'm going to kill her.* I was so not even on my period!

He stepped forward again and I took a deep breath. "So, are you feeling okay?" he asked.

I smiled. "Yes, listen, I'm really sorry about tonight. I wanted to go so badly. You have no idea."

"Yeah, I think I do. It's okay. I completely understand." He smiled. I watched in sheer pleasure as Trevor walked around my room. I took in his short-sleeved shirt that was fit snugly to his chest. The baseball cap he wore was on backwards and his short brown hair was only showing at the top of his head. His jeans were low on his hips and fit him perfectly. I pulled my shirt as far down as it would go while his back was to me. *God! Please just let my shirt grow three inches! I swear I won't be mean to the crazy religious guy out back!*

When I looked up Trevor was staring at me. I tried hard not to show the nervousness that was crawling up my body. "So, this is your room?" he asked.

I had not even been thinking about him looking at my semi-messy room, I felt my blush deepen.

"Yea, it's a little messy. I haven't had time to clean it up." I reached up to scratch my neck, even though it wasn't itching. Trevor had a smile on his face and a glint of hunger in his eyes. Apparently, he was having a hard time keeping his eyes off my legs. I couldn't help but let a warm mixture of pleasure and nerves swarm through my body.

He pointed to a picture on the wall. "That's your sister, Samantha, right?"

I nodded, clicking my tongue. "Yea, that's little miss diva."

He laughed. "My older sister couldn't be any different." His hands were tucked into his pockets and he swayed back and forth. He picked up my butterfly necklace which was sitting on my dresser, and glanced up at the butterfly painting on my wall. "You have a thing for butterflies?" he asked. "You never told me that before."

"Yeah, my mom gave me that necklace a long time ago and it just stuck."

He nodded. "It's nice."

Trying to change the subject, I said, "So, did you have fun at the party?" I bit my tongue as soon as I asked. I couldn't help but think he had been with someone else. *Holding their hand? Kissing them?* It made me sick to even think about it.

He glanced at me sideways and a laugh escaped his lips. "No, actually," he said while taking a few steps toward me. "It wasn't fun at all."

I gave a sigh of relief. "Why not?"

"Because I thought you stood me up." He was closer now, his voice low. "Because you weren't there."

A white hot rush flowed over me and my most personal spots warmed. I could see the desire in his face. The dark blue in his eyes glistened in the light of the moon. His pupils were dilating as he placed his hands,—one on the side of my neck, and the other on my hip. I felt a breeze on my leg when he pulled me in and my shirt climbed up. I gasped for breath. This was not happening. Trevor was going to kiss me. *Holy bananas, he is.* Not that he hadn't kissed me before, but this time was different. We were alone in my room and I was half naked. *Thank God I brushed my teeth!*

He smiled as he brushed a stray hair from my face. I couldn't breathe, let alone say one word. I was too nervous to try. It would probably come out as an incoherent blabber. He pulled us together, until there was no space. I placed one hand on his bicep and the other on his back, feeling the firmness of his body against mine. He was so close now. His peppermint breath on my face, he parted his lips and touched his mouth to mine.

Squeak!

Trevor and I jerked back. His eyes were huge. I pointed toward the window. He didn't even need an explanation. He ran toward it and climbed down the tree outside.

Squeak!

I ran toward my bed and jumped under the covers. My door knob jiggled and opened slightly. I closed my eyes shut. *Please don't let it be my dad or mom.*

"Child!"

Ah hell. I shot up and jumped out of bed. "What are you doing in here? You aren't supposed to be in the house! How are you getting in?"

Darrton's eyes narrowed and he brushed me off. "Everyone is asleep. I—what's that smell?"

I sniffed. "What smell?"

He turned his head toward the open window. "Who just came through that window?"

I stiffened. "No one."

"Do not lie to me, child. I am all knowing."

I jerked back. "You're not God."

Darrton's eyes grew wide and his jaw clenched. "Shut your mouth. Do not speak of things you know nothing about."

"Sure, says the guy that is all knowing!" His fist tightened and the muscles in his arms jerked. I wouldn't want to be punched by that guy. "What are you doing in here, anyway?"

"Answer my question and I shall answer yours."

I sighed and held the bridge of my nose. "Trevor."

"Is this a male?"

"Yes, your highness, he was of the male gender."

"Do not mock me, child."

"Stop calling me child! I am not a child."

"You're acting that way."

"Oh my God in Heaven. What do you need? I answered your question, now spit it out."

"I need more water. I am parched."

I gritted my teeth. I watched Darrton's eyes and noticed again the sinfully, pale blue color of them. They were hard to miss. They were the prettiest, scariest thing I had ever seen in my entire life. "Hold on, I'll be right back."

He pointed to my legs. "Cover yourself up. This is not the way a lady should be clothed."

"It's called sleeping. I was asleep, and it doesn't matter."

He watched me closely. "Water please."

I stomped downstairs to the kitchen. Turning the faucet on, I looked at the back door. I noticed the lock that was still broken. I stopped. *That ass.* I walked back up and Darrton was sitting on my bed. I pointed. "You!"

His sin-filled eyes darted toward me. "Yes?"

"You are the one that broke in last night?"

"Broke in? I was merely looking at my surroundings. I would never take what is not mine."

"Don't do that again. My mother was scared to death."

"Yes, I heard her bellowing all the way outside. What an awful sound."

"Please, drink your water and go back outside."

He grasped the glass and had turned it up to drink when he clenched his side. It was oozing blood and the cut seemed to be deep. I remembered the blood on the carpet we had seen this morning when we got up. *That's where the blood on the carpet came from.*

I took a step closer. "Are you all right?"

He backed away. "I do not need your help. It will heal itself." Pus oozed out of it as he drank the last of his water.

"Are you sure—"

"Yes, I will not say it again." His eyes, so pale, flashed toward me and I knew I wouldn't ask again. "Now, thank you for my water, but I must get my rest. I have plenty of things to do."

I gaped at him. He had started to pace my floor. I watched in amazement as his black wings, laid in a perfect pattern, folded against his back. *Those couldn't be fake, could they?* "I thought you were leaving,"

He ignored me and continued to pace, his wings shuttered to his back. I gasped. "Can I touch—"

I was reaching for his wing when his hand stopped mine.

"Under no circumstances may you ever touch my wings."

I swallowed hard and flinched at the shot of pain in my wrist. "They're real, aren't they?"

He released my hand. "I told you they were, and I will not tell you again. Goodnight, child."

I crawled back into bed and listened as his footsteps faded into silence. I didn't know what the hell was going on but I intended to find the hell out.

CHAPTER 2

Darrton

I walked back up to the place where the child had left me. My mind was racing and my side was scorching as I climbed the ladder. Lying down on the bed, I tried to calm my anxieties. There was nothing making sense in my brain. The child was so incompetent, but I had to use her, the best I could. I needed help. I held my side and closed my eyes, trying to make my head stop spinning. My thoughts traveled back to the moment where I awoke to this awful place.

❡❡❡

My senses were returning slowly. All I could make out was the blue of the sky and a humming sound in the distance. It had to have been a few hours before I was able to comprehend what was going on around me. My head was throbbing and when I tried to sit up, a sharp pain thundered through my body. Looking down at my side I noticed there was a fresh wound oozing blood. When I fell, I'd landed on my side. I hadn't been able to catch myself in time to land properly. The rocks, a few feet away in the garden, had broken into my skin, leaving a nasty looking gash in my side. A dark shade of hatred flashed through my mind. Trying to sit up, I fell back toward the ground, panting. This cannot be happening. *Where am I?*

I knew the answer to that. I was on Earth. I also knew why. I had been damned to Earth for my sins. It was my brothers and my punishment for trying to start The Apocalypse before Father told us to. We wanted to start our jobs. We wanted to make Father proud. Reaching back to feel my wings, I sighed. They were still there. My surroundings were…strange. It had been so long since I had been on Earth, everything had changed. I hadn't been on earth since 1898. When I had lain dying, I thought this was the end of everything, until Father gave me the title of a Horseman when I got to Heaven.

It had to have been midday, and all I could see was the building in front of me. It looked like a home, but I couldn't be sure.

There was a sudden noise at the back of the building and I looked up. A woman was coming toward the door. *I guess it is a home.* Pulling myself, I crawled with every ounce of power in me toward the side of the building where a shrub was growing. I made it to the bush just as I heard the door handle turn. Panting and lying down, I felt my blood drizzle onto the ground below. I wish my brothers were here. They weren't my real brothers, but our bond had strengthened over time. We were each other's brothers now. We were all each other had, the only family we had left. I hoped they weren't injured like I was. My three brothers would be in contact with me soon. *We have a mission.* I tried to sit up but my body refused. I lay back on the grass and closed my eyes.

When I came to, I wanted nothing more than to beat my head against the ground. There was an obnoxious sound coming from the house next to me. That music had words so ill-bred, it had to have been another language I had never heard. But regrettably it was the English language. The lyrics meant nothing, and I could hear the footsteps across from me, hopping around to the ignorance. There wasn't a language on this damned planet that I couldn't comprehend.

I moved, or tired to, but a significant pain struck me again. I cringed, holding my side in a tight grip. I would recover. I knew I would. *Only in time.*

My injury was from my fall. My fall from Heaven to Earth. I was damned by God. I was a Horseman. *It's time now. We've waited long enough, Father.*

The home beside me had been quiet until later in the afternoon, I guessed there were children by the loud voices and irritating music. *Damned children.*

People drove by, so oblivious to their surroundings. Take the people in the house beside me. I had been on Earth for a mere eight hours and not one of the fools had noticed a prowler. Even though the large shrub hid me, they should never close their eyes without checking. The Earth was full of dangerous predators. Not just humans existed, and there were far more terrifying things to fear than a murderer.

Girding up my loins under the almost unbearable pain, I moved. The solid earth was no comfort below me. Silently I held my tongue as I stood up.

My eyes searched the unusual ground below. There was hardly anything green around us, beside the pathetic excuse of a bush. The ground was filled with rigid rocks and some concrete.

I tried not to be distracted by these alien things. I had to move. I pulled myself up on the side of the house with my hands, but stopped moving when I caught a glimpse of something unfamiliar behind me. I reached back, searching for my pure white wings that used to surround me and protect me. They weren't there. Well, they were, but they were no longer an unpolluted white. They were a raw, dark, and hatred-filled black.

"Damn!" I yelled, stretching my arms and then falling to the concrete, cringing at the pain from the gash in my lower side.

Tears. Crying was something I had not done since the time of my former life on Earth. Years had passed since I had died and been chosen as one of the Horsemen. However, Heaven doesn't keep track of time like the Earth. A lifetime can seem as only a day to the Father. The time seemed to drag on for my brothers and myself.

I brought myself back up to my bare feet. Continuing around the wooden house, I heard the sounds of the mortals breathing inside. They didn't even realize I was entering their home. Their pathetic lock was nothing. All I had to do was turn the doorknob until it broke. Even with the gash in my side, leaking my blood, it took little effort to accomplish.

The house was full of objects of different shapes and sizes. Everything seemed so outlandish. Examining my surroundings, I could smell something not human. It was animal like. I saw something to my left move closer to me. The little creature was not much bigger than a rat, but its sounds were fierce and canine like. Its fur was fluffy and brown, and its barking continued.

"Silence!" I commanded.

With that one word the animal tucked its tail and ran. *Coward.*

I continued looking, stepping across the floor and toward the large white sitting place. It looked like a large seat. *Oh how times have changed.* Books, something I could relate to. I picked up a book labeled American History. Then a smaller book with a lot of blank pages. I read the lines. *My favorite part of school would be lunch. It's definitely not this class.* Whoever wrote this was apparently not that bright. The lameness of the words made my stomach heave. The world had come down to pure ignorance and it was infectious.

"Baby, baby, baby, oh."

I dropped the book, and my head jerked toward the stupid melody from the floor above me. It was around midnight and everyone except whoever was playing that ignorant music was asleep. I knew no one else could hear it. My hearing was better than any mortals. I took the steps two at a time and rounded the corner, seeing a door slightly cracked, with a bright light shining through. I hadn't seen such a bright light since I had walked into one many years before. And this light was indoors, of all places!

The music became louder. I carefully glanced around the corner of the door, folding my blackened wings tight against my back. The light seemed to be formed in a hard tube, hanging from the ceiling. There in the center of the room a mortal stood a young mortal. Her shirt was incredibly long and hung loosely to her knees. She hopped around with a hairbrush before her mouth and sang along to the obnoxious music. "Thought you'd always be mine," she sang over and over again. I quickly snuck back, away from the intolerable human that I could only want to kill. If only I could rid the world of this ignorant mortal. But calling attention to myself would only cause infinite problems.

The light that caught my eye from the end of the hallway was not as bright and the sound was lower. I entered the room and froze. This human girl was older and in a tight-fitting shirt and pants. They enfolded her every curve. Her hair was matted to her face and she twitched. Taking my gaze from her I looked at the flickering box. Walking toward it, lowering my head, I listened. It was speaking, softly, and the pictures were moving so quickly, as if there was a life in a box. *A picture box*? How bizarre. I heard a slight moan and the girl moved, but I was gone before I knew if she had awakened or not. Leaving the mortals' loathsome and unfamiliarly bizarre house behind me, I felt my side. It was still bleeding. I couldn't comprehend why it wasn't healing any faster.

The night air was crisp and cool against my bare back. My wings spread out wide and I tried to not notice the pain in my side. I heard a twig snap and glanced to the right.

A figure emerged from the bush where I had just been. The hood of his coat was over his face so I could not tell who it was.

He eyed the second story and then the door. I watched from the shadows as he picked the lock. If he were smart he would have checked the back door, I had already broken it. The door clicked.

I didn't know this family, and I had no reason to care what happened to them, although it was my job to kill those who did not serve Christ. My brothers and I had made a pact— we would start The Apocalypse, no matter what it took. We were Famine, Death, War, and Conquest. What were the Four Horsemen to do rather than take out the ones not of the Lord's honor?

It wouldn't hurt to go ahead and kill one child that didn't seem to be missed. His mother didn't even care enough to check on him during the night.

He opened the door and I caught him by the shirt. "What the fuck!" he shouted and took a swing at me. Stupid mortal.

"What business do you have here?" I asked.

"Okay, Miss Fairy, why don't you go get done in the ass…ahhh!" he screamed as I gripped his arm. "I was here to see Lizzie. She is my friend."

I laughed without humor. "Yes, I see. She waits up for you and everything." I leaned closer to his ear. "I think you want to die tonight."

Tears began to swell over his horrid face. "Please, don't—"

Snap. *Easier than I thought.*

I stripped the boy of any belongings on his body. He had a leather bound wallet with a few dollar bills and some odd objects that said, *Trojan.* After dragging the body until I found a junk yard a mile or so up the road, I went back to the mortals' house, eyed the bush, and walked toward it, pulling my wings into my bare back, until they were completely gone. I curled into the patch of dirt and tried to push the hard days to come out of my mind. The thought of being back on Earth both excited me and sickened me. The people around me were fools, but to think we would finally get to go through with The Apocalypse, which we had been chosen for, sent excitement through my entire body.

There was so much to do but I was entirely too weak to do it. I lay on my back against the rocky earth and closed my eyes, silently twisting the ring around my ring finger. That's when my ring burned into my skin. It was happening. One of the other Horsemen was trying to contact me. I closed my eyes and focused. My mind went blank and words appeared in it. It was Warren speaking to me. *The time is coming, Brother. I will not tolerate you not being here. You only have a scarce amount of weeks to get your priorities together. Get better. The time is coming. Satan will not wait much longer. We have to have Death of the Horsemen to perform.*

The words stopped. It was more like getting the wind knocked out of me than words appearing in my mind. I gasped for breath. Our rings were the only way for us to keep track of one another. It was painful to contact each other mentally, but a necessity. The time was getting closer—my brothers could not complete the ritual without me. I had to go. I had to find them. Pushing myself up, I tried to move but my side ached too much. I fell back to the ground, breathing hard. Time was running out. They would come for me if I didn't get better soon. I wanted to be better by the time my brother's found each other. They would be mad if I delayed any longer. *My brothers are waiting for me.*

෬ඁ෬ඁ

I opened my eyes and gritted my teeth. There wasn't much time at all. I had to hurry and get well. *My brothers are waiting for me.* I closed my eyes and tried to will myself to sleep. I needed rest for the upcoming days.

CHAPTER 3

Lizzie

P lease tell me that a meteor came to your house and blew it up, you had no clothes, you had no car to drive last night, and your cell phone was crushed?" Millie said, bursting through my door Saturday morning. *Well, she got the cell phone part right.*

I opened one eye slightly. She was looking straight at me. *Damn, she sees me.* I sat up. "Please, tell me you have a great explanation for telling Trevor I was on my period!" I demanded.

Millie tugged her black hair into a ponytail and tisked as she walked toward me. "Yeah, my best friend gets asked out by her crush and then doesn't show up for her date! That's my excuse, oh, I needed a good one! You better have a good one too." She was pacing back and forth, pointing her finger at me. "Come on, out with it. What was the big reason why you couldn't show up last night?" I opened my mouth to talk but she cut me off. "He was miserable last night. He had this poor puppy dog face the entire night. Not to mention, that little slut,

Rachel trying to get back with him! You weren't there! Oh! You weren't there."

The door swung open and my heart skipped a beat. *Please don't let it be Darrton.* "Listen here, Millie!" Sam shouted. "Please shut the heck up, I'm trying to sleep. If ya don't mind, hon." Sam glanced over at her. "And please, change those hideous shoes that so do not go with that shirt!"

"Get out!" I screamed.

"These shoes so do match!"

"Says who? I'll tell ya, no one. Someone call the fashion police. Millie is on it again!"

"Take that back. These were in *Seventeen* last month!"

"Sam, get out!" I yelled, this time getting up and pushing her out.

She went the entire way making cop siren sounds saying *fashion police, fashion police*!

"I hate your sister," Millie said calmly.

"Yeah? Try living with her," I said as I sighed against the door.

Millie pointed her finger. "Don't think you're getting out of this one! Where were you? What happened?"

A flash of panic rushed over me. I tried to think of anything I could to distract Millie. "Trevor climbed in my window last night," I blurted out.

Millie stopped and popped her gum. Her black ponytail swung with her head as she whirled around. "Get the freaking-a out of here!" she squealed and plopped down on my unmade bed. "Oh God!" She grabbed her chest and flung herself back on my bed. "Did you kiss?" She gasped. "No! You two did it! You lost your V-card, didn't you!?!"

I rolled my eyes. "No! We didn't kiss or do it."

Millie stopped and shot up. "Why the hell not?"

"Because, he just came by to talk to me. See if I needed anything for my period."

Millie laughed and I couldn't help but laugh with her. I snorted and that only made it worse. "Okay, I'm sorry. I got put on the spot I had to make something up quick. I'm only one girl. It's hard to entertain two guys!"

I smiled at Millie. I couldn't ask for a better friend in the world. My stomach growled and we looked at one another. "*The Picnic Basket.*"

Millie waited for me while I tugged on an old T-shirt and jeans. The sky was overcast, and it looked as if it might rain. I pulled on a grey hoodie and some Converse. "You ready to go?"

"Hells, yeah, I'm so ready for some of Momma's fudge!"

I laughed and we went downstairs to where the drama queen was eating her cereal. "Are we quiet now?" Sam asked over her spoon.

"Are we not a bitc—hi, Mrs. Laurence," Millie smiled and darted her eyes at Sam while Mom yawned.

"Good morning, my darlings. You two headed out?"

"Yep, going to *The Picnic Basket* for some fudge. You want us to pick you up some, Mom? It's the only place that is open this early that is decent and not fast food. Besides, we want some fudge."

"I want cookies and cream!" Sam shouted. "And don't smash it. I have needs and something sweet is on the list for today."

I heard Millie grit her teeth. She narrowed her eyes and spit through her lips, "Of course, Samantha."

Sam smiled. The way Sam and Millie fought, you would think they were sisters.

"Umm, fudge sounds nice," Mom said. "How about some mocha swirl for me, and pick up some dark chocolate raspberry swirl for your father?" She pushed around in her purse and was saying something to Millie when I glanced out the window.

I stopped. *Damn it. I can't just leave him here.* I clicked my tongue and taped my foot.

"Oh hey, Mom, I think I'm going to need a new cell," I said.

She glanced up, an eyebrow rose. "Why is that? We just got you that Android thingy."

"It's an awesome phone, Mom, but I accidently smashed it the other day at school. I don't know what happened it just fell out of my pocket and shattered on the concrete outside."

She snorted. "When we bought you that phone, the sales person said it was indestructible. Lies, all lies."

Yeah, they didn't test it on a Horseman of The Apocalypse.

"I'll get you one but I can't promise it will be as nice."

Of course not.

"Hey, I'll be right back," I said. "I left a sweater in the tree-house the other day."

"Why were you in there? Tree houses are for little kids."

Millie smiled. "Like you, Samantha?"

Samantha darted her eyes to Millie, and her lips firmed into a hard straight line. Mom continued to rummage around in her purse for money as I dashed toward the clubhouse.

It was quiet when I climbed the ladder. There wasn't a bird singing or a passing car. The air was humid and I could smell the rain. "Darrton."

He was nowhere to be seen. A shiver of panic crept through my body. *Where could he have gone*? Oh God, what if someone shot him? *A neighbor*? *A policeman*? *We would know about it wouldn't we*?

"Lizzie! Did you find your sweater? I got moolah!"

"Uh, no, not here, just a minute." I staggered down, trying to clear my head while mumbling to myself. I placed my Converse on the last step and my foot slipped. I landed awkwardly on my side. "Shit."

I heard Millie call, "Are you okay?"

I pulled myself up. I felt a pain in my wrist and, glancing down at it, saw the blood trickling down. "Damn it," I mumbled. "Yes, I'm fine. Let's just go."

Millie was not a safe driver. Never had been. We often wondered if the Department of Motor Vehicle's employee that was in the car with Millie, during her driver's test, was drunk.

Millie sang along to Trains' "Hey Soul Sister," and talked about how hot Brett had been the night before and how much fun they'd had. Unlike me, she had actually gotten to spend time with her date.

"You want to eat ours here?" Millie asked, already half way through her divinity fudge.

I pointed toward the open booth in the corner, catching a glance at the cut on my wrist. It would leave a mark. We had just sat down when the bell on the door rang. We both looked over and a petite woman with short, dark hair walked in. She had dark circles underneath her eyes, and she looked straight ahead, zombie-like.

As she stood at the counter, a man walked up to her.

"How are you, Mrs. Johns?"

Millie looked at me and widened her eyes.

She sniffed. "The best I can be during a time like this."

He patted her back. "Just know that I am praying for you."

She nodded. "Thank you. We are still looking for any clues we can to find him. There was no struggle at home so they are ruling out kidnapping." She was obviously holding back her tears.

The man shook his head, looking horrified. "Good God. I hope you guys find him."

Millie coughed and I looked back at her. "Poor woman," I said.

She nodded. "Yeah. I mean he was mean, but I don't think he deserved to go missing."

"Me either."

The mocha swirl was sliding down my throat when I saw a shadow cover the table. I turned and choked on my fudge. "Darrton!"

"Where have you been? You left me to myself and I am starved. I had to go look for nearby woodlands for food. I couldn't find any close enough. Why haven't you provided me with any food? I waited for you until I couldn't stand not having any food any longer."

Maybe because I'm trying to stay away from you. You freak me out.

Millie blinked. "Hit the road, creep. Who is this, Lizzie? Do you know him?" She glanced down at his bare chest and mouthed "hot."

Please don't let us get kicked out of here because of him. Someone shoot me. "What are you doing here? Haven't you ever heard of 'no shoes, no shirt, no service'?"

"Do I need to repeat myself once again? Are you hard of hearing? And what is that? No shoes…"

I gritted my teeth. "Outside now!"

Millie grabbed my arm. "Who is that and why the hell don't I know him? Can you say hottie? He so has that Steven Strait look about him."

I held the bridge of my nose and glanced over my shoulder. He was standing outside glaring in at me. "Listen, Millie…" I began to whisper and Darrton reached for the door to come back inside. *Damn.* "Darrton is my older cousin."

"Cousin, whoa, can I have him?"

"No!" I yelled out, not even meaning for it to slip through my lips. I bit my tongue as soon as I said it.

She grabbed her heart in an overdramatic Millie way. "Ouch, all you had to say was he is taken."

I huffed. "I'll be back."

Darrton met me and gripped my arm. "That's the second time I've had to warn you, child. Do not tell anyone what I am."

"I don't even know what you are!" I yanked my arm from his grip. "Some kind of fallen angel or Horsemen or dem—" I stopped myself. "Where are your wings?"

His eyes were boring into my head. "They are retracted. Would you like for me to take them out?"

"No, I would not like that," I snapped. "Why are you here? You're hungry? What do you eat?"

He snorted. "What a senseless question. What do you think I eat?"

Clicking, my tongue, I tried to calm myself. "I don't know? Clouds?"

He laughed. It was the first time he had laughed and I was taken aback by it. The musical harmony of it sounded almost…angelic. "No, child, I eat anything you eat. Maybe some fish, bread, broth."

I let out a long breath. "Okay, we have to talk. First, I will make you a peanut butter and jelly sandwich when we get home, because that is the extent of my cooking. Secondly, you have to wear clothes. You can't walk around half naked, okay?"

Darrton snorted and crossed his arms across his chest. "I do not have any clothes. I had to steal these trousers just to have them. I came nude."

A blush traveled across my check, and I dodged my brain away from picturing him naked. Darrton's eyebrows shot up. "Does that make you uncomfortable, child?"

I ignored him. "We will go get you some clothes, okay? I have a credit card my mom lets Samantha and I use, but for now I need you to go home. And try to take lonesome streets, you know, without people."

"I don't need to walk. I fly. Why would I walk? Hah!"

I slapped my head. "Silly me. Of course, you flew."

Darrton stiffened and suddenly grabbed my wrist. "What happened?"

I snatched my wrist away. "I fell from the clubhouse looking for you."

His eyes seemed to lighten and he gripped my forearm. "Be still."

"What are you..." I trailed off and watched in amazement. The slit on my wrist was slowly healing until it was gone. "How did you do that?"

He cocked his head to the side. "It's one power I command."

"Right," I said slowly, glancing at my wrist.

"Mommy, Mommy! That man's not wearing a shirt!" I heard from behind me.

The woman made a sound of disgust and covered the eyes of her little girl, who was pointing at Darrton. "Sir, you should have more respect for people than to walk around half naked, in a public place."

Darrton took a threatening step forward, and I pulled him back. "Sorry, lady. He didn't take all of his medication today,"

I said making a slow circle around my temple. I turned back to Darrton. "We need to go get you dressed."

I pushed against his chest and tried to get him to leave when I heard, "Lizzie." I stood in an uncomfortably, frozen-shitless position for what seemed like an hour. *Maybe if I stand still he will think that I am only an illusion.* I shut my eyes as tight as they would go. "Lizzie." I felt Trevor's hand on my back, "Is that you?"

"Yes, it's her. Speak to him, child."

"Who the hell are you? Is everything all right, Lizzie?"

Shit it didn't work. I turned around. Trevor had a wide-eyed look on his face. "Yes, everything is fine."

"You're white as a ghost? Are you sure?"

I nodded. It was a small nod—hell, I wasn't even sure if my head made enough movement for him to see. Numbness crept up my body. "Everything is fine, I promise," I repeated.

"Aren't you going to introduce me to your friend?" Trevor glanced over to Darrton who was looking at us in an intimidating way.

"This is Darrton," I mumbled. "He is my cousin."

Trevor's stance relaxed. "What's up, bro?" Trevor offered him a fist pump but he dropped it when Darrton didn't return it. Not like the man understood what that meant anyway.

"That is a very loaded question, son. There are many things that are up."

Trevor cocked his head to the side, and his mouth opened a bit in confusion. *Gheesh.*

Darrton opened his mouth to speak, then he closed it and sniffed the air. "Rain," he said.

"Yea, it's supposed to rain," Trevor said, moving closer to me. "You want my jacket?"

A small smile rose on Trevor's lips and I couldn't help but let the giggle, that was bubbling up my throat, out. "No, it's okay."

"Here take it," Trevor said. He slid off his jacket and draped it over my shoulders.

When I looked back, Darrton was staring and almost snarling at Trevor. "You're the boy that trespassed into Lizzie's chamber last night? I can smell it." Darrton's eyes traveled down Trevor.

Trevor froze. "No," he said slowly.

"Do not lie to me, boy!" Darrton turned to me. "You won't be needing this young lad's jacket. I have stopped the rain."

Trevor leaned in and let out a low whistle. Indicating what he thought about Darrton: that he was nuts. That made two of us.

"Darrton, I'll meet you at home. Do you remember where home is?"

"Of course. You act as if I'm a lost child. I know my way."

"Well, taketh your behind that way then," I gritted through my teeth.

Darrton ran his fingers through his long hair and sighed. "When will you be home? I am hungry."

"I will be home soon!" I said a little too loudly.

Darrton opened his mouth to say something but then stopped and gripped his hand. Before he fell to his knees I noticed the ring on his finger give off a slight glow. "I must go."

"Are you all right, dude?" Trevor asked.

Darrton had already darted behind the building.

CHAPTER 4

Darrton

The vacant lot behind the food store was empty when I reached it. My body convulsed once more before I fell to the hard rocks below me. My ring had glowed. It had seared me. *They're here.* A gust of wind hit my face and I knew it to be true. Which one was it? *Could it be War*? Was he firing up rebels against one another? Or was it countries against other countries? Families against families? His mission was to make people slay one another. He felt no mercy. I could imagine the *Red* around him, a blazing, deathly red. When I closed my eyes, I could see him. His part was to start wars. The thought of him made me miss my brothers.

Another ache shot through my hand. Famine's face appeared in my mind, I could see the *Black* in his eyes. Even in my vision, I could feel the eagerness that radiated off of him. *Famine.* It could be he that was starving the people of a country, or killing off anything edible. His mission was to starve the people before him, that not one soul should have nourishment, and not one soul should continue. He would look unto the world around him and create hunger, thirst, and heartache. Famine was closest to me, and I could only wait with impatience to see him. He was the strongest.

A severe pain slashed my side. My wound was bleeding and all I could see was *White*. Not a pure white. A ghastly white that would scare anyone that had the nerve to look. It would blind their eyes with ghostly essence. He was sent to *Conquer* and he wouldn't stop until we ruled the Earth.

Then my ring shot energy through me one last time. This time it differed. This time it did not burn me. This time it sizzled through me like ice through my veins. This time it soothed me. I pushed up off of the hard ground and looked around the empty alley. War was leaning up against the side of the brick wall. "Darrton. Brother, it's nice to see you."

I smiled. "Nice to see you, too, Warren."

Warren walked toward me. He had cut his hair and was dressed modernly. He shook my hand. The contact sent electric bolts through my body. Our rings touched and I felt a connection with him that no one on Earth would ever have with one another. A brotherly bond that would put any other blood-bonded brothers to shame.

"We've tried to connect with you, Brother, and you haven't answered."

His words seemed to snake around me. I lifted my arm and pointed toward my wound.

Warren nodded. "You've been wounded, but I see that it hasn't stopped you from getting out. You still fly. We can all feel when you do," Warren said.

"I cannot help it, Brother. I've been...distracted. I've been trying to get better, I was too weak."

Warren narrowed his red-tinted eyes, and a smile rose to his lips. His face was far more feminine than the rest of us.

"Oh, Brother. I believe I understand what you call your distraction. I believe her name is Lizzie, is it not?"

Anger surged into my throat and I snarled, "I care nothing about that child. She has given me shelter and promised me food. How dare you say she has distracted me?"

Warren threw his head back and laughed. "Brother, Brother, how defensive you get." He looked down at my side. "You have to be well to perform the ritual. Satan wants you in the best physical shape you can be. I will give you until you are healed to kill off the girl. She knows too much, and she is distracting you from what we were damned for. Get away from the house and away from her. Since she has helped you, it would be easier to leave, let her guard go down, and then come back to kill her. She won't see it coming. Be ready, Darrton. The time is coming."

Warren didn't say anything else. He turned, broke his wings from his back, and lifted himself up. He was gone before I could process everything.

My wings were begging to rip through my back so I set them free. My shadow covered half the walkway. I let my feet lift from the ground.

The only one that was left was *me*. The only one that was left was a pale blue *Death*.

There were only two things I had left to do. First was to heal. I had to be ready for the ritual. Secondly, I had to bring death upon her. I had to make sure no one found out. I had to do what I was given to do—kill.

CHAPTER 5

Lizzie

You're cousin has major issues," Trevor said as he opened the passenger side door of his car for me.

'*Who are you telling?*' I glanced up in shock. Sure enough, the clouds were gone. The air was a warm paradise and the rain…well, it wasn't raining.

Millie laughed from behind me. "Yeah, but he is ridiculously H–O–T. I want me some of that!"

Trevor raised an eyebrow and I darted my eyes to her. "Millie, stop," I breathed.

She raised her hands in surrender, while our bag of half-eaten doughnuts swung in her hand. "Just saying, comrade. Anywho! I will see you at your house, Liz," she said. Then glancing over her shoulder while Trevor walked around the car, she moved her eyebrows up and down. I held up my fist and she puckered up her lips.

I stepped into Trevor's Lexus and sank into the leather. "Hard day, huh?" he asked, cranking his car and putting it into gear.

I nodded. "Harder than you will ever know."

"Your cousin Darrton seems…"

"Like a crazy-ass?" I asked.

"Exactly."

"Yeah, well, I think he might be. I haven't known the guy long but he is driving me crazy."

Trevor pulled out of the parking lot and headed toward my house. "Yeah, I really didn't want to say much but he is odd and huge. I mean I thought I was big, but this guy is like a damn pro-athlete."

I twisted in the seat. He was rather large and built. He was freakishly accurate, too. *'I will stop the rain.' Gah, could you get any freakier? If I did believe he was a…Horseman. Does that make me crazy?*

Trevor's hand brought me back to the present. It landed on my knee and I stiffened. He pulled it back. "I'm sorry I…"

"No, you just surprised me, that's all. I was thinking and it just caught me off guard." I forced a smile. *Come on, Liz, pull yourself together. Do not blow this with Trevor because of some wacked-out, religious guy.*

"I see," Trevor said, grabbing my hand and intertwining our fingers. There went that flash of heat again. *Holy Moly, he is so cute!*

"So, I was wondering about next weekend?"

What about next weekend? I tried to focus my thoughts. "What about next weekend?"

"There is a Kings of Leon concert that I want to go to. I've already asked Millie and Brett. They said yes."

I smiled. "I would love to go. I love Kings of Leon."

He nodded. "I know, I remember."

My heart thudded. I had plans with him. *He isn't mad about last night.*

Trevor pulled into my driveway. "Where is Millie?" I asked turning around. Trevor laughed. "What?" I asked.

"Millie is smarter than she acts."

"Millie is an evil genius. She is like plankton, small but evil."

Trevor laughed. "That is so her new nickname." We both laughed and he turned to me. "I think Millie is giving us some time alone."

I felt my insides prickle and fidgeted in my seat. "Sounds like Millie," I mumbled. I glanced around at the house. Mom's car wasn't there and Dad was at work. *Should I invite him in*? Mom had never said anything about being alone with a boy. But I had never asked to be alone with one, either. "Would you like to—"

"I would love to," he answered impatiently and then laughed at himself.

I couldn't feel my legs, when I walked toward the door. Grabbing my keys seemed like an easy task but when I tried to do it, I dropped them on the ground. Trevor was now standing behind me and when I bent down to get the keys at the same time Trevor did we collided.

"Ouch!" I stumbled back and landed on my butt on the concrete step.

Trevor, laughing and holding his head, reached his hand out to help me up. "I'm so sorry. I try to be a gentleman and end up pushing you down."

I groaned. *God, please show mankind how to make an efficient time machine.* "No, it's okay. I'm just a little nervous."

Trevor stopped. "If you don't want me to come in—"

"No! I do." I fumbled with the key and opened the door, "I'm just out of my mind right now."

Trevor was so close behind me when he said, "Right," I could feel his breath on my neck. Muffin barked and I turned quickly around. "Hey, puppy," Trevor said, picking up the dog and laughing while he licked him.

"That's Muffin," I said, moving around him to go sit on the couch. *The couch is safe. Right?*

Trevor followed me and sat down. "So, this is your living room." He leaned in. "I think I like your room better."

I laughed but it was a nervous laugh. A drop of blood was beside his foot on the floor. I stood up abruptly. "You want something to drink? I'm so thirsty." I almost ran to the kitchen. I started to fumble around in the refrigerator. This wasn't like last night in my room, where there was nowhere to run and I was half asleep. He was right here. I had invited him in. I took out a bottle of water and sucked half of it down. *Breathe.*

I shut the door and Trevor was standing behind it. His baseball cap was turned backwards and his short sleeve shirt hugging his torso. I looked up at him and smiled, trying to swallow the gulp of water in my throat.

"Are you okay?" he asked.

"Yea," I said while my foot shook irrationally on the floor. "Why do you ask? You want some water?"

He glanced down at my foot and smiled. "No, no water, Lizzie. Are you that nervous?" He took another step forward.

"Nervous? Who said I was nervous?"

Trevor sighed. "Lizzie," he said. "I can leave if you want me to?"

I shook my head. "No! Don't please, ugh, I'm sorry, I just…I'm not good around boys. The only reason I was half-calm the last night was because I was half-asleep. I was like this, this summer, too, remember? It's just I've never had a boy really—"

He kissed me.

His lips were so soft against mine. His fingers found my waist and his other hand found the back of my neck. A peppermint taste filled my mouth. I let out a moan. Without thinking, I gripped his shirt and pulled him into me. My water bottle fell to the floor, spilling water everywhere, but I couldn't have cared less. There was no space in between our bodies. Our breathing was hard and heavy on each other. Trevor pushed me up against the counter. I felt his fingers tighten around my waist then lower to my belt loop. This excited me and I ran my hand along the bottom of his shirt. *I wonder what he looks like without it.*

Trevor's hands lowered to my butt and he lifted me up on the counter in one swift motion. *Oh God.* He positioned himself between my legs and dug his tongue into my mouth. When he pulled back, I felt myself wanting to grab him again. I looked up. His dark blue eyes were boring into mine. He leaned in again and touched my mouth once, then twice. His lips touched the corner of my mouth, then my check, and then my jawline until they were on my neck.

I had never experienced anything like this before. I'd kissed Trevor before but this was different. He was kissing my neck which had never happened before. When we had kissed, it was always sweet. It was pure, white hot pleasure. My fingers, without permission from my brain, dug into his back and pulled him as close as he could get to me. God that felt good.

"AH!" I heard someone yell. I opened my eyes as Trevor yanked me down to the floor. Samantha was staring at us with a bag from The Picnic Basket in her hand, her mouth wide open. "So, I guess someone does know what making out is? I thought she was clueless. Hi," she said, offering Trevor her hand. "I'm Samantha. Call me Sam, or beautiful. Whichever you prefer."

I wiped my mouth just as Trevor took Sam's hand and Mom rounded the corner. "Lizzie!" she said, then looking at Trevor, she stopped. "You must be Trevor."

Shoot me.

"I am Trevor, nice to meet you. You have a lovely—"

"Mom? What are you doing here? Why do you have those bags?"

Mom gave me the "you're being rude" look. "Well, since two girls were supposed to bring us back fudge and never showed. You two must have left before we got there, so we went ahead and got our fudge. We thought you two might have forgotten. We can never have too much fudge, anyway."

"Oh, Lizzie and Millie did go get the fudge but Darrton showed up."

I bit my lip and nearly slapped my hand over Trevor's mouth.

"What? Who?" Samantha said, tossing her hip to the side.

Mom passed us and placed the fudge on the counter, where Trevor and I had just been making out. Samantha walked passed her. "Don't think you want to put those there, Mom, Trevor and Lizzie were...ouch!!!" she screamed as I took the water bottle that had fallen from my hand and hit her over the head. She pushed me back. "What the heck!"

"Lizzie!" my mother yelled.

All of a sudden Millie burst out laughing and I stumbled because I didn't realize she was behind us. "Way to go, comrade."

"Say you're sorry to your sister," Mom ordered.

"Sorry," I mumbled.

Sam was glaring at me. She snatched the fudge bag from Millie and went into the living room.

Mom sighed and held her head. "And what is all this talk about a Darrton?"

Millie shrieked. "Oh! Mrs. Lawrence, he is H–O–T. He came looking for Lizzie earlier.

"We don't know a Darrton, do we Lizzie? Who is it?"

"Darrton your cousin?" Millie said.

"Who? I don't think so—"

"Ouch!" I yelled and grabbed my shoulder.

"What's wrong?" Mom asked.

"I have a cramp in my shoulder. We have to go, Mom, I have to go get some pain reliever from the car." I pulled Trevor along and Millie followed after.

Sam was sitting in the living room glaring at us on the way outside.

"What the hell, Lizzie? Were you that desperate to get away from your mom?" she asked.

"Uh yeah! You've met my family."

"Point taken."

Trevor stepped closer to me and I blushed. Everything that had just happened hit me and I suddenly felt like floating. Millie was staring at me, and she raised a perfectly plucked eyebrow. "So you two have fun?"

I closed my eyes and gritted my teeth. "Sorry for all of this, Trevor. My family barging in and my rude friend and crazy ass…cousin."

Trevor eyed me. "You're mom doesn't seem to think she knows him."

"He said he wasn't closely related," I lied.

Trevor nodded. "Well, as much fun as this was, and I truly mean it, I have to run. My little sister has dance practice and I have to take her."

"Okay, I guess I'll see you later then?"

He smiled and leaned in and pressed his lips to mine once more. "Yea, of course."

ℰ⁊ℰ⁊

I was utterly surprised. Millie waited two whole minutes while Trevor was backing out of the driveway before she started jumping up and down and asking for details. I gave them to her, down to the smell of his breath and the placement of his hands. His jacket was still snugly around my shoulders. I was on cloud nine. Which reminded me...*Darrton, angel, Horseman whatever. Where is he*?

Millie excused herself and it wasn't a minute too early. I had to find my "cousin," and see if he was okay. He had just run out of there and that glowing ring was freaking me out. I made two peanut butter and jelly sandwiches and, after getting a shirt from my dad's drawer and grabbing a warm wash cloth and a large bandage, I went to look for Mr. Horseman.

He was sitting on the twin size cot in the tree house when I came up. He glanced over at me.

"Got you this." I threw my dad's old Columbia T-shirt to him. He didn't speak but stood and rolled the T-shirt onto himself. It fit...well...sort of. It was so tight that it seemed painted on. His arms looked as if they might pop out of it.

"Much obliged. It is a tight fit."

I dragged my eyes away from his chest. "Next week we will go get you some clothes. I have an American Eagle credit card my mom lets me and Samantha use."

From the blank look on his face, I knew that he had no idea what I was talking about. I pulled the sandwiches out of the Zip-Lock bag and handed both of them to him. Obviously, food was something that was the same all over—when you are hungry, you're just hungry. He seemed to inhale them.

Wiping his mouth, he pulled his hair from his face. "I need to bathe."

"Well, you'll have to wait until tonight when everyone is sleeping."

Darrton stood there for a second. "That will do."

Trying to steady myself I said, "Sit down and I'll wash your wound off."

Darrton's eyes caught mine and I paused, waiting for him to snap at me. "Okay," he whispered.

He sat down on his cot and lifted his arm. Trying not to look at him, I raised my dad's shirt and pressed the warm cloth to his side. He flinched and his body tightened. "Are you okay?"

He nodded. "Yes, proceed."

I wiped the rest of his wound off, the best I could, and placed the large bandage on his side. It only covered the bad part of it, but it would help from getting anymore dirt in it. I stood and offered him a smile. He nodded as he glanced at his side.

I was trying to think of something to make the moment a little less awkward when I noticed he seemed distracted as if he was debating something. He finally said, "That Trevor boy is not good for you."

I scoffed. *Too bad for a nice moment.* "Excuse me?"

"I said—"

"I heard you," I said. "Why would you think that?"

"He isn't honest. I can tell."

I laughed. "Okay, Darrton, whatever you say."

He cocked an eyebrow. "You don't believe me. You think I lie?"

"I think you don't know him."

He smiled but it looked forced. "I know enough."

"Can we please talk about something else?" *Ugh! The nerve. He doesn't even know Trevor.*

"As you wish," he said,

Shifting my feet, I tried to think of a reasonable way to ask him what I wanted to.

"Ask your question."

I cocked a brow. "Well…" I cleared my throat. "I wanted to talk to you about what you are exactly. I mean, I know you said an angel or Horseman, but why would you be here? Is this The Apocalypse?"

"It's not The Apocalypse."

"Then what is it?"

Darrton's demeanor stiffened. "Child, you wouldn't understand.

"Try me. I'm smarter than I look."

"Doubtful."

I laughed without humor. "Whatever." I got up to leave and Darrton grabbed my arm.

"Sit." When I opened my mouth to argue, he said, "Do you want to know how I got here or not?"

I shut my mouth and sat down across from him. His eyes were hard and he seemed to be zoning out. "I am one of The Four Horsemen of The Apocalypse."

"So you've said. Is that kind of like a fallen angel?

A shrug. "Yes and no. I am one of The Four Horsemen. I resided in heaven like an angel, but I'm technically not."

"Yes," I said leaning closer. "And…"

He raised his head and his pale blue eyes made a shiver run down my spine. "I was damned to Earth."

I could barely get my voice over a whisper. "Why?"

"Have you ever been to church, Lizzie?"

I nodded. "On Easter, and when I was younger."

"Did they teach you about The Apocalypse?"

I shook my head and picked at a fringed hole in my jeans. "No, we were too small. It would have scared us."

"It should." Darrton laughed without humor. "Do you know about it now?"

I shrugged. "Yeah, I think."

He stared at me for what seemed like forever. "Well, child, it seems I might need to enlighten you. The Apocalypse is after Christ comes back for his people. After The Rapture, all the people that are not believers in God would be here during The Apocalypse. It's those who do not know God who will suffer."

There was that knot in my throat again. "Suffer how?" I asked, my voice breaking in the end. I had to pull my eyes away from him. Focusing on a crack in the floor of the room, I tried to steady my ragged breathing.

"That is where my brothers and I come in. We..." He sighed and stood. "...come to bring famine, war and death upon the earth. We perform a ritual that unleashes it all. They can only initiate what they represent before the ritual. Under normal circumstances, God would send us down and we would have the power to start it. But now that we've been cast out, we have to go through Satan to start it." My lower lip trembled. "Warren starts war and Famine starts famine. We each have a part to play. Although, that is just the beginning of it. They have to have me to perform the ritual first."

I couldn't make my mouth move. *What if he is telling the truth? He is a Horseman?*

"What kind of ritual, Darrton?"

He didn't answer. He just stared at me and twisted his ring around his finger. "Do you know what all of the Four Horsemen represent, Lizzie?"

He never looked away from me. There was a worry line in his forehead, and I felt a shiver.

"No," I whispered so low I wasn't sure if I even heard myself.

"We are War, Famine, Conquest, and Death."

I sucked in a breath and sat back away from him. "Darrton," I whispered, clearing my throat and speaking up, "which one are you?"

He titled his head and licked his lips. A cold shiver ran from my head to the tips of my toes. When he laughed, I felt bile coming up from the pits of my stomach. "Darrton, which one?"

His demeanor changed. There was no smile on his face. "I am—"

"Lizzie!" My dad yelled from the bottom of the tree house. "Come on in for dinner, sweetheart."

When I glanced back up Darrton wasn't in the tree house.

"Lizzie?" my dad yelled.

I glanced out of the back window. Darrton was gone.

My heart was drumming hard in my chest. *He is a Horseman. Which one?*

"Lizzie, is everything okay up there?"

No. I shook my head. "Um…coming, Dad." I climbed down the ladder and hurried off into the house. I couldn't bear to look at my dad. I knew if he looked me in the eyes, he would be able to tell that something was wrong. He wouldn't understand or believe me if I told him. I still wasn't sure if it was all happening. When I opened the door Mom and Sam were gathered around the TV in the living room and they were silent.

"What's going—"

"Shhh!" They both turned around and gave me death glares. Over their shoulders, I saw the commotion on TV. "It just happened out of nowhere. People are going mad!" my mother yelled.

"It is the craziest thing I have seen, Scott. People are going crazy and fighting one another for no reason! There you see it." The weatherman on Channel 7 pointed toward a child with a gun in her hand. "That is a dad and his daughter. They are trying to kill one another! The red—it's hazy. Everything seems to have a red glare—what is going on?"

"Jesus," my dad said from behind me.

"We have to get out of here," the reporter said. "This is Lance Grimms, reporting from Dafna, Israel." The screen went blank.

Any doubt in my mind seemed to trickle away out of my ear and down to my feet. I might as well have stomped on it. It was real. *This is real.* War was breaking out, War of The Four Horsemen.

Sam was uncharacteristically quiet at dinner, and Mom and Dad seemed to pick at their grilled chicken salads. No one knew what to say. I did, but I couldn't. I was going to throw up. *He was in our backyard. Only a few feet away from our home. How could this be happening?*

After diner when everything went quiet, I pulled open my laptop and clicked on *Google*. My fingers shook as I typed in *Apocalypse.* I scrolled down and clicked on *Bible Prophecy— Apocalypse.* The page was never ending. I scrolled down and stopped on a random spot. It read...

> *These events which are about to be unleashed upon this world, even though global in nature, will focus on one thing – the nation of Israel. One tiny piece of land. A speck of land when compared to the powerful enemies that surround her on all sides (look at a map). A*

> *land God calls His own. God says He owns it*
> *and the sons and daughters of Israel are His...*
>
> *I will bless those who bless you (Israel), and*
> *curse those who curse you. (Genesis 12:3)*

I shut the screen. My body felt rigid and bile was edging its way up my throat. *I have to find some answers.* Jumping up, I ran toward my closet and started rummaging around. I pulled out a *Precious Moments* light-pink Bible from underneath loads of quilts. I hadn't opened it in ages and it was practically brand new. My knees buckled beneath me as I began to skim for *Revelations.* It took about five minutes before I found something that might help. It didn't make me feel any better.

> *Now I saw when the Lamb opened one of the*
> *seals; and I heard one of the four living*
> *creatures saying with a voice like thunder,*
> *'Come and see.' And I looked, and behold, a*
> *white horse.*
>
> *And he who sat on it had a bow; and a crown*
> *was given to him,*
>
> *And he went out conquering and to conquer.*
> *(Revelation 6:1-2)*

My mouth was getting dry. I remembered Darrton's earlier words. *'Conquest.'*

Right below it, it read...

> *When He opened the second seal, I heard the
> second living creature saying, "Come and
> see."*
>
> *Another horse, fiery red, went out. And it was
> granted to the one who sat on it to take peace
> from the Earth, and that people should kill one
> another; and there was given to him a great
> sword." (Revelation 6:3-4)*

There was such an aura of truth about the words it made
me think that it couldn't be made up. *Red.* A red horse. The red
haze that seemed to be everywhere on TV today. My body
shook and I had to bite my lip to stop crying. This was going
to happen…this was happening. *Darrton said this wasn't The
Apocalypse. Was he lying? Why was he damned?* Maybe he
couldn't tell anyone.

I skimmed down farther.

> *When He opened the third seal, I heard the
> third living creature say, "Come and see."*
>
> *So I looked, and behold, a black horse, and he
> who sat on it had a pair of scales in his hand.*
>
> *And I heard a voice in the midst of the four
> living creatures saying, "A quart of wheat for
> a denarius, (A denarius was equal to about a
> full day's wage) and three quarts of barley for
> a denarius; and do not harm the oil and the
> wine. (Revelation 6:5-6)*

Food. This was something no one could live without. How could someone starve innocent children? If anything made me sick it was the fact that everyone would be hungry. This could lead to cannibalism. The tears had flowed down my face and started to soak bits of words up on my page.

I wiped my nose on my hand and turned the page.

> *When He opened the fourth seal, I heard the voice of the fourth living creature saying, "Come and see."*
>
> *And I looked, and behold, a pale horse. And the name of him who sat on it was Death, and Hades followed with him.*
>
> *And power was given to them over a fourth of the Earth, to kill with sword, with hunger, with death, and by the beasts of the Earth."*
> *(Revelation 6:7-8)*

Something about this struck a nerve. Not that I didn't believe *Death* would come, but I had a sick feeling it was near. Something was picking at my brain. Something familiar about this part…pale. I let out a sickened cry and slid the book away from me. *Maybe if I close my eyes, it will disappear. Pale.* The pale blue, almost white, in Darrton's eyes was the only thing that was making its way through my thoughts. It had consumed them. *Death.* Darrton was Death. Death was in my back yard, within reach of my family.

I could see Darrton's shadow from the closet floor where I was sitting, and I froze. I couldn't make myself move. "What do you want?" I asked.

Darrton stood deathly still and tilted his head. "Do you regret helping me?"

I didn't answer.

"Thou that helped me would not be harmed. I will leave your family safe." He looked me in the eye but it looked like he was hiding something. "Why are you here?" I demanded. "You said it's not The Apocalypse. You said you were damned—why?"

He smiled but there was nothing about it that comforted me. I slid farther toward the wall and scrunched myself into a ball.

"I was damned because my brothers and I made a pact to destroy."

"Heaven?" I asked.

"No, child. Everywhere. It's our time. It is our time to destroy."

My eyes were starting to feel heavy and it seemed that there was nothing I could do to stop this. Darrton walked toward me and bent down. His eyes—pale, his pale eyes—were so close. Reaching out to touch me, he lifted my face to look at him. Something pierced my heart. A warm shiver made its way up my spine. "I won't hurt you. You have to believe me. You sheltered and fed me. You've saved me. I'm not sure I would have been able to survive otherwise. My condition is getting better because of you. My injury is only healing because you have helped me." A piece of dark hair fell into his face.

I didn't believe him. "You're evil, aren't you?"

He shook his head. "This is what I was chosen to do. Kill."

"Kill the ones that aren't for Christ. Not everyone. It's supposed to be after The Rapture."

His eyes darkened. "The time is come, child. You can't fight it now. This is the time no matter what anyone says. It's time to unleash everything," Darrton said, gripping his ring. "We've waited so long."

"So, you're plan is to what? Just start killing everyone?"

Shaking his head, he knelt down before me—on both legs this time. "No, I must get with my brothers. War has started his part of this, but they have to wait on me to perform the ritual. I have to be there and so does at least one of the other Horsemen. He has to make the oath while I let the demons out. There has to be four in all. If it is not all four Horsemen, then there would have to be two other beings: fallen angels or demons. Whoever it is has to be of another world to open the seal."

"Get out," I breathed.

Darrton's eyes narrowed. ""Make me."

"I'll call the cops…" I trailed off not sure why I thought cops would solve anything.

"You want me to leave?" he asked. "I will leave. But not before Trevor gets what is coming to him. I see who he really is, where you don't." He turned to leave.

"No!" I shot up. "Please, don't!"

"He is bad news." Darrton stopped and turned toward me, shaking his head as if he was talking himself out of something. "I need to bathe." I stepped toward him, grabbing at his arms. He flung me against the wall. His breath was coming in harsh beats upon my skin. "Why do you help me, child?" His brows were furrowed in fury between his eyes. There was confusion radiating from his face.

"What?" I said, between gasp.

"Why did you shelter me, feed me, and clothe me?"

"Because you needed help…everyone deserves a chance." Darrton's wings broke from his back and my dad's Columbia

T-shirt fluttered to the floor in pieces. "Are you going to kill me now? Is that what you have been planning all along? Were you going to kill me so I couldn't tell anyone and then leave?" I was talking loudly now but I prayed no one could hear.

"Yes!" he said. "I am going to kill you!" His words slashed like daggers in my skin. *Why did that hurt so much?*

"Do it," I breathed. "Just leave my family alone. No one knows anything. They will never know you were here."

Darrton placed his hands on the side of my face. I saw the muscles in his arms flex. A slight growl escaped his lips and he lowered his hands to my shoulders. Without trying he picked me from the ground, where my feet dangled and bounced off my bedroom floor. Closing my eyes, I prayed to live, to be left alone. He dropped me and pinned me up against the wall.

The silence seemed to go on forever. He still had my arms pinned against the wall. I was still breathing heavily when he leaned toward me. "I can't now."

Relief, wonder, and anger seemed to bombard me. I managed to steady my voice and asked, "Why?"

Darrton pushed his head toward my face. I smelled the warm dark hunger of his breath. He stopped and released me. "I have to go now. I will take my bath while everyone is asleep and go back to my chamber. I will see you Monday."

I was gasping and I had no idea why. "Tomorrow is Sunday?"

"I won't be here."

CHAPTER 6

Darrton

Ill-bred fool!" I shouted into the night. Anger was swarming through my body and my wings took charge. There wasn't any excuse for not killing her while I had the chance. *Why did I tell her anything? Why did I tell her my plans? Why did I threaten to kill Trevor, when it meant nothing to me? You lie.*

My body felt frigid in the air. There had to be an underlining reason why I couldn't kill her. A reason why I wanted to touch her ivory skin. I was so close. *Damn!* So close to ruining any chance of contacting my brothers. I could fight this attraction. She was merely a child. A child who needed to grow up and mature. A child who was nothing more to me than a place for me to stay until I got better. I flapped my wings higher and felt my side. It was healing now.

I was healing now.

It wouldn't be long before I could leave.

It wouldn't be long before I killed her.

It wouldn't be long before the ritual began.

It wouldn't be long before there was nothing left of the world but my brothers and I. The Horsemen. The thought made my stomach tighten. *That's why I was chosen, right?* I knew it was but it made my body quake and I wasn't sure why?

e∕∋e∕∋

Lizzie

"Earth to Lizzie," Millie said, waving her hand full of Cheez-Its in front of my face.

"Huh?"

Trevor squeezed my hand from under the lunch room table. "You seem a little out of it today. Are you okay?"

"She's seemed out of it since Monday. It's Wednesday, Lizzie, time to get better, comrade."

I faked a smile. "I'm fine, just tired."

Brett chugged down the rest of his chocolate milk and wiped his milk mustache off. His shaggy blond hair moved when he shook his head. "But we were talking about the game Friday while you were in some other world. Do you want to go with Millie and meet up for the tailgate afterwards?"

I nodded. "Of course, that should be fun."

Not that I didn't think it would be fun to spend time with all of them, but I couldn't stop thinking about Darrton. I hadn't seen him since Sunday. He had been eating the food I set out, but I never saw him. It made my stomach feel sick. *Where was he? Was he off killing someone?* The entire situation was making my head hurt but just knowing he was roaming around scared me. What scared me more was that his "brothers" had to have his presence to perform this ritual. *What if his brothers come here?*

"Also," Millie said. "I was thinking it might be time for a movie night. My parents are going loco about my room so maybe we could do it at your house?"

I choked on my Kool-Aid. "My house? I'm sorry, have you met my family?"

Millie rolled her eyes. "Your dad is never there, your mom doesn't care, and Samantha...well we can handle that little wench."

I sighed and covered my face. "I can ask my mom tonight."

Brett nudged Millie and she gave him I'm-getting-to-it glare. "Um how about you call her now and ask?"

"You want to do it tonight? Why?"

She shrugged. "I have a Spanish test coming back tomorrow that I failed. If we wait until Thursday, they will say no. But by Friday they will have forgotten so I can go to the game. Just call her, Lizzie."

Trevor glanced around and put his hand on mine to stop me from pulling out my phone. "Mrs. Ought's at two o'clock. Maybe go to the bathroom?"

I looked over my shoulder. Mrs. Ought was patrolling the cafeteria. "Okay, guys, you owe me."

"Oh, comrade, you know we love you."

"You better," I mumbled under my breath as I walked toward the bathroom.

There was no one in the bathroom. I checked like three times, looking under the stalls.

I dialed my mom's number. "Hey, Mom."

"Hey, Lizzie. Is everything all right? I'm kind of getting groceries right now. Did you start your period again and forget a tampon?"

I groaned. "No, Mom. I had another question. Do you think it would be okay for Millie, Trevor, Brett, and me to have a movie date tonight at the house?"

She giggled into the phone. "Of course, Lizzie. Why wouldn't it be? Oh! I can make some of those asparagus cookies you guys liked so much last time."

Gag me. "Uh, maybe some chocolate chip ones instead? Millie is allergic." *A little lie won't hurt.*

"Damn and I know you and your sister liked those so much. I'll just make some of those, too!" she said.

I rolled my eyes. "Okay, Mom. I have to go. I'm in the bathroom talking to you. See you when I get home."

"Bye, bye, hon."

Whew. Thank God, that's over.

"Bravo, Lizzie."

Oh shit.

I turned around and glanced at Rachel. She was standing near the doorway. She was tapping her high-heeled toe on the floor and clapping her hands. "Got a date with Trevor tonight, huh?"

I slid my phone into my pocket and shrugged. "What's it to you?"

She smiled and took a step toward me. "Trevor doesn't belong with someone like you. He is just confused. Don't get your feelings hurt when he comes back to me, crawling on his knees."

"Okay, Rachel, when he does, I'll even let you say '*I told you so.*'"

She gritted her teeth and pushed her platinum hair from her shoulder. "Listen here, you little bitch. You keep thinking that he won't leave, and you'll be crying in a few weeks when he comes back."

I rolled my eyes. "Okay, Rachel. Have an awesome day," I said, walking past her.

She pushed her shoulder into mine, walked toward the stall, and slammed the door.

Freak.

Millie was feeding Brett Cheez-Its when I got back. "Oh, hey what did she say?"

I sighed. "Just pretend to be allergic to asparagus cookies."

She threw her head back and laughed. "That a girl, comrade."

ℯ❀ℯ❀

"He is *not* too old for me!" Samantha shouted at Millie.

I banged my head up against the wall mirror in my room. Samantha was red-faced and had her hands clenched around a Justin Beiber CD.

Millie smiled. "He is, Samantha. He is so too old for you and would never even think about dating you."

Samantha stomped her foot. "Take it back!" she screamed.

Millie crossed her arms and shook her head. "Nope."

Samantha ran over to my bed and snatched Millie's cell. "Well, let's see how Brett would like to find out that you're in love with a guy named Jake!"

Millie's face turned serious. "I don't know a Jake."

Samantha smiled. "But he won't know that," she said, dangling Millie's cell in front of her.

"Give it back, you little brat."

Millie chased Samantha around my room for a while before I stood up, grabbed the cell phone, and kicked

Samantha in the butt, out the door, and shut it behind her. "How old are you?" I asked.

Millie snatched her cell. "She is the devil, Lizzie."

I nodded. "I know, but just cut it out."

Millie rolled her eyes. "You've been so grouchy lately."

I sighed. *I have been.* The truth was I was worried to death. It was Wednesday night and still no sign of Darrton. *Where could he be? There is still war breaking out in Israel and it was only getting worse. This is real.*

"Are you okay? Is there something you want to talk about?"

I looked over at Millie. She was sitting on my bed, her black hair in long curls. She looked so honest. I wanted nothing more than to get down on my knees and tell her. To tell my best friend what was going on. To tell my best friend that Death, one of the Four Horsemen was living in our tree house. But I couldn't.

"No, I'm just tired and sick of school."

Millie nodded. "Are you pms-ing?"

I sighed. "Yes, that's part of it."

Millie nodded. "It's okay. We all go through it."

I nodded and pulled on my necklace. "Yea we all go through it." At seven, there was a knock on the door. Nerves were roaming all over my body, and I couldn't seem to keep my feet still. "Come on, comrade," Millie said and pulled me down the stairs.

Mom was already opening the door. Trevor stood on the other side of it. He shook my mom's hand. "Nice to see you again, Mrs. Lawrence."

"Oh nice to see you, too, Trevor. Come on in. Oh hey, Brett! How are you?"

Brett bent down and kissed my mom's hand. She giggled and let him in. Millie rolled her eyes and elbowed him.

"So, what are you kids watching tonight?"

I looked over toward the TV and Samantha was sitting on the couch, watching Justin Beiber's new movie. "Samantha, get up. We are watching movies in here."

She sighed and stretched out, hogging the entire couch. "I was here first."

"Mom?" I asked.

Mom narrowed her eyes and pointed toward the stairs. "Up to your room, Samantha, now and don't start."

Sam stood up abruptly and stomped up the stairs. Millie snickered under her breath.

"Okay guys," Mom said. "I'm going over to Sally's. It's book club night."

"You're leaving?" I asked, panicked.

"Yes, sweetie, just keep an eye on Samantha. I'll be back later tonight. Both batches of cookies are on the stove for you guys."

Millie coughed as if it was her cue. "Oh thanks for making the chocolate chip, too. I'm deathly allergic to asparagus."

"No problem, dear." She grabbed her keys and walked out of the door.

Millie laughed. "You so have the best Mom ever."

Millie grabbed Brett and pulled him to the couch. She grabbed the remote and turned the channel. I felt as if I couldn't move. *She left us*? I sighed. "What are we watching tonight, ladies and gentlemen?"

"How about, *Just go with it*?" Millie asked.

Brett snorted. "That's a chick flick."

Millie pouted out her lip. "Please," she mumbled into his ear.

"Okay," he said, pulling her closer to him. "You guys going to sit down?"

Trevor grabbed my hand and pulled me along to the love seat next to the couch. Trevor sat down first, placing his arm on the back of the couch. Millie winked at me and nodded her head.

I sat down beside him and he pulled me closer. The movie started and my nerves were all over the place. *Why am I so nervous? I've dated him before.* He was just a boy. Trevor placed his hand on my shoulder and pulled me as close as I could get, without being on top of him.

Brett, not wanting to watch the movie in the first place, couldn't keep his hands off of Millie. She would swat at them but before long she and Brett were lying down, cuddled up and whispering in each other's ear. "Who else thinks this movie is lame?" Brett asked.

Trevor laughed and raised his hand. "I do."

Millie elbowed Brett. "I like it. Don't you, Lizzie?"

I smiled. "I do. I really like it."

Brett snorted. "You two always team up on me. I'm glad Trevor is here to even out the score a little bit."

Trevor leaned up and fist pumped Brett. "Oh yeah, bro. We got this."

Millie and I laughed and she lay back down.

The movie was almost over when Trevor leaned close to my ear and whispered, "Lizzie, you want to go get a cookie with me?"

Alone? A heat was rising up in me. It had been so long since I had been alone with him. "Um, sure."

Trevor rose and I ran my gaze over him. His white button-down shirt was opened two buttons down on the top. I noticed how tight his chest looked underneath it. There was a smirk on his lips and his blue eyes were so intense on me. Millie and Brett were too enthralled with each other that they didn't even notice. He offered me his hand and led me to the kitchen.

The cookies were on the stove with aluminum foil covering them. "I'm guessing you want the chocolate chip?" I asked, looking back and smiling at him.

He was leaning back on the cabinet, a crooked smile on his face. "I don't want a cookie, Lizzie."

A shiver ran down my spine. I furrowed my brows. "Then what do you want?"

He smiled and leaned forward. His thumb brushed against my bottom lip. "I want to kiss you again."

My breath caught in my throat. His fingers slid down my side cupping my hip. His lips touched mine, and I let myself melt inside. I don't know what it was about the kitchen but it seemed we were drawn to make-out in there. Trevor pulled me against him, while he leaned back against the cabinet. He dug his fingers into my back and slid them up the back of my shirt. When he pulled back from me he moaned. *Moaned.*

"I've missed this," he said, his mouth brushing my lips.

"Me, too."

He kissed me again, this time deeper. Trevor turned me around and his lips trailed down my neck. I opened my eyes when I heard something from outside. Darrton was standing in the window, his eyebrow cocked.

Embarrassed, I pushed against Trevor. "Excuse me, Darrton is outside."

Trevor groaned and pulled me to him. "Just leave him out there. He can wait a minute."

"It won't take one minute." I didn't give Trevor a chance to stop me. I went out the back door.

Darrton was leaning up against the back of the house. He had an apple and was nonchalantly eating it.

"Where the hell have you been?" I asked.

"Isn't that Trevor, the one that I told you was bad news?"

I rolled my eyes. "I asked first, where have you been? Killing people?"

Darrton rolled his eyes. "Foolish girl. You think I would tell you if I were? And you wonder why I don't think you are very bright."

I clenched my fist. "Darrton, you can't just come and go. Someone is going to see you coming in and out of our tree house."

He pushed off of the house, tossing the remains of the apple out into the yard and stood in front of me. "I know how to be sneaky and hide and so does your boyfriend."

"What do you have against him?"

He shrugged. "Don't listen to me. I really couldn't care less. I was just trying to help you out since you've helped me out." Darrton turned on his heels and walked toward the tree house.

"Are you staying? Will you be here when I get done?"

He turned and looked at me. "Probably not. Don't worry about me, Lizzie. I can take care of myself. The problem is that you can't."

"Darrton, come back down here! Right now!"

He didn't answer and he didn't come back down.

"Ugh!" I yelled and ran back into the house. Trevor was standing there his arms crossed over his chest.

"Are you okay? You look mad."

I shook my head. "Darrton. He just…" I trailed off not really sure what to say.

"If it's Darrton, then I understand completely." Trevor laughed. "Now, where were we?" He pulled me in and just as his lips brushed mine Millie and Brett walked in.

"Oh! Are we interrupting?" Millie teased.

I pulled away, my face burning, and glared at Millie.

"We came to get some cookies."

I smiled and grabbed both plates. We all walked into the living room. We sat down and passed out the cookies. "So, I can't wait for the concert," Millie said.

Trevor looked over and smiled at me. "I can't either. It's going to be fun." He squeezed my leg and it sent a warm sensation over me.

Millie moved her eyebrows up and down and took a big bite of her cookie. I tried not to let myself blush but I could feel the burn across my cheeks.

"It's going to be kick-ass, dude," Brett said. "Just like that party you missed the other night, Lizzie."

I blushed as Trevor looked out of the corner of his eye at me. We had almost kissed that night. "Next time Aaron has a party, you have to come no matter what," he whispered.

I nodded and smiled. Millie's cell phone made me jump. She rolled her eyes. "It's my mom."

Trevor sighed and glanced over at me. "So I had fun tonight. I really did."

"I really did, too."

I could hear Millie talking to her mother, and Brett laughing, but I couldn't take my eyes off of Trevor. He leaned in and brushed his lips against mine, his hand running along my neck.

I pulled back when Millie said, "I hate to be the bummer but my mom is freaking out. She said the movie should have been over ten minutes ago. The weird part is that the movie was over exactly ten minutes ago. I swear she has an alien in my brain."

I laughed. "Well, are you leaving?"

Millie nodded. "Yea, sorry, Trevor, we have to go. I hate to cut your smooching short and all."

Brett pulled Millie out of the room. "Leave them alone, Millie." He gave us a thumbs-up over their shoulder.

When I looked back at Trevor he was staring at me. "I had fun tonight really, Lizzie. I hope that we can do it again soon."

"Me, too," I whispered, my face turning red.

Trevor pushed my honey-colored hair away from my face and softly kissed my lips again. I'll see you tomorrow at school, all right?"

I smiled, weak-kneed. "Okay."

I watched as Trevor walked out of the kitchen.

"Bye, Lizzie," Millie yelled before shutting the door.

I was a little light-headed when Samantha walked into the kitchen. "About freaking time!" she said, then turned around and went to the living room.

Whatever.

I took my time before I went out to the tree house. I showered, did a little homework, and finally decided to go out. Mom was in bed. Dad had called and said he wouldn't be home until late. Samantha was dancing and singing in her room, so I didn't have to really sneak out.

When I climbed the staircase no one was there. It aggravated me. He was just coming and going as he pleased. I wasn't sure why that bothered me, but I knew it did. He was always gone. *Damn Horseman.*

CHAPTER 7

Lizzie

The next day my history teacher Mr. Shay stood over me, his shadow dropping over my paper, which was filled with nothing but the swirls and doodles I had been drawing during class.

"Ms. Lawrence, I appreciate art as much as the next person, but doodling won't get your classwork done."

I sighed and nodded. "Sorry, I'm getting on it…" I trailed off into silence. There was no concentrating on my work. What I really wanted to say was, *"If you had Death of the Four Horsemen in your back yard you wouldn't be doing you work either, hon!"*

Of course, I didn't say that.

"Does anyone know what the major current event, happening in the world today, is?" Mr. Shay asked, leaning back on his desk and taking a bite out of his apple.

From the front row, a girl's arm shot up. "There is a war in Israel and no one knows the cause."

He nodded and slapped her desk. "Yes. Thank God, one of you watches the news."

"Yeah, better be doing more than thanking God, better be praying to him," I mumbled below my breath.

The rest of the day went by in a blur. Millie got grounded that afternoon so I couldn't hang out with her, Trevor had football practice for the game the next day, and Darrton was...well not at home. All I could do was homework and watch TV. When you had Death of the Four Horsemen in your backyard...TV started to get really old. He never left so suddenly. I wasn't sure why he had. *Maybe he was gone forever?* The thought made my stomach hurt, and I wasn't sure why. I hated that I cared, but I did. He was still injured. His side was in bad shape. *Why would he leave? Had I made him mad? Why the hell did I care?*

It was already Friday and I hadn't spoken to Darrton since Wednesday. Although he sure as hell ate the stuff I left for him, I never saw him. He wasn't there when I went to school, or when I went to bed. There was a nervousness building because of the situation that was starting to make me shake. *Where could he be? Why did he leave? And why the hell did I care?* My phone beeped. I pulled it out and read the text from Trevor. No telling when Trevor had actually sent it. My mother had gotten me a new phone, and it took three freaking hours to get a text message. She'd said, *"This phone is better than no phone."*

See you after the game 2night?

Of course.

You ready to go tailgating afterwards?

Can't wait.

I wasn't lying. I would love to go. But there was this nagging feeling in the back of my mind, and I couldn't put my finger on what it was. *Fear? Loss? Hurt?* None of those were it. It was something deeper, more imbedded in me. The torture of it was that it was right there, roaming around my mind, touching ground, and then speeding off right when I thought I knew what it was. It others words, it was a tease.

Millie had her face painted half red and half white, and had a shirt that said, *These seagulls won't leave anything but skulls!* I cocked an eyebrow as she pointed to her back which had Brett's number painted onto it.

"Where is yours?" she asked as she pulled out of our driveway, clearly not looking behind us at the motorcycle that was slamming on its brakes to keep from hitting her. She flipped him the bird out of the window.

"Mine is back at home with your dignity."

"Funny, comrade! You know you want to rep yo man!"

No matter what the situation was Mille could make me laugh. Even if our world was actually spinning to an end and I couldn't tell anyone about it. I laughed anyway. "Okay, Malibu, let's just try to get to the game in one piece."

"I've got this, babe. I am an excellent driver."

I snorted. "Right."

The stadium lights were shining brightly as we pulled into the parking lot. "Whoa! Game time, bitches!" Millie yelled, and I secretly wished to be any place else. "We are so going to get—Hey!" she screamed as a white motorcycle skidded toward us, stopping only a foot away. "Listen, punkass, I can fight and I'm not afraid to beat your ass!"

"Millie," I whispered. "It's the guy you flipped off. I would tone the gangster shiznit down a bit, hon."

The rider kicked out the kickstand, propped his bike up, and tossed his helmet on the back of his bike. "Ladies, I think we might need to learn some manners. Girls are not supposed to act like that, now are they?" the guy asked. His light eyes were squinted and looking directly at us. He then flashed a brilliant smile, stood up, and walked toward us, his long, lean body graceful and nonchalant.

Millie scoffed and rolled her eyes. "So, 'big dog,' you think you're a charmer, now do you? Why don't you go get some ass or smoke a joint?"

He narrowed his eyes and cocked his head to the side, stroking his chin. I tried to make a mental picture of him. He had short blonde hair, a ring on his ring finger. He had a wide nose and was good looking. "You're not very nice, now are you? Lucky for you, I don't like nice."

"Not so lucky for you that I am about two seconds away from keying that nice little white bike over there."

He tossed his head back and laughed. It was sing-song like. "You," he said, nodding in my direction, "why is a pretty, respectable—" He looked at Millie. "—girl like you hanging around with a hoodlum like that?"

My mouth felt dry all of the sudden and I felt threatened. There was something off about this guy. The way his smile seemed to creep up his face. He took a step forward and my body shivered. He was bad, and somehow he oozed menace, but I couldn't put my finger on how I knew. I picked up a piece of gravel and threw it at him. "Leave us alone!" I said, loudly.

Millie gawked and the guy, with his bright eyes, grabbed his jaw and glared back at me.

"Hey, is there a problem over here?" A police car from the school crept up beside us, with its window rolled down.

"None at all, officer," the guy said. "Just going to watch these Seagulls whoop some tail."

The officer moved off. The guy gave us the finger and left.

"Jerk," I mumbled.

Millie slapped my back and laughed. "Remind me not to ever get on your bad side you might hit me with a rock."

The stands were crowded with high school kids making out, throwing popcorn, or screaming at the top of their lungs. Rachel was a few rows in front of us. She and her "posse" would look back at us and laugh.

"I'm sure it's not that funny," Millie said, yelling over to them.

The team ran onto the field a blur of red and white, the crowd roared. Millie was screaming when the referee blew his first whistle. Then an utter silence fell over the crowd as the first play went down. I knew Trevor. How could I not? He was the tall and lean one. He was the fastest one out there. He ran, looking back over his shoulder, and caught the ball. Everyone began to scream again and, I can't lie, I was a little excited myself. Then he fell. The crowed groaned.

"Maybe next time," Millie said. And it seemed like she said that the entire game. There wasn't a play where Trevor didn't fall on his face, get tackled from out of nowhere, drop the ball, or get smashed by ten guys. I was beginning to think the only reason girls liked him was because he was cute. He was so not doing well.

Glancing around the crowd, I looked over at the visiting side. There were black and white shirts and cheerleading uniforms jumping up and down in the stands. It wasn't until I looked toward the field house in the near distance that I notice Darrton. He was leaning up against the fence leading toward the bathroom. Darrton's head was slightly tilted in an arrogant position. His shirt was tight to his chest and his jeans low on his hips Out of all the people in the stands, he was looking at me and smiling. It wasn't until Trevor tripped again that I realized what was happening. The douche bag was making him fall.

What an ass.

I had all the best intentions in the world to get up and go after him, but when I looked back over to the fence, he was gone.

My mouth opened to say something to Millie but I shut it, remembering I couldn't tell her anything. It tore a little piece of my heart out. She was my best friend and she knew nothing about what was happening right next to her. On the other hand I couldn't have said anything to her anyway. She was too busy in her own little football world. Mille was an awesome friend but not an awesome football partner. She laughed when the other team's players got injured and would stand up at random times and scream, "We love the Seagulls! Go, Number 35!"

She always wondered when she sat down why she had to scoot closer to me to tell me something. I'd been scooting away from her every time she stood up and screamed. She was steadily munching on Cheez-Its she'd brought from home and laughing every time someone fell or fumbled. I smiled to myself. *Maybe she is better off not knowing.*

I watched Trevor run back to the bench and take a seat. I frowned as the coach walked toward him and started yelling. Trevor had his head in his hands. "Poor, Trevor," I mumbled. When the whistle blew Millie started laughing. When I looked back at the field there was one of the other team's players lying on the field. "Millie, that's not funny."

She was bent over, laughing. "Brett tackled his ass."

I rolled my eyes and glanced around again, looking for Darrton. He wasn't anywhere to be seen. When I looked back over at Millie I noticed the crazy motorcycle guy sitting a few rows down from us. He was sitting by himself and eating some popcorn. A shiver ran down to my toes. *Something isn't right about him.*

Millie was still laughing when the guy turned around and looked up at me. There was a white glare in his eyes. I dropped my drink bottle, which was in my hands, and it snapped Millie out of her laughter. She followed my gaze and snarled. She flipped him off and yelled, "See that guy out on the field? My boyfriend did that to him. You're going to be next if you don't turn your ass around." She made a sound of disgust as the guy winked at us. Bending down, she picked up my drink, because I was still frozen in place looking at the guy. "Don't worry about him, he is a creeper," she said. "Oh hey, Trevor is playing again." She clapped her hands and yelled, "Go Trevor!"

I tried to steady my nerves. There was still something bothering me about that guy. He wasn't normal.

Trevor and Brett were high-fiving some of the other players and walking toward the field house when we met them on the field. Brett wrapped Millie into a bear hug and showed the same enthusiasm as she had been, minus the screaming.

Trevor was smiling at me and then he stopped. "What's wrong?" he asked.

I shook my head. "Nothing. Why?"

He took a step closer to me. "You seem down?"

"Ah! Some guy was harassing us in the parking lot earlier."

"Who?" he asked.

I shrugged and placed my head on his sweaty shoulder. "Have no idea and right now, I don't care. Let's go to this bonfire and have fun."

He kissed the top of my head. "I like the sound of that."

"Hey, are you okay?" I asked. "You seemed to be off tonight."

He scratched his forehead, pushing his matted, sweaty hair out of his face. "Yeah, it's like the ball was slicked with grease and so were my shoes. I couldn't stay up or catch anything. I kind of feel like an ass."

"It's okay. It doesn't matter to me, anyway."

He smiled. "That's what I like about you."

CHAPTER 8

Lizzie

The bonfire was in the woods on the backside of one of the team player's parents' property. The fire was blazing by the time we got there. All the vehicles were backed up toward the fire and everyone was sitting on tailgates or in fold-out chairs.

Trevor drove his dad's pick-up and he, Mille, Brett, and I sat on the tailgate and watched the fire. Trevor sat behind me, his legs dangling beside mine. Leaning back against his chest I took a breath. I knew I shouldn't be thinking about Darrton but I couldn't help it. *Where was he*? I couldn't help but to be worried, even though I tried not to be. I shook my head and focused on the fire that was making a miniature firework show in front of us. *This isn't what I should be thinking about right now.*

One of the team members was singing along on the hood of his truck to some crazy rap song and everyone was falling over laughing about it.

A guy with short spiky hair walked over to us, a red plastic cup in his hand. I'd seen him around before but really didn't know him. Trevor fist bumped him and he smiled. "You were a little off tonight, bro," Red Cup said.

Trevor laughed and nodded. "I have no idea what the hell happened."

Red Cup shrugged. "It happens to the best of us."

The guy took a swig of his drink and furrowed his brow. "Funny how nice and quiet it is over here and all those people overseas are killing one another."

I grimaced. *I wish everyone would just stop talking about it.* "Wars happen all the time," I said, trying to reassure myself more than the others. "We are always at war with someone."

The guy focused his bright eyes toward me and said, "Yeah but people are killing their own family members over there for no reason. We sure as hell don't do that in my family. There is something up with it. Something is wrong and I feel it."

I gritted my teeth. I didn't want to hear another damn word about it. "Why would you think that? You have some kind of psychic ability where you know something is wrong?"

Trevor tensed behind me and squeezed my side. "Well," he coughed. "Liz, little kids are trying to kill their parents. You don't think something is wrong with that?"

I shrugged. *Stop talking about it*! Red Cup gave Trevor a what-the-fuck-is-up-with-your-girlfriend face and walked off.

Millie leaned over close to me. "What the hell is wrong with you, comrade?"

Sighing, I raked my fingers through my hair and leaned forward. "Nothing, I'm fine."

"Then what's up with the bitchy attitude, Lizzie? It's not cute on you."

I ignored her and wrapped my arms around my knees. Brett was wide-eyed and, pretending he needed some more beer, left.

Trevor leaned up, squeezed my thigh, and whispered into my ear, "Wanna' take a walk?"

I nodded and jumped down. Anything to distract me. Millie cocked an eyebrow. Her devious smile rose to her lips. "*Protection*," she mouthed and waggled her eyebrows up and down at me.

I sighed in relief. 'What's that?"

She laughed. Millie was the kind of person who would tell you how it was one minute and then forgive you the next. That filter a lot of people had in the brain that says, *Don't say that, it's mean*, well Mililani Rouse didn't have it. She also didn't have a grudging bone in her body, well at least toward me. She was the only person I've ever known who could call you a bitch and then turn around and give you advice or tell you she loved you in the same sentence. She was the one person I could count on to keep me in check. I loved that about her.

Trevor and I pushed our way through the tall grass and walked closer to the woods than I would have preferred. But he put his arm around me, and I felt okay. He pointed toward the moon which was shining brightly. "At least we can see. The moon seemed to know we wanted to take a walk tonight."

I smiled.

"Are you okay?" he whispered as I shielded my face from the wind with the side of his jacket.

"Yeah, I'm fine, why?"

He shrugged and looked off into the distance. "You just seem distracted lately. Not yourself."

"Just tired of school I guess," I lied.

"I feel ya there. Hopefully, this weekend will make you feel better."

I nodded. "I'm sure it will," I lied again.

I snuggled deeper into his side and walked with him. After about ten minutes, he stopped and we sat down by a creek that was trickling through the dark. Sitting down beside me, Trevor gasped, "Wow." He reached toward the ground and pulled up a huge black feather. "What kind of freak of nature would leave this behind?"

I stiffened. *Yeah, what could have? Why was he here? Is he here now?* I looked around and up in the trees. I didn't see him but I didn't have cat eyes either.

"Are you okay?" Trevor asked, holding the feather in his hand.

Just looking at it made that crazy feeling burst in my chest. I picked the feather from his hands and threw it in the creek beside us.

His mouth was partly open and his eyes wide. "Okay," he whispered.

"I just…" He was here. *I can feel him.* Pulling myself up to my knees, I pushed Trevor to the ground and straddled him. *Maybe this will make him so uncomfortable he will leave.*

I kissed Trevor with all I had. I let his fingers dig into my thigh. Taking over, he pulled me off of him and pinned me to the ground below. I was heated all over. I didn't care if Darrton saw or not. *I want him to see.* Trevor pulled off his shirt and his white, tight body was glowing underneath, in the moonlight. I pressed my hips upwards and Trevor ground his into me.

Am I really going to do this? Trevor kissed my neck, and his right hand cupped my left breast. I moaned. *Hell yeah, I'm going to do it.*

Before I knew it my shirt was off. Trevor was kissing my belly and sliding his tongue up my side. The ground below me felt rough but his tongue and touch was too arousing for me to care. Carefully, he slid his hands up to my zipper and peeled my jeans off. The air was cold against my skin but he covered me with his body for warmth.

I heard the howl of a coyote as Trevor unzipped his pants. The sound of the zipper made my body stiffen. We were going to have sex in the woods. Another howl. *No, this isn't right.*

I pushed Trevor off of me as I sat up.

He stared at me. "What's wrong?"

"I can't. Not here. We're in the woods. It's not the right place or time."

He sighed. "I've never brought a girl to the woods. It will be special."

That sentence irked me. *He has never brought a girl here, but he had brought a lot of other girls other places?*

"No, Trevor. It's just not right. I'm not ready."

"Come on," he said, kissing my neck. "I swear if it hurts I'll stop," he breathed into my ear.

Is he not hearing me? "Did you not hear me? I said I didn't want to. I'm not scared it will hurt. I just don't want to have sex."

He jerked his head back. "You're kidding, right?"

"No! I'm not kidding! I'm not ready. I do not want to have sex with you!"

He laughed. "Then why did you let me take your clothes off, Lizzie? Didn't you know what would happen? Are you that naive…"

I zoned out while he was giving me a long lecture about blue balls and all this stupid shit I didn't care about, when I heard a distant sound and it was getting closer. *What is that? Thunder?*

"...I really like you and if it hurts I can always stop. I'll pull it..." He trailed off into silence while a dark shadow was cast over the ground.

I shivered. *Please no.*

I didn't even hear him land but I saw him behind Trevor. His wings retracted and he had a crazy, hungry, dark look in his pale eyes. "When is it okay to try and force a lady into intercourse, son?"

Trevor jumped up. His eyes were wide in fear and surprise. "I've had all I can take of your crazy ass. Come on." He balled his hands up into fists. "Let's duke it out. Let's get this over with."

Ah shit! I stood up. "No, you guys, just stop. There is nothing more to talk about. I'm not having sex with you, Trevor. Get over it, take me home, and Darrton..." A shiver ran down my spine as I said his name. "You can just go home. Everything is fine."

Trevor looked as if I'd pissed him off a little more. "No, we're not done. This whole situation is messed up. This guy is your cousin and acts like he is a freaking prince charming coming to your rescue." He pulled his fists up and took a swing at Darrton. He missed. *What the hell is wrong with him?* A sickening vibe ran down my body. Why was he acting this way? *To think I'd really liked him.*

"Come on just stop—" I pulled at Trevor and he pushed me back against the tree. My skin above my underwear line hit the tree and I felt blood start to ooze out.

Darrton's eyes landed on mine and a snarl rose on his lips. The length of time it took Darrton to knock Trevor out was the time it took me to blink. When I looked back up, Trevor was lying, shirtless, on the ground, and was sound asleep.

Darrton didn't say a word to me. He bent down and whispered something into Trevor's ear. I stood up, suddenly aware of my clothing, or lack thereof, and even though I was freezing a burst of warmth surged through me. Darrton stepped toward me and picked me up. Without a word he broke his wings free and shot up toward the sky. I had no choice but to grab a hold of him. His dark, musky scent was intoxicating. The wind blew through our hair. We were above the trees now, watching the ground grow smaller and smaller. I was in the arms of a Horseman.

Darrton stood on the tree limb closest to the window and pulled both of us into the bedroom. When he set me down, I couldn't do anything but stare at him. The house was quiet and I could hear the crickets from outside, chirping. Standing there in my underwear and bra I crossed my arms across my chest.

My eyes were burning from the tears trying to escape. I wasn't one hundred percent sure why I was crying, but I knew it was mainly because of Trevor. I had liked him for so long, and he treated me like that. Not that I didn't take my clothes off, but no means no. *He tried to force me*? I tried to shake everything out of my head. Darrton was right. He wasn't right for me. I would never mention it to him or say anything about it. I couldn't. My heart hurt too much to deal with Trevor right then, I had other things to worry about anyway.

"Where have you been?" What a dumb thing to ask after he'd just kicked Trevor's butt and considering the current situation. "And what was up with the commotion today? You made Trevor lose any chance at a college scholarship, not that I give a damn now, but just saying."

He didn't answer. He just stood there, his wings tucked in around his back and his face an emotionless mask. I was secretly waiting for him to say *I told you so.*

"Don't you know where you have been?" I asked.

His dark hair fell in front of his face when he stepped closer. "Did you want to?" he asked.

"Want to what?" I asked.

"Sleep with him?"

My mouth gaped open. "You heard me tell him no. Why do you want me to say it again?" My face was a burning. I threw my hands up in the air and then pulled them back down when I remembered the cut on my back.

"I want to hear you say it," he said.

I shivered. "No."

He took a step closer. The raw-earth smell was musky and it covered him. "Say it. Say you don't want him."

"Why?" I yelled. "What's it to you?"

Darrton shook his head and sniffed the air. He walked around me and looked at the cut on my lower back. He knelt beside me. Ignoring me, he brushed his fingertips across my bleeding cut and I felt it start to heal.

I turned toward him and put my hand on his shoulder as he tried to rise, keeping him down on his knees. "Why? Why do you care? You left without a word. Ignoring me, not showing your face, just eating, and taking the clothes I set out for you? And then you swoop in and take Trevor out—"

"He would have talked you into it."

Shaking my head, I laughed without humor. "No, I don't want him anymore." It slipped from my lips and I bit my tongue.

"Why is that, child?"

"I'm not a child and you know it. Stop acting like I am, when deep down you don't see me as a child." My hand was shaking as I watched Darrton's jaw moved.

"No, you're not a child." He shook his head. "Not at all."

Darrton leaned forward and touched the side of my head. His mouth was very close to mine. Death was staring me in the face and I wasn't scared. I didn't want to move.

An irritated sigh slipped from his lips and he pulled back. "Maybe you should clothe yourself. I'm a Horseman, but I'm still a male."

My body quaked at that. *Yes, you are*! I stood there for a minute. *What just happened*? Had he tried to kiss me and changed his mind? Did my breath stink? I quickly thought back on what all I had eaten that day. *Or maybe he is trying to be respectful. Since Trevor did try and force himself on me, after I said no.*

I finally got off the bed and went to my closet. I pulled on a wife beater and a pair of sweats. Darrton had his fingers interlaced and resting on his knee when I came back out. "Something's wrong?"

He nodded.

I pushed my toe into the plush rug beside my bed. "Do I want to know?"

"Probably not."

"Well, I guess, tell me anyway."

"I found a trace of someone here. I sensed them again tonight at the game. They have all found each other. Now they're here to retrieve me." He twisted his ring. "This isn't the first time they have visited, but this time they haven't made themselves known. My brothers are checking on me."

I pointed down to his ring. "What is that? Can I see?" Grabbing his hand I tried to pull it off, but it wouldn't budge. "Have you gained weight?" I teased.

He rolled his eyes. "It's not meant to come off. It's forever there, engraved into me."

"Is that how you know they are here?"

He nodded. "Yes and no. I feel them when one of them is near. Also, the ring has been weighing down on me lately. It also has been scorching me. It's letting me know it's time. They connect with me through the ring. We can communicate mentally."

"Time to what?" He didn't answer. But I knew. *Kill. Destroy. Bring The Apocalypse.* "Have you seen them? How many? Which ones?"

Darrton reached over and patted my hand, "Don't you worry about it, okay?" he said, reassuring me. "I will make sure you and your family stay safe. You don't deserve what they will try to make me do to you."

I could see he was telling the truth this time. I didn't know how but I knew. He left and I wanted to grab after him. *Why, Lizzie? Why reach after...Death?*

CHAPTER 9

Darrton

The evening air was cool on my bare back but I had a heat rising in my body that I had never experienced before. I had stroked her, and it felt so damn good. Touching her face was like my own personal Heaven. Leaving her was my own personal Hell.

I climbed up the ladder to the tree house and sat on the cot.

"Bravo, Brother." I heard Warren's voice and bile tried to rise from my stomach. "Why did you stop? You could have had her." He seemed pleased when he walked out from the corner of the room. "She's an appealing little thing, too."

A shiver ran down to my toes. *He is here? So close to Lizzie?* God, there was a sickening feeling rising from my gut. It hadn't been long since I had seen Warren, but I hadn't done anything he had asked. I had not moved away from Lizzie or killed her. I was secretly hoping not to see him for a while longer. I couldn't kill her. There was something about her. She helped me. She didn't deserve to die, because I dragged her into this. *Why does it matter*? I couldn't understand why I cared but I knew I did.

I finally found my voice. "Brother," I said, standing. "You're here. Back so soon?"

He picked at his nail and smiled. "I'm here. Looks like you have a wonderful house here." He gestured around.

"It gets the job done."

He leaned his head back and really looked at me. "So, how are we to do it since you have yet to succeed?"

"Do what?"

"Kill the miss. She knows too much and it's time to go. Not that you have been looking for us. It's time for the ritual and you know the procedure. You have to be there, Darrton. It has begun to irk me that you have not killed this girl, or moved, and have delayed our plans. However, I am trying to give you the benefit of the doubt. Your wound seems like it has healed itself, brother."

Wrath built up in my chest. "Looks like you haven't needed my help. You have destroyed Israel." I tried to keep off the "Lizzie" subject.

"Ah, older brother. That is what is so great. One down, many more to go." He nodded and his face was anything but pleasant. A leather bound jacket was wrapped around him and he seemed so different.

"So, Brother, what will it be?"

"A stoning," Caden, *Conquest*, said from the window. He laughed and stepped inside. "Since she likes to throw rocks at people, I say a stoning."

Had he had an encounter with her? He held a motorcycle helmet in his hand and he tossed it onto my cot.

"That sounds great, Brother," said Warren.

Caden scanned the room. "Where is Ferdia? Have you heard from him?"

"He hasn't been here, I haven't heard anything from him," I said.

All the while Warren had been staring at me. "Something has changed about you, Darrton. Something's very different. I'm not sure if I like it yet or not." He picked up a bat from the corner, tossed it up, and caught it.

"Nothing is different, brother."

Caden laughed and pushed his blond hair from his face. "I think I see it, too. Maybe a good killing will get you back on your toes, dear brother. We wouldn't want you slacking on your job. You've only killed once since you arrived, if I'm correct. The little sneak trying to spy on the girl?"

I cringed and clenched my jaw. "I have changed my plans, brothers," I tried to say as calmly as I could.

Caden raised an eyebrow. "How so?"

"I do not plan to kill Lizzie."

Warren focused in on my face. "I see a little bit of a bond has built up. It's pissing me off a little, Brother."

"I just believe that she would not tell and there's no need to start here. We would go across the sea…"

Caden snarled, "You want to keep this girl safe? Why is that?' He walked toward me. "What could possess you to keep her safe out of everyone in the world? Do you desire to court her?"

Before I could answer, Warren said, "I believe he does, Caden. I believe he would like to do much more than court her, though. I witnessed a little scene before you arrived. I thought it might be too much for someone to watch without blushing. I believe Darrton has fallen in love with this mortal."

Caden grinned. "Too bad she has to perish. We will kill her, Darrton. No arguing about it. She has to die. We might give you some more time to spend with the child." Caden smiled and cocked his head. "Does anyone else know? That awful best friend with the vulgar mouth?"

My body was shaking too hard to answer. "Ah, who cares if she does or doesn't know? We can kill her, too," Warren added nonchalantly.

"We will not, and I won't say it again."

Caden raised his head, reached out, and gripped my neck with his bare hand. "What did you say? Are you trying to go back on our bargain? We do not take too kindly to that, Darrton. We swore to one another that no matter the consequences we would stick to the plan. Getting damned to Earth was hard enough, but we all stuck through it. Now, there is no turning back, my dear sweet brother."

I tried to reach out to him but his grip was so strong on my neck, his fingers crushing my airway.

"What shall we do to show him how we view traitors, brother?"

Warren walked closer and stroked his chin. "I'm sure we will think of something...ah! I think I have it...dear brother." My breath was coming in short gasps and I watched as Warren stepped toward the window. His hands moved over toward the house and I choked out a scream. "Let's see how much Daddy loves his children." Warren snapped his fingers and when I opened my eyes we were in the living room. Caden still held me by the shoulders and I watched as Lizzie's dad walked in from the hallway.

His eyes were glazed over and as much as I yelled at him he couldn't hear me. He slid past us into the kitchen without as much as a glance in our direction. He fumbled through the drawers until he pulled out a shining silver butcher knife. I yelled at him but he never stopped. Knife beside him, he walked zombie-like up the stairs. I cringed as I heard her door open. I tried to get away to follow and stop him, but Caden held me tight.

"Looks like Daddy just can't stop it, now can he? He can't fight the feeling within him to kill. What a pity." Warren snapped and we were in her room. The butterfly painting shimmered in the moonlight on the wall. Her chest rose and fell at a steady rate.

Her dad stood beside the bed. The knife in his hand, he was staring at Lizzie as though looking right through her. He held the knife up high above his head. I tried to move but couldn't get loose. He drove the knife into Lizzie's chest, and she let out a piercing scream.

"Okay, I'll go with you. I'll do whatever you want. Please stop making him hurt her."

She was convulsing at this point, a look of panic-struck confusion was written all over her pure face. Her blood was dripping down her white T-shirt and she was clinging to it. "Dad, what's happening to me?" He didn't answer, only stood there looking down at his murder weapon, before driving it into the other side of her neck. She screamed and fell to the floor.

"Make it stop, make it stop!"

Warren snapped his fingers.

The scene was gone.

Lizzie lay there, her chest rising and falling in perfect rhythm and her dad nowhere in sight. I dropped to the floor and coughed so hard and deep it drew up blood. When I looked back up we were in the tree house. Caden and Warren wore emotionless faces.

"You see what might happen when you don't keep up your end of the bargain?" Warren asked.

My jowl tightened and I nodded. Caden walked toward me and spoke low, "We meet tomorrow afternoon at Haystack Rock. Be there. And if the girl is not dead, we will know."

A splitting sound erupted and Warren drew open his wings. "Darrton," I turned and looked at him. "She better be dead."

Caden threw his head back and laughed while he jumped from the window. Warren burst from the open door into the sky.

Hearing Caden's motorcycle, I jumped down from the tree-house. I had to save her. I had to hide her.

CHAPTER 10

Lizzie

Saturday morning came bright and early. My bed had never seemed so comfortable, in like ever. I stretched and pulled my muscles as I yawned, sneezing when I felt something brush up against my nose. Then I felt something tickle my cheek. Turning my head, I felt something soft and little, brush up against my cheek again. Beside me a butterfly sat on my pillow, floating his wings on and off of my cheek. I gasped.

Sitting up, I examined it without touching it. It had black eyes on its wings. It was beautiful. Another tickle came from my arm. As I looked over, I noticed they were everywhere. The contours of my room stood out in a rainbow of different colored butterflies. *How did they get in here?*

I was laughing at myself when I heard a slight chuckle. Darrton stood by my window, leaning against the wall. His hair was pulled back into a low ponytail. He had on low-rise jeans and a snug white T-shirt. "Did you do this?" I asked, sitting up looking around the room.

He nodded. "Yes."

"Thank you," I whispered.

He nodded. "I have another favor to ask you, Lizzie."

I sighed. *Too good to be true. Shouldn't I be scared of you?* "What is it?"

"It is not really of the favor kind, but an order. We have to leave."

"We as in whom? You have a mouse in your pocket?" He glanced down into his pockets like he might actually look. "It's just an expression, Darrton. It means I'm not coming with you."

He furrowed his brow. "I've packed your bag. We have to go." He tossed me some clothes and stood waiting for me to dress.

"You're serious? You think I'm going to just leave my family to go with you?"

"You have no choice. They are coming to kill you."

"You mean them as in the Horsemen? Why would they want to kill me in particular?" I shrugged and walked over to the mirror to tighten my ponytail. A butterfly was perched on the side of the mirror, its wings fluttering in a smooth rhythm.

Darrton grabbed my arm. "We have to leave. They will kill you because you know about us. They will kill you because I won't."

I shivered. That was his job to kill, yet, he wouldn't kill me. *I'm not complaining!* Although, it made my stomach tickle thinking about why he wouldn't. He did almost kiss me last night and...

"Lizzie—" he said, interrupting my thoughts. "We have to go now. Get dressed, you have no choice."

"The hell I don't. I'm not going anywhere with you. What? I'll never see my family again? I couldn't just not ever see my family again."

"If you don't come with me, they will kill your family."

My heart fluttered. They would kill my family? Who would do that? I crossed my arms. "I don't believe you," I lied, "And I'm not going." *He is lying, isn't he?*

Darrton carried me out of the house, over his shoulder, while I screamed into his hand. "Let me go! Darrton, damn it, let me go!"

He tossed me onto his motorcycle and said, "I dare you to move." Bringing my leg over the side I tried to run, but he caught me.

Ugh! "I hate you."

"Good, it will make things easier." He didn't even look at me while he pushed my bag into the back compartment of the bike.

"When did you get this?" I snarled.

He cocked an eyebrow. "I borrowed it."

I sighed. "You mean stole?"

"Borrowed," he said, straddling in front of me.

"Do you plan on bringing it back?"

"Sorry, can't hear you over the sound of my new motorcycle."

I shook my head. *Thief.*

"Wrap your arms around me," he said through his helmet.

Hesitating I wrapped my arms around his waist. I locked my fingers and felt a snap. I tried to pull my hands apart but felt cold metal around them. Handcuffs.

"You let me go, Darrton," I screamed.

He shook his head through the helmet and revved the engine. Glancing back to my house, I felt a sting. *Is this it? Would I ever see my family again? Would I ever eat Mom's bad cooking, fight with Samantha, or eat pizza with Dad?* Where was he going to hide me? Was he really going to kill me? I shivered as the late August air brushed my skin. We were leaving and I didn't even know when or if I was coming back. *I guess I should be a little more upset.*

As much as I tried to be sad about leaving, as much as I tried to be scared…I just couldn't. I felt safe and I knew I shouldn't. I knew my family would be safer without me than with me right now. *I would be back, right?*

At some point I must have fallen asleep. When I awoke from a long and unpleasant ride on the back of the motorcycle, I saw the green population sign for Vancouver, Washington, population 161,791. Well, for the next few days it would be 161,793. *Well I think two days. Two weeks? Oh God! What if I never come back?*

"Are you awake, Lizzie?" Darrton screamed over the roar of the engine.

I nodded against his shoulder and nonchalantly tried to pull my hands free. *Damn it.* "Yeah, unfortunately."

"We have to pull in for some gas. We are almost there."

"Where is there?"

"There is a valley close by where we can setup camp."

"I'm not staying in a valley. What the heck? I'm not staying in the woods, either. We need somewhere else to go."

Darrton set his lips into a hard straight line. "Do you have taverns here?"

"A tavern, like a motel?"

His silence told me he had no idea what I was talking about. "Like some place that has rooms we can rent out for the night?"

I nodded. "A motel."

"Good that is where we are going then."

I stiffened. *Wait. Alone? No supervision. My mom would be freaking right now. Wait. I'm supposed to be freaking right now, too.*

Darrton pulled into the gas station and popped the kickstand up. I felt him as he unlocked the handcuffs and I grabbed my wrist and held them. He stood up and waited.

"What?" I asked.

He gestured at the gas pump. "Well, show me how to do it."

I lifted a brow. "You can drive but you can't pump gas?"

"The guy that sold me the bike showed me how to drive it. He thought I was crazy because I was an adult and didn't know how to drive. I didn't want him to think I was any denser, so I didn't ask how to get gas. Now, are you going to show me or not?"

I hid a laugh and talked him through the steps of pumping the gas. I pointed him in the direction to go pay and he disappeared inside. I was waiting for him beside his bike when I felt my phone vibrate. Making sure Darrton wasn't looking, I checked my phone. A text from Millie. *Where are you? Everyone is freaking out, comrade. Trevor is flipping his lid. Kings of Leon tonight?*

What the hell? Did Trevor think that I was still going to that stupid concert with him after he basically tried to rape me? I slide my phone back into my pocket before Darrton came back from paying for the gas.

He pointed toward the bike. "Get on. We only have ten more miles."

I crossed my arms. "Darrton, a couple of questions, hon. First off, what did you say to Trevor after you knocked him out? Secondly, what comes after the hotel? Are we going to run forever? I mean, I have to graduate, and these guys…Horsemen…things won't chase us, will they?"

Darrton held the bridge of his nose with his fingers and sighed. "First, Trevor has no memory of any of that ever happening. I made him forget. Secondly, I have a plan and you don't need to worry about it right now. I've asked directions and I know where I am going."

I placed my hands on my hips. "Tell me now or I'll scream."

He cocked an eyebrow. "Are we three?"

"Are we a kidnapper?"

"Nicely done," he smiled.

I bit my tongue to keep from smiling and gestured at him. "Well, tell me."

He leaned forward on the bike's handles. "Tell you what? I will make you a bargain. If you come without a fight, I swear to you, when we get settled I will reveal my plan to you."

I clicked my tongue and debated. "Deal," I said, offering my hand.

He shook it. "Now, get on."

I sat down and held on. He snapped the handcuffs.

Ass.

When we pulled up to the motel, I noticed the sign *Homewood Suites. At least it isn't a rat motel.* Darrton parked, unlocked my handcuffs and kicked his kickstand out.

I whistled. "Hope you're paying, babe."

"I wouldn't be a gentleman if I did not."

A warmth spread across my body. Darrton took my bag out from the back of the bike and began walking toward the doors. "Aren't you coming?"

I nodded. "Yeah," I caught up with him, "How are you paying for this? And how did you pay for the bike? How do you have money?"

He shrugged. "We have our ways."

I stopped. "You stole money!" I yelled out.

A man emptying his trunk glanced over at us, saw Darrton, and pretended to be looking at someone behind us.

"Of course not. I may kill but I'm not a thief. I earned it."

"Doing what?" I asked, hand on my hip.

"Playing cards."

I cocked and eyebrow. "Cards? When did you have time to play cards?"

"Texas hold 'em, and I had time when I was away for the few days. I may be a Horsemen but I am not stupid. I know how to get a ride, or fly where I need to go. Cards have been around for ages. I do pretty well for myself." He nodded and gestured for me to go ahead. *Hmm, a Horsemen that can play cards? What is the world coming to?*

The sliding doors opened for us and the brightly lit lobby was cozy and well sized. A lady in a nicely ironed polo smiled at us. "Welcome to Homewood Suites, how may I help you two this evening?"

"We need a chamber for the night."

She looked confused.

"He means a room," I said.

She smiled but I could see the hesitation on her face. It wasn't until I really looked at her that I noticed she was questioning Darrton and I being together. "May I see your license, sir?"

Oh no. He reached into his low rise jeans and pulled out his license. *Where on earth did he get that?*

She eyed it and looked over at me. "And yours, ma'am?"

Darrton glanced back at me and gestured for me to give it to her. *I'm only seventeen! She is going to call the cops!*

I pulled out my wallet and slid my card along the countertop. Darrton thumped his fingers.

The lady looked down at my card and sighed. "Okay," she said with a bright smile. "You look much younger than you are, ma'am."

Clueless, I looked up at Darrton but he acted like he didn't see me. *What did that thing say*?

The woman went to clicking on the computer and I glared up at Darrton who smiled. "I thought he had kidnapped you or something, dear," she said. "You do not look twenty-one."

That's because I'm not!

This should have made me feel better but I was wound so tight that a sigh of relief was so out of the question.

"Here you go, sir. Room 313. You and your wife have a lovely time."

Wife!

Darrton pressed the elevator button. He was looking everywhere but at me. He had a smile on his face that looked more like he was holding back a laugh.

My patience was running thin. "Wife, huh? So, you don't steal but you make fake IDs?"

Darrton glanced over at me, his eyes narrowed. "This is for your safety, Liz. I have to keep you safe now."

Wow who could argue with that? The elevator beeped and we both stepped in.

Darrton pressed three and I watched as the light moved up the wall. "You're different, Darrton," I said, pushing my toe against the floor.

"How so?"

I looked over at him. He was leaning up against the wall, hair pulled back into a low ponytail. He looked...normal. He never did at first. He'd looked...mean. He'd looked like...death.

"You're not mean. You're not scary. That black stuff around you isn't there anymore."

He cocked an eyebrow. "You're complaining because I'm not being mean to you?"

I rolled my eyes. "I'm not complaining," I said, while exiting the elevator. "I'm just pointing it out. Are you changing to…a human?"

He snorted and walked along the hallway stopping in front of our door. "That can't happen. I'm not here to turn human. I'm here to kill, Liz." He turned toward me and I could see it was a lie. "Don't ever forget that."

We walked through the kitchenette area. I dropped my bag on the chair and stopped. "Where is the other bed?" I gasped, choking on my words.

Darrton cocked his eyebrow and looked at the bed. "Maybe that was all that they had left? Or maybe because we are married?" He shrugged and held back a smile like it was no big deal or anything.

"But we're not."

"But they thought we were." He slide off his shoes and sighed. He looked like he hadn't gotten a lot of sleep or something. "I will sleep on the couch, Lizzie."

"What's going on that you're not telling me? And why are we here? Do we plan on running away forever? I have to go home, Darrton. I have a family and friends. I have to go back to school. I can't stay on the run for the rest of my life."

He pressed his finger to his lips and sat down on the bed. "Elizabeth," he said and it sent a shiver down my spine. My whole name coming out of his mouth made my stomach twist. "I'm keeping you safe. It's because of me that you're in danger and I should have never involved you. I will take care of everything. They aren't after your family, they will leave them alone. They are after you, but you're safe with me."

"Okay, so why are we here though?"

"I'm looking for someone."

"Who?"

He sighed and ran his fingers down the length of his face. I started to play with my nail. "His name is Ian."

"Is he one of the Horsemen? 'Cuz I don't think that is such a good idea."

"Of course he is not. He is an angel."

I stopped and looked up at him. "What do you mean, angel?"

"He is fallen. A fallen angel. I knew him before he fell. He is like us, damned. Ian died a long time ago. Every time an angel is damned, everyone in Heaven knows. It is a horrible punishment to be damned."

Leaning up against the desk behind me I watched Darrton's face. "Why was he damned? The same reason as you?"

He shook his head. "No, he fell in love with a human."

I gasped. "Is that against the rules?"

He shook his head. "Not exactly. He was watching her from Heaven and God damned him for wanting out of Heaven so badly to be with her."

"So God damned him?"

"Yes."

"When was this?"

Darrton tapped his chin and thought back. "I think the '20s."

My mouth dropped open. "She must be dead by now?"

He nodded. "I believe she died."

I felt my phone vibrate in my pocket but I jabbed my finger in there and ignored it. "So, he was damned to Earth, and now she died without him? Will he die, I mean can he die?"

He shook his head. "That's part of the punishment, he will never age. He can die, but it's harder for him to be killed.

He can never be happy with someone forever. He will always be the same."

"Will you always be the same?"

His eyes seemed glazed over and he shrugged. "I'm not sure, actually. God gives immortality for punishment. I'm being punished. All Four Horsemen are being punished for taking The Apocalypse into their own hands. So it's possible that I will stay the same."

I sat on the table and began to swing my feet. "So, were you always a Horseman? Or did you die and go to Heaven?"

Darrton's eyes were so pale against his tanned skin. "I was a human for 22 years before God chose me."

"How did it happen?"

Darrton opened his mouth to speak but he bit it back. He stood up. "Go take a shower and I will bring you something to eat from down stairs. Anything you prefer?"

I shook my head. "As long as it's edible. And no onions. I hate onions."

"No onions." He nodded and walked out.

❧❧❧

The shower felt so good. It was hot and the hotels soap smelled like lavender. I was enjoying the bath until the buzzing sound of my cell phone ringing brought me out of the bliss. "Ugh!" I stepped out of the shower and tied a towel around me.

It was from Trevor. *Hey, Liz. I haven't talked to you today. Are we still going to the concert tonight? It's a pretty long drive. We will need to leave soon. Lizzie? You there?*

Millie: *Where the fudge are you! Your parents have called the cops! Are you okay? I'm getting scared, Lizzie. Where are you?*

I shut my phone and tried to breath. I had 37 missed calls from my parents, Lizzie, Trevor, and Sam. *Would they move on with their lives if I never come back? Would they adopt another daughter? Would Samantha get my room? What about Millie, would she go off to her senior year and find another friend? Would someone else get to sit with her at lunch and eat Cheez-Its? I really don't care if Trevor finds someone else to try and seduce.*

My mouth became dry and I fumbled with the door knob and bolted out toward the sink. The cabinet door closest to the bottom didn't have any glasses and the one above I couldn't reach. I tried to step onto the counter to get but the cabinet door opened before I could. I gasped and turned around. Darrton was standing there behind me, a glass in his hand.

"Are you okay?"

Embarrassed, I grabbed the glass filled it up with tap water and gulped it down. I dropped the glass into the sink and placed my face in my hands. I felt a sudden breeze on my side and I realized I was still in my towel. "Don't look!" I screamed. I pulled it up from my waist where it had fallen and my whole body started to heat. "Don't look!"

"I'm not, Lizzie!" he shouted back.

My face was red and when I turned around Darrton had his hand over his face and was turned away from me. "Okay, my towels up now. You can look.

He turned back and cocked an eyebrow. "What is wrong with you?"

"Nothing...I was just...my parents called the cops, Darrton."

"I presumed they would. That is why I got you a fake ID. So that they couldn't track you down. Do not call anyone, either. They may be able to track you. We can't let them find us just yet, especially before tonight."

"Why tonight? What are we doing tonight that is so important?"

He looked like he was debating whether to tell me something or not. "I'll tell you later." He pointed toward a plate of food on the table. "That is yours. Eat up and calm down, okay?"

I nodded my head. Darrton grabbed his wallet off of the table and started toward the door. "Where the hell do you think you are going without me?"

"I have to find Ian. Or at least get a message to him somehow."

"Well, let me get dressed then, I'll come with you." I started toward the bed where my bag was but Darrton stopped me.

"You can't come. I want you to stay hidden and safe. If they find me with you it will only make it worse."

"You're leaving me alone?"

"I have to. You can't come. There is a swimming pool down stairs, TV, and food. I've programmed my number into your phone. Please, if anything happens call me. And please do not call anyone you know. Do not answer the phone, either. We have to stay hidden. Just for a little while."

"And how do you know how to use a phone?"

Darrton's lip pulled up into a smile. "The man at Verizon showed me how to put a number in my phone. He showed me how to take a picture also. He deserves a raise. I'm not a fast learner but he still was very patient with me."

"Well, someone is moving up in the world."

He smiled but then it turned into a frown. "This is serious, Elizabeth. If anyone knocks on the door, do not answer. Do you understand? Call me if anyone besides housekeeping shows up here. I doubt they will. I didn't see them following us, but they are sneaky."

I didn't say anything. I couldn't. If I wasn't scared before I was now.

Darrton sighed and walked toward me. His hand on my bare shoulder made my body weak. I bit my tongue to keep calm. "Do you understand, Elizabeth?"

There was that name again…Elizabeth. I shivered. "Yes, I understand."

"I will be back tonight and be ready when I am."

"I thought we couldn't risk going out?"

He smiled. "I have a surprise. It will be dark and easier to hide."

I nodded. "Okay."

He walked toward the door and shut it. I was alone.

ᴄ⁄ᴈᴄ⁄ᴈ

After drying my hair and getting dressed, I plopped down onto the bed and turned on the TV. My cell had been blowing up so I just shut it off. I couldn't see another text from my mother begging me to call her. I skimmed through the channels and it seemed news was on all of them. I stopped on a local news channel. There were pictures of the war that had been going on in Israel.

"We are speaking with a child that supposedly saw the cause of the madness," said a woman dressed in a business suit.

This pulled my attention. The child was battered and bruised. He had tear stains down his tanned face. He spoke in some foreign language, but a translator was beside him. "He was big. He waved his hand and everyone started screaming and hurting each other. He had wings," the translator said. I watched the child's face as he spoke. He was more than scared. He looked around as if someone would come and snatch him. "He was mean—he had red all around him." The little kid began to cry and ran from the camera and into the house behind them.

"As you can tell, the children have been traumatized and are hallucinating. These poor children," the lady said, shaking her head. The TV went to commercial.

I tried to move but I just couldn't. These people had no idea what was coming. I clicked to another channel and stopped. "People seem to think this is The Rapture. But no one has gone missing? These plagues have just come out of nowhere. No one has gone back to the promise land," the man said.

I turned the TV off. No one knew what was really happening. I couldn't seem to get enough air into my lungs. I stood up grabbed the door key and walked out. The hallway was empty and it was cool. I could breathe.

At the end of the hallway I saw the glow from the drink machine. When I rounded the corner, there was an old lady, sitting with her hands in her lap, staring at the wall. She didn't even look over at me. I pulled seventy five cents from my pocket and clicked Dr. Pepper.

"Crazy things are happening," the lady said.

I glanced back at her and she was staring straight at me. I gasped. One of her eyes was almost black and the other white. "Yes, ma'am, they are." I pressed the Dr. Pepper again. *Why isn't it coming out?*

"My mother always told me this day would come," the woman tisked.

I turned again and she was smiling. It wasn't a pretty smile, more like a menacing one. "What day is that?"

She cocked her head. "You don't know?"

"Umm." I licked my lips. "No, I don't."

"The day when they betray the Lord."

My body stiffened. "Who are they?"

My Dr. Pepper finally fell from to the bottom and I jumped. She smiled again, this time standing up slowly. She had a limp and walked sluggishly. "I believe you know more than you let on, Elizabeth."

"Ma'am? How do you know my name?"

She just smiled. *A creepy smile.*

"Who are you, ma'am?"

"I'm just an old woman. My mother always believed in these stories. I believe her."

"You know they're here?"

"Who, darling?" She smiled and started to walk off.

"Aren't you scared?" I called after her. "Do you have any spells to keep them away?" *What a stupid thing to say.* "Maybe garlic or silver bullets?"

She turned and looked at me. Her eyes were uninviting. "Darling, I'm not scared. I know my time is coming before it starts. I won't be here for it. But—" She coughed. "I do pray for those who will be here when it spreads. I pray for you, darling. There isn't anything we can do about it. No silver bullets. My mother always told me to pray every night that when the time came I would be taken before Hell was let loose on this place. My mother was right. My time is coming shortly."

"Wait, ma'am! What do you mean?" I called after her but she was gone. *Why would she think that she would be gone? Was she going to die? Did she know how bad it was going to get*? I ran to the corner and looked down the hallway. She was gone. Grabbing my Dr. Pepper, I walked back to the room.

ᗉᗅᗉᗅ

It was late and Darrton still hadn't come back. Cable was getting boring. I couldn't leave, even though I really wanted to. My phone seemed to be laughing back at me. *You can't use me*, it was singing. I turned it on and it flooded with texts. *Where are you, please call me baby. Let me know you are okay*?

I dialed Millie's number. I was checking the peep hole when she answered, making sure Darrton didn't bust in while I was on the phone. He would flip his lid.

"Hello! Hello! Lizzie, are you there?"

I choked up at her voice. It had only been one day but it seemed like a week. "Millie."

"Thank God! You're all right? We've been worried sick, Lizzie! Where the hell are you?"

"I can't—"

"You're mother has been throwing up! You're dad hasn't said one word, and even Samantha seems concerned. Trevor has been so worried. We were supposed to go to the concert tonight. If you get home in tim—"

"Millie!" I screamed. "Shut up and listen," I said, peeking out the peep hole. "I can't come home. I can't go to the concert, either."

"What the hell do you mean you can't come home? You have to come home."

"I can't. We're all in danger okay. You'll thank me later. Just go to the concert. Tell Mom and Dad I'm okay and tell Trevor…to go to Hell."

"What the hell, Lizzie—"

"I have to go now—"

"No don't hang up—"

"Bye Millie." I shut the phone and let it fall to the floor. I felt a lump form in my throat. *I can't believe I just did that.*

My stomach was hurting so bad. I couldn't keep doing this to my family. What did Darrton expect me to do?

I picked up my phone and tried to call Darrton. It rang and rang. He didn't have a voicemail so I couldn't leave him one. I sent him a text.

"Where are you? Please call me."

He never texted back.

Ass.

CHAPTER 11

Darrton

The address took me to downtown Vancouver. It was rather late in the afternoon and the town reminded me of a ghost town. I parked my bike on the curb of a closed warehouse that had boards nailed up over its windows.

There was a creepy feeling washing over me. I could feel another fallen. Ian had to be here.

The alley to the left reeked of crime. It was the dark and gloomy nightlife that criminals looked for. A man down at the end of the alley was curled up in a box, singing an old western song. He was three sheets to the wind and didn't even know I was only a few feet away from him. I stopped in front of the door. It had three bullet holes. I knocked three times.

It opened. A man poked his head out and gave me the once over. He then unlocked the door all the way, giving me just enough space to walk in. I slid in and was hit in the face with smoke, I could smell the alcohol. It burned my nose. The man who let me in sized me up then gestured for me to follow him. His arms were covered in markings and his head was almost shaved. We walked past a few people who were playing pool, with girls hanging on their right arms. They weren't fallen but I had a gut feeling that they knew something about us.

The area was a tight fit but there were a number of rooms off to the side. We walked toward the back. He stopped at a door and knocked three times.

"Come in," someone called.

The man gestured for me to go in. The room was completely different than what I had expected. It was light, modern, and had a huge desk in the middle. Ian was sitting behind it.

"My brother!" he said, rising up and coming to greet me. I noticed he hadn't lost his deep southern twang. He'd had it ever since he died.

"It's been a long time, Brother."

He grabbed me in a hug and squeezed. "It's been way too long, Darrton." He studied me. "You look great. Besides being here on Earth and everything. But of course I would never point fingers."

I took him in. He looked…so human. His hair had been cut. He was wearing khaki pants, a button-down shirt, and sandals. "As do you. You look rather human, but good."

He winked. "Being down here for over eighty years, it starts to wear on you after a while."

"Has that much time gone by?"

He nodded and gestured for me to sit down. "Have a seat, son. I guess we got some business to take care of?" He rummaged around in his cabinet, brought out two shot glasses, and poured bourbon into both. He threw his shot back and sighed. "I'm actually surprised to see ya' here at all. I'm guessin' something has happened. Am I correct?" He poured himself another drink.

"We were damned."

He looked over his drink at me, placed his shot down, and sighed. He was rarely serious, always laughing, but now his eyebrows drew down in the middle. "Darrton, what in the hell did you do?"

"We tried to take over. We knew—"

He laughed but it was without humor. "Did you not learn from me? The punishment is so great. I will never see Emily ever again. I have to live every day without her. For what? Forty years with her and forever without her?" Ian looked me dead in the eye. "The Apocalypse is beginnin' and it's without His permission. You've sinned greatly 'gainst God."

I nodded. "I did not come here to be patronized, Ian."

He leaned back, his dark eyes unpalatable. "Why did you come here, Brother? Would you like me to help you kill? 'Cause I won't. I refuse."

"I'm not asking you to do that."

"What exactly are you askin' me? To help the others?"

I shook my head. "I've only seen Warren and Caden. I haven't seen Ferdia."

"Are you not with them now? I would have thought y'all would have been together? What is goin' on Darrton? Are you even looking for them?"

I looked down, unable to face him. My actions were too shameful.

"Ah!" He threw his head back and laughed. "I know that look." He tisked and shook his head. "You're in love?" He smiled.

I jerked my head up. "I am not. I feel bad for involving Elizabeth—"

Ian stopped me. "Elizabeth?" He began shaking his head again. "Darrton, you have to get over her that was a long time ago."

"It's not her, it's another. She is merely a child and I have involved her. They want to kill her. I'm supposed to be meeting them now. I just...can't. I can't let them kill her. They say she knows too much, but I don't care. She wouldn't tell. She hasn't yet."

"You have feelin's for this mortal or you wouldn't think twice 'bout killin' her. That is what you were chosen to do. Kill."

I slammed my hands down on the desk. "But not her. She has done nothing wrong. She is merely a child, Ian."

"Let me remind you, Darrton, that when you were taken you were merely a child yourself. You were 22, if I recall."

I looked the other way, out of the window. I felt my phone buzz in my pocket and tossed it out on the desk. "This imprudent thing buzzes and I have no idea why. It's not ringing, no one seems to be calling, and I can't stand it. I haven't been back on Earth but for a couple of weeks, and already I want to rip my hair out. Why do we need cell phones, anyway?"

Ian laughed. "Oh, how the years have changed. You have a text, Darrton. It's from Elizabeth." He read it over. "Is she with you?"

I snatched the phone away from him. "I had to bring her along with me, Ian. I couldn't leave her at her home to die. They were going to kill her if I didn't. I had to."

Ian crossed his arms. "Do you have a plan, Darrton? You can't live your past through this girl. She is not your Elizabeth..."

"I know she's not. She's Elizabeth Lawrence and I have promised to take care of her. I won't let her die in vain." My head began to throb. I knew she wasn't my Elizabeth. She wasn't the one I'd left behind.

"You're head over heels for this girl," Ian said, smiling. He puckered his lips.

I shook my head and took a step toward him. "Unbelievable!"

He raised his hands in surrender, then his face turned serious. "What do you plan to do? We have to do somethin'."

"We? Are you saying you will help me?"

Ian placed his hand on my shoulder. "I wouldn't have it any other way. I can't let this happen to the world when it's not ready."

I nodded. "I regret it now. Getting damned. If I had it to do all over again, I wouldn't have."

"Me, either."

It was silent for a minute as we thought about what we left behind. It was stupid and selfish, but we couldn't fix it now.

Ian broke the silence. "So, what's the plan, friend?"

"They will come after me. Once they are sure I didn't show tonight, they will come after Lizzie and me. They will try to kill us both."

Ian nodded. "We need help. We can't take on both of them alone. I'm not as strong as the four of you. I will have to find some friends of mine."

"Did you find any more fallen?"

He nodded. "Yes, over the years. Some are here, others have lost touch, but I'm sure I can dig them up."

I nodded. "I will have to try and find Ferdia. He hasn't contacted any of us. Although, I'm not even sure if he will be willing to help us. He did make the same pact as the rest of us did."

"We won't know until we try?" Ian glanced at the bourbon. I knew he wanted another shot. Especially after this. "Any idea where he could be?"

I nodded. "Yes, actually I think I might know. He always talked about going to the Pacific Ocean. I think California."

"Well, we are going to Cali then, right?"

I shook my head. "Not yet. I might be able to speak to him through my ring. And I can't just leave the girl here by herself."

Ian stroked his chin. "She can stay at my place. It's heavily guarded. I'm a very wanted man these days."

"Why is that?"

Ian cracked a smile. "I've been involved with some drag racing, fixing horse races, and the normal stuff."

"Of course, the normal stuff. Where is your house, anyway?"

"Upper east side. A few miles from here. It won't take use long to get there especially if we fly. So, she can spend the night there and she will be safe. We can leave tonight."

I shook my head. "Tomorrow. We have plans tonight."

He cocked an eyebrow. "A date?"

I looked back over my shoulder and shook my head. "An outing, she deserves it."

Ian yelled after me, "She deserves the truth. You care 'bout her, partner."

I was half way to my bike by the time he yelled. My ring had begun to burn and I was waiting for their words to hit me. They knew I had fled.

Warren's laugh hummed in my head first. *'You can't run, Brother. We will find you.'* An ache ran through me. *I'm fighting my own brothers. There is no other choice.* I shook his words out of my head and got on my motorcycle. I had to get back to Elizabeth. My three brothers were coming for her. I had to stop them.

CHAPTER 12

Lizzie

I was slipping into my boots when Darrton barged in the door. More than annoyed, I jumped up. "Where the hell have you been?"

Darrton froze. His pale, compelling eyes skimmed down my body, like snakes slowly wrapping around my thighs. I squirmed. When his eyes met mine they were heated. "I told you where I was going." He grabbed my bag and changed from the shirt he had on.

"I tried to call you, like you told me to and you didn't answer. I thought you were dead, Darrton. It scared me."

He pulled the shirt over his head and retied his ponytail. "It would take a lot to kill me. I am Death, Lizzie."

I blinked. He was Death. This made a shiver go down my spine. Even though I already knew this, hearing him say it again made me quake.

Placing a hand on my hip and taking a deep breath, I said, "Where are we going tonight? I'm ready to get out of this room. There is nothing on but news of the War. And a crazy lady thinks she is going to die so that she doesn't have to endure the things that are coming. And I have millions of texts from people I would really like to talk to."

He cocked an eyebrow and slipped on a leather jacket, which I didn't know he had. "Are we finished? Are you ready?"

Shrugging, I gave him a once over from the corner of my eye. I knew I should be scared out of my mind, but I had a bubbly feeling in the depth of my stomach. *Why was I nervous? Where were we going?*

"Elizabeth, are you ready?" he asked again

I nodded my head and took another deep breath. "Yes, I'm ready. Let's go."

He didn't tell me where we were going. *Go figure.* He just told me to hold on. We were on the bike for quite some time. I figured it to be over two hours. The green Seattle sign made me sigh. Seattle was where the Kings of Leon was playing. Hopefully Millie had gone. I hoped she had. There was no reason for her to worry about me and not go. It wouldn't hurt my feelings. It just sucked that I couldn't go. *Trevor better not have gone with her, though. That ass better stay the hell away from my best friend.*

"Are you all right?" Darrton asked as we stopped at a red light.

"Yeah, why?"

"You're tense that's all." He revved the engine and sped along.

I guess I *was* kind of tense. I tried taking a breath. My lungs filled with cool crisp air. We rode for about three more miles before he pulled over behind what looked like a huge stadium. He jumped off and offered me his hand.

Pointing to the stadium, I asked, "What's this? Are we going to a football game?"

"Do you like football, Elizabeth?"

"Well, not really."

He cocked an eyebrow. "Then why would I take you to one?"

The look in his pale eyes made me shiver. I took his hand and felt a warm impression in my palm. We walked around the stadium. The street light was out. We stopped where the traffic was scarce and the moon was hidden behind a building.

"Is this the part where you kill me?" I whispered, close to him.

He let out a slow chuckle. My body stopped moving when I felt his hand on my lower back. The other one wrapped around my hip bone. "Do you trust me, Elizabeth," he whispered low into my ear, and the warmth spread deep inside of my stomach.

I nodded. "I know I shouldn't, but I do."

He let out a soft moan and pulled me tighter. "Do not let go. Hold on to me."

Doing as he said, I held on. The wind wrapped around us. I heard his shirt rip and his wings spread from his back. My feet left the pavement, and I held tighter to him. We shot up, his wings taking us higher. When I felt my feet hit something solid, I kept my eyes closed. I could hear a crowd roaring in the background.

"Elizabeth, open your eyes."

When I opened my eyes, my mouth dropped in awe. We were on the top of the stadium. I estimated that around a million people were below us, fists pumping.

I looked up and the sky it seemed so close. The stars danced out from around us and the air was so much cleaner up here. "Where are we?"

"I didn't want you to miss your concert. It wouldn't be fair."

"How did you know about it?" I asked.

"I overheard you talking to Millie about it."

I cocked an eyebrow. "So, in other words you were eavesdropping?"

Darrton smiled but ignored the question.

Grabbing Darrton, I hugged him. He seemed surprised at first, but then I noticed how firm his body was against mine. The heat was undeniable. When I pulled away, he was staring down at the crowd. Kings of Leon entered and everyone roared.

"Let's have a seat. He gestured toward a blanket that was already laying there. I sat down next to him and I watched as the band started to play.

"Thank you, Darrton."

He didn't say anything at first but finally, he said, "You're welcome, Elizabeth."

We listened to the band play for hours. When a slow song hit, the crowd pulled out lighters and cell phones and waved them back in forth.

"I wonder if Millie is here."

He shrugged. "Maybe, her and Trevor."

"Ugh," I groaned.

"You not too fond of him, now?"

"He basically tried to force himself on me."

Darrton was quiet for a second. "I wanted to kill him."

That thought had crossed my mind. The way his eyes had flared so intensely, I was afraid he actually would kill him. "Why?"

Darrton glanced over at me and his eyes flashed with hunger. "Because he was trying to talk you into something you didn't want to do."

My body was enflamed. I had to change the subject quick. I wasn't supposed to feel like this. "Well, he wouldn't be the first person to go missing this semester."

Darrton sat back on his hands. "Oh yes, the boy who was trying to break into your house."

I jerked my head back to him. "Excuse me?"

"The boy who was trying to break into your house."

A lump formed in my throat and the cool air didn't seem so cool or inviting anymore. "You took Lucas?"

"I didn't take him. I killed him. He was trying to get to you, Elizabeth." Darrton looked down. I knew that wasn't the only reason but I was too close to crying to care.

He had killed Lucas. I tried not to think about his mother crying at The Picnic Basket and at school. *What would have happened if he hadn't killed him? Would Lucas have killed me?*

I nodded and curled my knees up to my chest. *Would he have raped me? Killed me? Cut me?* A flood of unruly emotions dashed over my skin. Lucas had been trying to hurt me. Not that I expected any less from him but it still made me quiver. I let out a shiver and Darrton slowly wrapped his arm around my shoulder. Even though I should have been scared shitless of him, his warm arm smelled so good and felt so soft against my skin. He shhhed into my ear, and it was then that I realized he really wasn't the same. He was comforting me. He kind of…cared.

The rhythm of the song changed and a slower song came on. I felt his lips brush up against my ear and I couldn't think.

"Would you like to dance?" he asked.

He clasped my right hand and drew me up to my feet. My heart rate was picking up, and I couldn't feel my legs. Darrton pulled me so close to his body that I thought I might melt into him. His left hand was on my lower back and the other clasp with mine out to the side. We just swayed back and forth for a little while before he took my hand and placed it onto the back of his neck. I held onto him. He gripped my hips as if he wanted to make us one. He wasn't wearing any cologne, but he smelled so terrific. There wasn't anything holding me back anymore…there couldn't be. I leaned into him and he let out an "hmm."

His body language and the way he moved, so sexy and smooth, reminded me of dancing from a different time era.

"Darrton," I said into his chest.

"Yes," he replied, his voice deep.

"Who were you before you were a Horseman?"

He body tensed as he swayed back and forth with me. "Jacob."

Jacob. "What happened?"

He spun me out and twisted me around, dipping me and bringing me back up to him. "I was in the Spanish-American war in 1898. I was a solider for America."

"You were killed?"

He nodded. "Yes, I was courting a girl. Her name was Elizabeth."

Strange. His eyes glazed over and I felt uncomfortable even being there. "You don't have to talk about it—"

He squeezed my side. We had stopped dancing. "No, I want to. You deserve to know." His finger intertwined with my belt loop and he pulled me closer. "I was a killer back then, too. I was a great shot and it did not pain me to kill a Spaniard. That's what my father had done when he fought and that was how I was raised. To fight. To kill. To win.

"Well, I was shot by a man who, as I was dying, prayed that I went to Heaven. It sickened me that he was praying for his enemy. I did go to Heaven. I went and that is when I was given the title of *Death*. I would be one of the Horseman that brought God's people home and destroyed the ones that were left. All the Horsemen are given their titles after death. God sees something in the person and they are given their title. And then God comes when it is time for The Apocalypse." Darrton sighed. "That's why we were damned, because we took matters into our own hands. We did not wait on The Rapture. We wanted to go now. We wanted to start The Apocalypse. God damned us to earth. We have to have the ritual to release Hell. We have to go through Satan to release it. If we would have waited, God would have given us all the power we needed without having to perform the ritual."

"So did you all meet in Heaven? Is that where you met?"

He nodded. "Yes. We were all given our titles at different times as we died. God gave us each the separate titles. We were together in Heaven, waiting. We bonded like brothers during that time. Warren first brought up the idea of having The Apocalypse sooner. Ferdia and I were iffy at first. Caden was always going along with Warren. He looked up to him." Darrton sighed and closed his eyes. "It's just that we had been waiting for so long for The Rapture, and we started to crave it. God had given us these powers and these titles. We wanted to fulfill our purpose. We wanted to do what we were chosen to do. So we made our pact to do it. When we presented our plan to the Father, he cursed us for going against his will. He damned us to Earth and stripped us of our powers for starting The Apocalypse. That is why we have to go through Satan."

"So if you were stripped of your powers how come you have wings and can heal? You did heal my cuts? Since you healed my cut, shouldn't you be able to heal your own?"

"No, we can't heal ourselves, only others, and we only lost our powers to start The Apocalypse alone. Hell will not follow me, because I do not have the power any longer. We had to make a deal with Satan for it to happen. And everyone in Heaven has wings. All the fallen angles keep them after their fall but they are turned black. That is a sign of their punishment from God, along with living forever."

I felt something for Darrton that I had never experienced before. *Pity.* I had never thought to ask why and how he felt about anything. He had gone through so much. I could not imagine being taken away from someone I loved.

I cleared my throat. "Elizabeth was left alone. Did you miss her?"

He nodded. "Every moment of every day."

"Do you still?"

His pale blue eyes danced in the moonlight. "No one will be able to replace her in my life, Elizabeth, but I've moved on. That was over a century ago."

I nodded. "I'm so sorry that happened."

"I'm not."

The song ended and the crowd began to roar again. Kings of Leon went backstage for the intermission. It sounded like a stampede of people running toward the bathroom.

"I have an idea."

"What?" I smiled.

He held out his hand and I grabbed it. "You better trust me."

I shrugged. "It's worked so far."

He pulled me off the edge of the stadium roof, that opened into the stadium with no ceiling, and we fell toward the bleachers below. Gravity was pulling our bodies to the ground, the wind whirling around us. We landed. I was holding on to him so tight I was sure I was cutting off circulation to his brain.

"Let go, Lizzie. We're fine," he said and seemed to laugh.

When I opened my eyes we were in the back row of the bleachers. The couple in front of us were too busy sucking each other's faces to see us. Darrton pulled me toward the aisle and we walked down to the bottom of the stands.

"Where are we going?"

He just turned back and smiled. The stairs leading up to the stage were protected by bodyguards and they didn't look too friendly. The one on the left had a scar on his left cheek and the other one was so pale I thought I might be able to see through him. Darrton didn't seem too fazed. He walked up to them and in unison they pulled together blocking the way with their big bodies. They had sunglasses on, even though it was night, and their leather jackets were tight around them.

"Where do you two think you are going?" the guard with the scar asked. Then he looked down at Darrton and saw he didn't have a shirt. "And why don't you have a shirt on? It's September chilly."

Stepping back down the stairs, I tried to pull Darrton away but he just looked down at me and shook his head.

"I think we are going backstage to see the band, sir."

The one on the right, that really needed some sun, pulled down his glasses and cocked an eyebrow. "And what made you think you could do that?"

Darrton shrugged, his muscles moving with every minuscule move. He dug in his pocket and pulled out two slips of laminated paper. "We have these."

Scar picked up the paper and examined them. He gave us the once over and nodded toward the other one. "Before you go—" He bent down, rummaged through a box that sat below the stage, pulled out a shirt, and tossed it to Darrton. "This isn't the barn, son. Wear some clothes next time."

Darrton smiled and slid the shirt on. "I'll remember that." Darrton pushed past the guards and pulled me up to his side. "Ready, Lizzie?"

I gulped. "I guess I'm as ready as I will ever be."

The lights backstage were brighter than I'd imagined them to be. There were people, important people, running around acting as if they were on speed. You could tell the backstage fans from the people that worked there. For one thing, the workers didn't have faces that were drooling over the band members, and two they weren't wearing "We love you, Kings of Leon," shirts. I wasn't wearing one. I looked over at Darrton and the shirt, that was a tad bit snug, said "Kings of Leon, Rules," on it.

Darrton looked and saw me looking at his shirt. He rolled his eyes. "Come on, or we will never meet them."

Darrton pushed through a ton of people and stopped at the front. There was someone in my way. I couldn't see but I could hear someone yelling, causing a scene. "Please! Just one more question. I'll never get this chance again!"

The drummer Ivan said, "But there are so many other people who would like to ask a question."

I heard the girl huff. "But you don't understand! This is like a do or die kind of thing. I would even stop eating Cheez-Its for you just to answer one more."

"Listen, what's your name?"

"Millie," she said.

I froze. Millie. I knew I recognized that voice. Annoying, yes, pushy, yes, my best friend yes! I pushed past another person and saw her standing there, hand on her hip, mouth in a hard straight line. It wasn't until I noticed the drummer Ivan and the lead singer Caleb had given each other glances and pointed over in the distance, that I saw Trevor and Brett. I felt Darrton pull me closer to him, keeping an eye on me.

His breath was warm on my neck. "We need to go. They can't see you."

I was two steps ahead of him.

We pushed through the remainder of the crowd and were at the curtain when I heard, "Lizzie! Is that you?"

Brett was standing there, with his face squinted up, hitting Trevor on the shoulder, trying to get his attention. Trevor's dark blue eyes darted to mine, and I swear I heard his sigh of relief from across the crowded stage.

"Hey! Over here!" Trevor shouted.

Darrton was pulling me along when I heard Millie scream, "Lizzie! Oh my God, it's you! I was so scared…" Her voice trailed off as we took two steps at a time and pushed through the guards.

"Hey! No running!"

We were halfway through the crowd by the time they left the first step. We didn't stop or look back, even to see if they were chasing us. The exit sign was red and shining above the door. Darrton was impatient with my speed so he swept me up and almost ran with me.

He rammed his shoulder into the door and we scampered to a stop in the alley beside the stadium. I was out of breath and my shirt clung to my body with perspiration.

My feet hit the pavement and I dropped to my knees. "Whew, I'm not ten anymore."

Darrton moved quickly and pulled me up. "We have got to go Lizzie. They were trailing us."

The exit door slung open and Brett and Trevor ran out into the alley. Millie came through only a second later holding her side. "Oh God, Lizzie," she said limping her way to me.

She gripped me in a tight hug. I was starting to get a little panicky.

"Where have you been?" she screamed. "We've had cops looking all over for you. And you just show up at the concert un-freaking harmed?" Her black shirt was glistening from the glitter she had put on it. It said *I Love You, Ivan.* Her mascara was running and her mouth was in a hard line.

I tried to think of some logical explanation as to why I had just vanished for the day. Trevor stepped forward and I cringed. His hat covered his eyes but I could still them underneath the shadow. "Lizzie, are you all right?" He glanced at Darrton, jabbed his finger at him, and tried to whisper, "Did this guy hurt you?"

Darrton snorted. "You're a fine one to talk about that."

Trevor looked at Darrton with narrowed eyes. "What the hell is that supposed to mean, asshole?"

Darrton took a step forward and I felt myself take a step toward *him*. I was begging and pleading in my mind for him to stop. *Please! Do not kill him.*

Brett stepped behind Trevor and crossed his arms over his wide chest. *Oh yeah, two against one. Sorry to say both of you are going to get your asses kicked tonight.*

"That means you are the only one trying to take advantage of Elizabeth and we both know it."

Trevor threw his head back and laughed. "Says the old ass 'cousin' that shows up and takes her away for the day?"

"You're the one who tried to harm her."

Trevor looked puzzled. It was then I remembered Trevor did not remember anything about trying to talk me into sleeping with him. I coughed and stepped toward Darrton. "Maybe we should go."

"Go?" Millie screamed. "You just got here. Why would you go? Your mother is throwing-up-sick, worried about you."

Brett slid around Trevor and grabbed my arm. "I think this guy has you brainwashed."

Darrton stepped closer. "Let go of her arm and leave us now."

Brett gripped my arm tighter. "Hell no, Brother. She is going with us and you are going to go back to molesting children or whatever it is you do."

Darrton snarled. I think I might have pissed in my pants. Millie became awfully, and uncharacteristically, quiet.

Trevor stepped forward and I could tell he was about to do something stupid. He turned his black cap on backwards and took a swing at Darrton. He had barely moved when Darrton reached out and grabbed Trevor's fist.

If I had ever heard a cry of hurt, it would have been then. Trevor cried out the most dreadfully agonized cry ever and fell to the ground holding his hand. I tried not to look but I could see his knuckle bone through his skin. He scrambled to his feet and put up his left hand, his good hand, and tried to swing again. This time Darrton moved and Trevor hit the air.

Brett's feet made a loud, crunching sound on the pavement as he stepped toward Darrton. In the same moment, Darrton picked Brett up and slammed him onto the pavement. Brett let out a murderous scream.

Millie, who'd never moved during this whole entire scene, whispered to herself, "Please be dreaming. Let me wake up in Ivan's arms and let this all be a dream."

I bit my lip as she looked at Brett on the ground. The emotion on her face changed to anger and confusion. She clenched her fists and looked up at Darrton who was standing without an ounce of emotion on his face. Millie stepped forward and took a big long kick at Darrton's shin. "Take that, freak!"

Then she dashed back behind me and looked over my shoulder at him. His eyebrow was raised as he bent down and whispered into Trevor and Brett's ears.

"Millie," I said.

She didn't answer.

"Millie, are you okay?"

She didn't answer.

"Damn it, Millie," I said, turning and shaking her, "are you okay?"

She looked dumbfounded at me and screamed, "Hell no. Greek God over here just beat some ass, and you've been missing with him for the last 18 hours! I am *not* okay!"

Darrton and I both looked at each other and he sighed. "Millie, I'm sorry you had to see that."

"Don't come near me! I will mess you up, guy!"

"He isn't going to hurt you!"

"Horse shit!' she screamed. "He is going to kill me! You've killed them." She pointed to Trevor and Brett's limp bodies.

"They're not dead, Millie."

She raised her fists and looked over them at the bodies. "No?"

Darrton shook his head. "No."

"Wake them up!" she shouted.

"I will." He stepped toward her. She turned, screaming, and tried to run the other way. Darrton caught her, whispered into her ear, and laid her body close to Brett's.

eↄeↄ

Darrton didn't say one word to me the entire way home. He didn't even tell me he was leaving. He just began to walk down the alley that was getting darker by the minute. I was struggling to keep up. I had to basically jump onto the back of the bike just to get a freaking ride home.

Darrton walked swiftly to the room with me behind him. The ride in the elevator was quiet and all I could here was the clicking of the floors and the soft sound of jazz in the background.

Having to catch the room door as he opened and shut it, I was boiling mad.

"Darrton!" I said, slamming the door and looking at him.

He ignored me, walked toward the bed, and started taking off his shirt and shoes.

"Damn it, Darrton! Talk to me!"

He turned on his heel and I could see the dark pit of hate in his eyes. His jaw was set in a hard line and his fist was clenched. "We have nothing to talk about."

I scoffed. "The hell we don't. You whoop my friend's asses and you storm off and try to leave me."

He shook his head. "And you call Trevor your friend?"

I stopped for a moment. "Is that what this is about? Trevor? I want nothing to do with him, Darrton. I can't help that he was there tonight. I can't help that we ran into them. I can't help that he swung at you. Is that why you are mad? Because they tried to fight you?"

He let out a slow and uneasy laugh, without humor, as if he was trying to control his temper. "This has nothing to do with him trying to fight me. I couldn't care less about their pathetic attempts."

"Then what is it, Darrton? Are you mad because we were found by them?"

Darrton let out a sigh and ran his fingers through his long hair. His bare chest rose and fell with each heavy intake of breath. "Never mind, Elizabeth. It's nothing important." He turned back around and reached for his clothes.

"Damn it," I said, walking toward him and giving him a shove. "You're going to tell me, so help me God! What is it?"

The movement was so quick, I almost stumbled backwards. He grabbed my wrists and held them tight along my side. "I said it was nothing, Elizabeth." He lips were tight and his eyes were ravenous.

"Tell me, now," I said, biting off each and every word. "Tell me now or I will leave, Darrton. I'll leave and tell everyone."

He gripped my wrist tighter and let out a long breath.

"Tell me!" I screamed.

"I can't stand the way he looks at you!" he yelled, letting go of my wrists.

Darrton backed away from me and up against the bed. The pale blue of his eyes was wild and hungry. I felt my breath catch in my throat. I let out a deep sigh. Those words set off a fire deep down in my core.

"Why?" I asked, barley above a whisper.

His shadow loomed over me and I was too aware of his body so close to mine. "Why, Darrton?"

His full lips opened and I watched as my name rolled off his tongue.

"Elizabeth."

"Why, Darrton?"

"Because I want you for myself." His words were velvet running along my body.

I didn't even have time to respond. His lips found mine. In the middle of all the madness going on in my head, I relaxed and let my body fall against his. He gripped my lower back, brought his other hand up, and twined it into my hair.

The way his lips moved was…heavenly—aggressive and ravening. He pulled away and let out a moan. It sent shivers down to my toes. He backed me up against the wall, pinning my hands above my head. His lips were soft and his body hard against mine. When he let my arms down, I found myself wrapping my hands in his hair, letting it flow through my fingers. He lifted me off the floor and placed me on the bed. His warm body hovered over mine as he let his lips travel along my jawline. My head was spinning, my eyes dazed. The warmth of his lips on my neck made my back arch in pleasure. I'd never been kissed like that. His tongue slipped into my mouth and I tasted the sweetness of his mouth on mine. Every hollow part of me filled up with a bright heat that was begging to swallow me whole. It was a red hot, dangerous heat that was begging to be released.

"Elizabeth," he whispered into my ear.

"Hmm."

He let his fingers dance across my arm and up to my neck where he held my head so tenderly, as if it might break. "I've wanted to do that way too long, Iofiel."

I smiled as he traced the curve of my side. "What does that mean?"

The corner of his lip pulled up into a smile. "Angel of Beauty."

I blinked trying to make sure all of this was real. Darrton placed his hand on my chest where my butterfly necklace lay sprawled out in slumber. When he lifted his hand a butterfly was flapping slowly and rhythmically along my chest.

It flew off and when I looked up Darrton he was staring at me, his eyes brilliant, inviting, and beautiful. "What are you thinking?" he asked, pushing my hair from my cheek.

"I…I'm not sure I'm thinking of anything. I can't really think straight, right now."

He cocked an eyebrow. "Is that good or bad?"

Smiling, I rolled over on my side. "Extremely good."

"Thought I might have lost my touch after all of these years."

I imagined his touch, all over me. *Oh he has definitely not lost his touch.* I shrugged. "Ah, you're okay."

Darrton let out a laugh, an honest, raw, earthy laugh that seemed angelic at the same time. His eyes turned serious all of the sudden. "Elizabeth, I have to keep you safe."

My stomach churned. "Ah, the dark light in every conversation. Reality."

He nodded and pulled me onto his chest. "Reality is, Iofiel, that they are coming after you now. They know you now. They have to have me, Death, to perform the ritual. They won't stop until I'm there. They will try to take you, to use you to force me do the ritual. They won't stop unless they are killed. I will have to do it. I have to kill them before they kill you."

I rested my head and, I'm not sure exactly how, relaxed into his chest. "Will they hurt my family, too?"

He shrugged. "Not sure. Probably not. They might use them as a trap to get you home."

"Will you protect my family?"

Darrton was quiet for a moment. I felt his finger lift my chin. A tear escaped my eyes and he smiled. "I wouldn't let anyone harm your family. We will deal with that, if and, when that time comes."

"What is the plan then? What is our next move?"

He pulled me close to him and I felt his warmth over me. "I'm leaving tomorrow with Ian. You'll be safe at his house until we return."

"You're leaving me here alone again?" I gasped.

"Not alone. Ian has guards that will protect you at all cost. You won't be harmed."

"Where are you going?"

"To California."

I almost laughed. "On vaca?"

"Yes, because a vacation is exactly what I need right now." I could hear the smile in his voice.

"Ah!" I sat up and looked at him. "You understood our lingo! Someone is rising on the popularity scale."

"A dream come true."

I sighed, pulling my legs up to my chest. "Why are you going?"

"We have to find Ferdia."

I wiggled my toes, trying to keep myself calm. "Which one is he?"

"Famine. I haven't heard from him, I'm not sure why. I normally can reach all of my brothers but Famine seems to be blocked."

I pointed to the ring. "Have you tried to use that? It seemed to help you earlier. Well, it shocked the hell out of you at least."

He shook his head. "No luck. All the activity through the ring has been from Caden and Warren."

"What normal names."

"They were taken later in life than me. Famine was first and I was second. Famine welcomed me into Heaven and showed me how to leave my life behind. He became like a true brother to me. He has always been there with me, always, through every turmoil I have ever had."

"Yeah, hence the name Ferdia. I would have pinned him to be the first. No offense, his name sounds like a girl's name. Just saying."

Darrton looked over at me. "Yes, we know. But if you ever get the lovely chance to meet him, don't mention it. He doesn't take to kindly to it."

"No wonder."

We were quiet for a minute before Darrton stood up. "We better get some rest. We have a long day ahead of us tomorrow. You need sleep."

"Yeah, a long vaca for you and a long day of being babysat for me." I rolled over and started to work my way under the covers.

"I have to keep you safe, Elizabeth."

I nodded and looked up at him. His shirt was off; the dark faded jeans were hanging low on his chiseled hips. He even had the V. *I think I'm going to faint. I just kissed him*! "I know, Darrton, and I appreciate it."

He didn't reply. He walked over to the light switch and turned it off before going to lie down on the couch. "Goodnight, Elizabeth."

I held the covers tight around me. "Darrton."

"Ummm."

"Can I ask you a favor?"

"Yes."

"Can you sleep over here?" As soon as I said it, I was embarrassed that I had. A heat spread along my cheeks.

"Would you like me to?"

Flame engulfed my body. "I think I would."

I didn't hear him get up from the couch, but the bed moved I stiffened. Darrton reached over me and pulled me into his chest. He spooned me and slid his fingers through my hair.

"Goodnight, Iofiel. We will keep you safe," he whispered, and knowing that it was true I closed my eyes and drifted off to a peaceful sleep.

CHAPTER 13

Lizzie

"Room service."

I heard a southern twang and sat straight up in the bed.

A tall, lean man with short dark hair was staring at me. He was smiling and leaning against the desk on the other side of the room.

Darrton stirred beside me and sat up. His hair was ruffled, his shirt off, and his eyes were narrowed. "Ian, nice surprise."

Ian? The fallen angel Darrton had been talking about? Suddenly, I realized what it looked like. Darrton and I in the same bed? My face heated.

"Aw, good mornin', sunshine." Ian leaned forward, his gaze so deep, I could feel it in my bones. "Cute," he said.

I was too embarrassed to respond. I dug my elbow into the bed and swung my feet over the side.

Darrton sighed. "Leave her alone, Ian."

"Just makin' conversation with the lady in the room, Darrton. I wouldn't be a gentleman if I didn't." Ian walked, well rather staggered over to the side of the bed and grabbed my hand. He pressed his lips to it and I could smell the alcohol on his breath. "It's a pleasure to meet you, darlin'."

"Please to meet you," I said quietly then jumped when I noticed the guy in the corner of the room.

Ian laughed. "Oh, my, what a dunce. I forgot to introduce Scotty." He pointed to the young guy standing silently in the corner of the room. He had blonde hair cut short and tanned skin. He smiled and I noticed his teeth were perfect. "Scotty will be watching over you while we go on our trip."

Scotty walked toward me. He couldn't have been over nineteen or twenty. He was dressed casually and didn't look as if he could defend himself. But if I had to guess I'd bet he could.

"Nice to meet you, Elizabeth."

"You, too. You can call me Lizzie."

Darrton reached over and shook his hand. "I wish you would have called before you came over, Ian. We could have been ready."

Ian's smile was amused. "Yes, y'all would have had time to cover up the evidence." Ian pointed to the unmade bed and Darrton's shirt lying on the floor.

I gasped. "We did not!" I knew my face was flushed and I had all the reasons in the world to smack him across his smiling face.

"Guilty dog, dear," Ian said, still smiling.

"Leave her alone, Ian. Damn it."

"I'm only pickin' with you, sweetheart."

"Picking what?" I asked.

Ian laughed, throwing his head back and holding his stomach while bending over. "I'm telling you a joke."

Nothing is funny. "Oh."

Darrton sigh and looked over at me. "He was originally from Georgia, before he died and became an angel. Excuse him and his drunkenness. He has a problem and does not know how to stop it."

"It's called AA." I wrapped my hand around my stomach noticing I did not have a bra on. I'd shed it late last night.

Ian pointed his finger at me and swayed side to side. "Yes, dear, and they are deadly wrong about me. I have no problem. They have the problem. Who are the ones sitting around, cryin' and feelin' sorry for themselves?" He winked at Scotty. Scotty rolled his eyes.

"Right," Darrton said, then turning to me, "would you like to take a shower before we leave?"

I nodded. "Please, I'm barely awake now. Actually, I'm hoping I'm dreaming."

Darrton nodded, grabbed my bag, and handed it to me. "Believe me, Elizabeth, you're not dreaming. Wishful thinking."

☙❧

My hair was a hot mess. There were strands standing up all over. It looked like a rat had taken a bath and had babies on the back of my head. I stripped off my clothes and waited for the shower to turn hot. My phone beeped from the counter. I leaned over and opened the text.

"Where are you? It's been two days. We haven't heard a word." It was from Millie. She really had forgotten about last night. A strange sharp pain hit my side. She didn't even remember seeing me. I was thankful and utterly devastated at the same time.

The water was hot on my skin. It felt like heaven to wash away my thoughts and worries from last night. At least for ten minutes until I would have to get out. I lathered up my hair and let the warm water rinse it clean. The hotel soap smelled better than it had the day before. After bathing, I jumped out and wrapped the towel around my body. Sliding down against the cabinet, I relaxed and kept my eyes closed. This was the most miserably wonderful trip I had ever been on in my life. My family and friends were left with nothing, War and Conquest of the four horsemen were after me, but spending time with Darrton made it tolerable.

The door creaked open and Darrton slid inside. His brow was furrowed. "What's wrong? Are you sick?"

I shook my head and held myself tight. "I'm afraid, Darrton."

The lines on his forehead disappeared and he relaxed. "I know, Elizabeth. But I'm not going to let anything happen to you, I promise.

"Don't make promises you can't keep."

He slid his fingers underneath my chin and lifted it. "I'm promising you will be safe and back home soon."

That sent a surge of energy through me. "What will happen to you afterwards?"

He didn't answer. "You need to get dressed. We need to leave as soon as we can. Ian and I have to hurry, so we can find Ferdia."

I nodded. Darrton got up and left. I cried silently. He was going to go. I could see it in his eyes. He was scared, too, even though he didn't want to admit it. He wasn't sure what was going to happen, but I knew he would try and I was sure it would be worth it

છળછ

Darrton, Ian, and Scotty were standing outside, talking in the hallway, when I walked out. Of course, the conversation stopped and everyone looked at me. *Oh brother.*

"Are you ready?" Darrton asked.

I nodded. "Yeah, let's just go."

"Well, that's no way to treat the day, young lady," Ian said, taking a sip out of a flask that he pulled out of his pocket.

"Neither is that." I pointed toward the flask.

"Oh, how the youth have changed. Does no one get a little tipsy around here anymore?"

Scotty laughed. "Yes, but you're not a little tipsy, Dad."

Dad? How could Ian have kids, especially one that young?

Darrton exchanged a glance with me but it didn't tell me anything. I was so out of the loop on everything. We left the hotel and walked toward the parking lot. There was a stretch limo waiting on us.

"Driving fancy," I whispered tersely to Darrton.

He shrugged. "That's Ian."

Ian swaggered over to the door and drew it open. He waited until we got in before he did. I thought he was just being nice, but then I noticed this put him closest to the bar. I wasn't sure which reason was the right one.

He had poured himself a drink before we even left the parking lot. I had never been inside a limo. We had talked about getting one for senior prom since we were freshman. I wasn't sure if I would ever get back to go when it was time.

Ian smiled and shot down his gin and tonic. "Let's watch some news, shall we? I'm sure there are interesting things our brothers are doing."

I cringed. I didn't want to see one more effin thing that their brothers were doing. They were putting me in a crappy mood. Ian flicked through the channels and stopped on some news station. There was talk about Israel and the war there but then Ian turned it up. He had a serious look on his face.

A man was being videotaped. His eyes were white and his face smooth and angelic. "Everyone, if you follow me, all will be fine. Everything will pull through. This war that is spreading, we will find a way to stop it. We will stop this disaster." Next to him a man stood. His hands in his pockets and a red glare in his eyes. War.

"Those bastards," Ian mumbled below his breath. "Warren will get them all on their side and have each and every one of them doing their biddin'."

Darrton hadn't moved since the TV started. He sat beside me, still and quiet. His hands were gripping his knees. I wasn't sure what was going on in his mind but it wasn't good. I could tell.

Ian sighed and placed his arms on the back of the seat. "Well, we have our work cut out for us, Darrton. We have to get those bastards."

Darrton nodded. "They are moving quicker than we had planned."

Ian looked over at me and then over at Darrton. "She will be fine, my boy. She will be fine."

We were only in the limo for a few short miles after that. The driver pulled up to the gate and I looked out the window at Ian's house. My breath caught in my throat. It reminded me of an eighteen-hundred. Savannah, Georgia, Victorian home. The giant columns on the porch were as big as my bedroom. Ian jumped out and swaggered over to the gate. Darrton helped me out and we followed closely behind Ian. He pressed the button on the brick wall.

"Yes. Who it is?" an Asian voice asked from the other end.

Ian sighed. "Who is it always? It's Ian, Yuki."

"No. Do not sound like him."

"Ah! You blasted fool. Let me into my own house!"

Darrton was holding back a brief smile. I couldn't help but notice Scotty was leaned up against the brick with a cocked eyebrow.

"Yes sir, what is the parsword?"

Ian held the bridge of his nose and sighed. "It's golden boy."

"Goldern boy?"

"Yes! Fool! Let me in!" He threw ups his hands. "My God in Heaven above, that bastard does this to me every damn night. I swear I will have his head before it's over with." The iron gates opened and we pulled onto the paved road leading to Ian's home.

The wooden porch was beige and there was a swing to the right that I swear could hold twelve. Ian opened a door that was made of a deep dark wood, and I smelled lavender breeze by me.

It really wasn't a home, it was a mansion. The ceiling was at least fifteen feet. The foyer was well proportioned and a huge spiral staircase led up to a skylight.

"Welcome to the home of Ian Mercer, a former southerner and still one at heart. I couldn't leave my house behind once I was back here. I had another one built." He glanced up at his masterpiece. "I think we did a pretty damn good job."

"I'd say," I mumbled.

Ian smiled. "Scotty why don't you show our lovely guest to her room for the time being? Darrton and I have business that needs to be discussed."

Scotty pulled himself away from the doorframe and jerked his head toward the stairs. I quickly followed him up toward the second story. He walked smoothly across the marble floor, ignoring all the dynasty mirrors hanging elegantly on the wall. We passed several rooms before he stopped in front of a door with angels engraved into the frame. *Ironic? I think not!*

Above the door, painted in a perfect cursive script, was the word Iofiel. Scotty was watching my face. "It means Angel of Beauty."

I nodded. "I know. I just…I've heard it before."

He smirked. "Darrton requested this room for you."

A rush of heat burned my face. "Yeah, that's where I have heard it before." I passed by Scotty into my room and noticed instantly the fireplace in the far corner. A skylight was open to reveal natural light and the bay windows overlooked the close cut lawn below us. The bedposts were so huge, I couldn't even get my arms around them. Not to mention a comforter that looked like clouds was placed inside them.

"Here is your bathroom." Scotty pointed toward the second door. "I hope this is okay?"

I tried to keep my laughter down but it slipped. "Okay? This one room is nicer than my entire house. Shit! My entire neighborhood."

He laughed and pulled his hands from his pockets. "Yeah, well Dad always likes to do things big. He is drunk a lot but he means well."

"I didn't think he wasn't. He seems funny, yes, drunk often, but he seems like an all-around good guy."

He shrugged. "They'll be gone a couple of days, so you want me to show you around, so you can get used to the place?"

"Of course."

Scotty led me around the upstairs. There were several rooms and bathrooms and he showed me his dad's collection of Civil War guns. One room even had an old car in it. I'm not sure what it was. But it was cool as hell.

"This is where I like to hang out with friends."

"You guys have a theater?" I asked, enthralled with the large screen and rows of black, theater-reclining seats.

"Yep. Mom had always loved going to the movies, so he thought he would bring a reminder of her to us."

Biting my lip I smiled at him. I wanted to know more about his Mom and how exactly he was even here and only looking around twenty but I didn't ask. I couldn't. When my phone began to ring, Scotty looked down at my pocket.

I groaned. "Trevor."

"Boyfriend?"

"Uh no. Thank God. He is an ass and I can't stand him."

Scotty nodded. "So, is Darrton your boyfriend?"

I nearly choked on my own tongue. Pushing my toe around in the carpet I said, "Well, I mean. We just met and everything so I don't really…"

"I understand. One of those, 'it's complicated' things?"

"Very complicated. I'm not even sure if I'll be alive next week, so I'm trying not to make anything more complicated than it has to be."

"Understandable." I guess he felt my awkwardness as he said, "Let's go downstairs, surely they are done talking."

I followed Scotty back downstairs and into the kitchen. I could smell something cooking. It smelled delicious. It smelled like chicken.

The kitchen was more modern than the rest of the house but still had an elderly vibe about it.

"Hello, darlin's, just in time for some food," Ian said. "We southerners love us some food."

Darrton was staring at me when I walked through the door and I watched as he watched me walk. His eyes moving with every move I made. "We are leaving soon," he said.

"Yeah, I figured."

Ian passed a plate and pointed for me to sit down. "Now, you eat your fried chicken or my feelin's will be hurt and I will go all drunk southerner on you."

"You're not drunk now?"

Ian cocked an eyebrow. "Sweetie, this is just an early mornin' tradition. I'm just a happy person."

Scotty sat down across from me. "He's drunk."

I nodded and laughed. "For some reason, I think it could get much worse."

Ian held his hand to his chest. "I'm offended. You think I'm a drunk, young lady."

"If the shoe fits."

"Well, actually the shoe is a size too big."

I snorted and took a drink of the tea that was waiting for me beside my plate. "Ewe! What is this?"

"It's sweet tea, love."

"Sweet, why?"

"It's the southern way. Kids these days do not appreciate anything." He smiled and went off into the kitchen.

Darrton sat beside me and shook his head as Ian walked off. "We're getting ready to leave soon, Elizabeth." He looked at me. "Everything will be fine, I promise. No one will hurt you or your family. You have my word."

I took another bite. "Yeah, I know."

"You will be fine here with Scotty."

Scotty looked up at me. "I wouldn't let anyone hurt you."

Even though I believed them, and I knew they would never let someone hurt me intentionally, I was scared, anyway. I nodded and put on a fake smile. "Yeah, I know. I'm fine."

We finished our diner and then followed Ian into the living room, I mean living house! Because the size could have been someone's home. He sat next to an end table and lit a cigar. "I have to calm my nerves before we leave, or I might go ballistic."

I had many things I wanted to say to that but I felt a sudden turn in my stomach. They were going to leave me here with only one person to defend me against two fallen Horsemen who were designed to end the world. Not that I didn't think Scotty would try to fight them, I just wasn't sure if he could take both of them.

"Don't worry, darlin'," Ian said, tapping the end of his cigar in the crystal ashtray. "We have security cameras on every corner. Believe it or not, I've had robbers before."

"What happened?" I asked, not really caring to know but just trying to get my mind off of my possible death.

"They are buried in the backyard."

This caught my attention. "Say what?"

"Yes, we buried the bastards in the backyard."

Darrton let out a laugh. "My God, Ian, you're a criminal and a murder. What has become of you, Brother?"

Ian swung one leg over his other. "I'm a murderous criminal mastermind, friend. You forgot mastermind." He winked and Scott rolled his eyes.

It was quiet for a few minutes before Ian stood. "I am going to pack a few things. Scotty would you like to help me?"

"Uh, no?"

Ian kicked him and grabbed his ear. "Get in here, child."

"Ouch, Dad, okay, stop."

"Damn it, you fool, I'm tryin' to give them some privacy. Have I taught you nothin'?"

Scotty's mouth was shaped like an o and he turned a dark shade of red. "My bad."

I placed my head in my hands and shook it. "My God, help us Lord because I am about to kill myself."

Darrton sighed and placed his arms on the back of the couch. We didn't say anything for what seemed like a long time. We hadn't even had a chance to talk about all of the stuff that happened last night. The whole making out and stuff. Which there wasn't really much to talk about. It had been amazingly perfect and I wanted more. Period. End of sentence.

"Elizabeth, don't be scared. I know you are."

I shrugged. "I'm not scared." I started clicking my tongue and picking at my shoelace.

His hand fell over mine. "Yes, you are."

I shook my head.

"You're clicking your tongue. You are scared." He turned my face toward his. The chiseled outline of his jaw tightened. "Elizabeth, please, just be calm and trust me. If anything happens to you, I would kill myself if I could. I will not let anyone hurt you. The truth is that I would rather be damned to Hell than to let you die. I couldn't stand it. I'm the only reason you are in the position you are in now. I'm the reason Caden and Warren will try and take revenge. I'm the reason we have to run away like cowards, and I'm the reason any of this happened, because I broke the bond. But I will not be the reason you die, Elizabeth. I refuse. I will sell my soul many times to keep you from death. It's not your place or time."

I choked back tears. "Did you practice that speech?"

Darrton laughed. "Ah, Iofiel. Just promise me you will stay strong? Scotty will take care of you. He is a good kid. We won't be gone but a couple of days, maybe not even that long. Can you manage to stay out of trouble?"

My shoulders lifted and fell. "I will try my damnedest."

His eyes softened. He raised his hand to my necklace and let a butterfly appear out of his hand. "It's funny, huh?"

I watched in awe as the butterfly flapped his wings.

"That your favorite insect has wings?"

I glanced up at him. "I'd never thought of that."

He nodded. "Maybe you were thinking about me before you even knew it."

"I'm sure I was." My answer came without hesitation. "Do you think Warren and Caden would really kill me?"

His eyes darkened and he frowned. "I know they would."

"Well, you two better go find Ferdia. Because I don't want to have to whoop some Horsemen ass today."

Darrton pressed his lips to my forehead and I felt his breath roll down my face. His hands were holding me so tight; there wasn't space in between us. Burying my face in his chest, I said a silent prayer. We needed more help than we ever could imagine. I wasn't sure if God was listening but I utterly hoped he was. There was something pushing at my stomach. There was something wrong with all of this. I didn't want them to leave but I knew I had to let them go. They were going to find help, which was a step in the right direction.

"Elizabeth, be brave," Darrton whispered into my ear. "Scotty will keep you safe. Just calm down and try to relax. You deserve it."

Ian's drunken swagger emerged from the stairs. "Now, I believe that it's time to go find a friend, am I correct?"

Darrton sighed. "And this is who is helping me?"

"Darrton, you've hurt my feelin's. I am taking the time out to help you and you talk about me being drunk?"

"No one said anything about being drunk, Dad."

"I believe they did. Where is my flask?"

Scotty sighed and rolled his eyes. Darrton wrapped his arm around my waist and for the second time he kissed me. This kiss scared me. It was urgent, hard, relentless, and strong. It was a kiss someone gives to a person before going off to war, or when they're scared they won't come back.

When he pulled away, I wasn't breathing normally. "Be safe, Darrton."

"Always."

Ian walked up to me and even though I smelled the whiskey on his breath his eyes showed no fear. There was a hint of hardness around them. "I will keep him safe, darlin'."

"I trust you, Ian."

He winked. "Of course, you do."

CHAPTER 14

Darrton

It took all the strength in me to walk away from that house. Elizabeth was biting back tears and I could feel her heart beating erratically. We all knew that if worse came to worse, Scotty would not be able to protect her from both of them. Ian said there would be no way for them to get in without Scotty seeing it or the alarm going off. *So what*? The alarm would go off and they would have her with them in less than two minutes. Before she could see straight.

My stomach was full of bile and it was trying to push into my throat. Ian walked silently down the pavement toward the limo. He was quiet because we both knew. He had been drinking because he knew there would be a chance of something happening. I prayed they would follow our trail to Ferdia and think Elizabeth was with me. That was the prayer that had been in my heart since the moment we left.

Ian opened the gate and I braced myself. The driver opened the door. We both slid into the back.

When the driver was behind the wheel again, he asked, "Where to, boss?"

Ian was chugging down another shot. "To the nearest cliff, Evan."

"Yes, sir."

Ian crossed his legs and looked at me over a narrowed glare. "We will find Ferdia and we will fight them, Darrton."

"I know. But that doesn't necessarily mean we will win."

He tipped an imaginary hat at me. "That is something we will have to risk. Do you love her enough to fight for her?"

My heart thudded. It almost hurt to hear that word. Love. Love wasn't something that we thought of as Horsemen. We thought of disaster, death, winning, bad and monstrous things.

"I will take that as a maybe..." Ian trailed off, taking another swig.

"I'm not supposed to get distracted. That was God's rule."

Ian cocked an eyebrow. "I believe God had a rule about waiting on His call to start The Apocalypse, too, right?" He leaned forward, a serious expression on his face. He had stubble growing on his cheeks and I knew he was tired. He was scared, he was helping me, and he didn't have to. "We all make mistakes, Darrton. You've made a handful. You've been damned to earth because of it. You don't have to make any more. We can fix this. It won't be easy but we will have to fix this. And I don't mean this in an overdramatic kind of way, but the fate of the world depends on it." He managed a smile and leaned back.

"That's what frightens me. We could lose and everything would go to hell. It would all fall on my shoulders because I did not stop them. I shook hands with them and promised my loyalty to them. I'm just as involved in this as they are."

Ian stroked his chin and shrugged his shoulders. "Where I'm from, promises are meant to be broken."

"Where I'm from, promises not kept, end in death."

Ian cocked a brown eyebrow. "Why would you have to worry about Death? You are Death."

We arrived at the cliff. The driver pulled slowly up to the bare, desert-looking sand. The mountains were huge in the distance and the air was crisper, here up this high. Ian leaned over to his driver and said, "I have bags in the back. Have them sent to this address." He handed him a piece of paper. "And when you get back, if Scotty or Lizzie want to go anywhere, take them. I want her to feel at home, and I want her to not worry, is that clear?"

Evan, the driver, nodded and the window rolled up.

Watching the black limo drive away, I asked, "How much does Evan know? He seems rather calm about dropping us off at a cliff and leaving."

Ian shrugged. "He never asks any questions. I treat him well. His kids are set for life and he and his wife are happy and have plenty. That was our bargain. He doesn't ask questions and I will take care of anything he needs."

A cold shiver shot through my arm and grabbed my ring. "Damn."

"Which one?"

"Cold...I would say Caden. He has always had ice in his veins."

"That, my dear friend, means we'd better gettin' goin'. We have a Horseman to find." He walked to the edge and looked down. "Are you sure he will be willin' to help us, Darrton?"

I shrugged. "I'm hoping he will be. That isn't a promise I can make you, but I can say that if any of them would help, it will be him."

Ian nodded. "Well, that's good enough for me, partner. Let's fly," he said, winking and stretching his arms out. His shirt ripped from his body and his wings sprang out in a gush of wind. His wings, like mine, were black. Being damned will do that to an angel. Ian smiled at the wind and looked over at me. "Beat you there."

Smiling, I watched as he bent his legs and soared up toward the sun. I felt my wings ripping from my back before I even realized they wanted out. My body always felt free when my wings were open and I was flying. But as I bounded off the cliff and soared toward the sky, I had a sick feeling in my stomach. This time, "free" wasn't a part of my mind. Saving her was.

CHAPTER 15

Lizzie

My first conscious thought after the door shut was that I had no idea who this guy standing beside me was. Yeah, I knew what Darrton and Ian said about him. *But hell. Do I really know Ian, anyway?*

"So…" Scotty said, leaning against the now shut door. "This is a little awkward, now isn't it?"

I let out a laugh. "You're telling me."

"You like pool?" he asked.

I shrugged. "Never really played."

His mouth opened in awe. "Well, dear friend, it's never too late to learn."

An hour and twenty painful minutes later, I had a semi-good idea of how to play pool. The rules…yes. Was I good? Hell, no.

Lining the pool cue up, I pushed it against the ball. It missed. "I think you're winning, Scotty."

He shrugged and took a swig of the Miller he had in his hand. "Who's keeping score?"

Eyeing the drink, I glanced up at him. "Are you old enough to be drinking that?"

Scotty's lips crawled up his mouth into a smile. "Yes, officer, I turned twenty-one a couple of decades ago." He took another swig.

"Good to know." I stopped and watched him. How could he be so young and so…old?

He bent down, eyeing the ball, and shot it right into the hole…thingy. He leaned back and admired his work. "How old are you?"

"Unfortunately, I'm only seventeen."

"Ah," he said. "The teen years. Drama, drama, drama."

Nodding, I shifted my feet, "Yeah, tell me about it. Fallen angels, Horsemen, boyfriends trying to screw you, and a best friend you can't even talk to.

He cocked an eyebrow and leaned on the table. "Sounds like a teen soap opera."

"It is." I tried my pathetic attempt at making the shot and it actually went it. One out of thirty seven tries. *Go figure.*

He tipped his glass. "Lucky shot."

"Scotty."

"Ummmhmmm," he said, squinting one eye and making a clean shot. "What is it, girl?"

I was trying not to click my tongue since Darrton said I always do that when I got nervous. Instead, I played with a string hanging off the end of my shirt. "You know earlier when you said Ian was your dad?"

Scotty laughed, leaned back, and crossed his arms. "Well, he is."

"Yeah! I mean, I believe you…I just don't understand how…"

He coughed. "Well, friend, when a man and a woman get horny, they…"

"Hey! Cut it out," I said with a smile. "You know what I mean."

He nodded and finished the rest of his drink. "Yeah. I know what you mean. Sit down, kid. I'll explain the unbelievable to you."

We walked over to the couch sitting in the corner of the room. Scotty sat and propped his feet up on the table in front of us. His face looked...tired. I hadn't noticed before but there were black circles underneath his eyes.

"What are you?" I asked before I registered what I had said.

He laughed and pushed his hands through his blond hair. "I'm a half-bred, Lizzie. A mutt."

"Should I call you mutt?"

He glanced out of the corner of his eye at me. "I'm a Nephilim."

I had never heard the word before but it gave my spine a chill. "What exactly does it mean?"

"There is a story behind it. In the beginning of time when Lucifer and his followers were cast out of Heaven, they would 'mingle—'" He gave me a sideways glance. "With humans. That is how Nephils are made. They are half-human and half-angel."

I furrowed my brow. "So, you're half?"

"That's right." He pointed to himself. "In the flesh."

"So you're an angel?" I asked, with a smile.

He cocked an eyebrow. "I sure as hell look like one." *That's right.* He laughed and it was just as heavenly as an angel's. "But how do you know I'm one of the good guys? What if I'm on the bad side?"

"There are good and bad sides?"

"Aren't there always?" He stretched his arms out on the back of the couch. "Since the beginning of time there has been good and evil."

"What determines whether someone is a 'bad' angel or a 'good' one?"

He sighed and sat forward, his hands clasped between his legs. "First, it could be on how your parents raised you. Secondly, it could be because someone close to you isn't a good guy. Or thirdly, you always have a choice to do good or bad. It's within yourself that matters."

"How could a fallen angel not be good? They're angels?"

"Think about what you just said, kid. They're fallen. They would've had to have done something to fall. None can be truly good if they have fallen."

That made me cringe. *None could be truly good if they had fallen?*

"The truth is stranger than fiction sometimes, kid." He winked and stood up. "Enough with the heavy. We need to go eat. I'm starved." He offered me his hand. "Can you cook?"

I looked up and raised an eyebrow. "This isn't the 1800s. You can cook."

"Well, we're shit out of luck." He led me up toward the door. "Better yet, let's just go to Philly Bilmos. I know they can cook."

"Where is Philly Bilmos?"

"Down town."

"Are we supposed to leave the house?"

He shrugged. "I'm hungry, you're hungry. We have an excellent excuse." He smiled.

⤳⤳⤳

Scotty drove a Jaguar. Not that I didn't expect it, since his dad seemed to be loaded. I whistled as I saw it sitting underneath the side carport. "This is nice, Scotty. Could Ian adopt me?"

He unlocked the car. "I bet he would."

"What kind of car is this?" I asked, sitting down in the passenger seat.

"It's a Jaguar XKR-S. It goes 0-60 in less than 4.2 seconds, and it can get up to 186 miles." He started the car, with just a button, I might add, and it purred underneath us. The smell of leather filled my nose and I suddenly envied him. My Honda wasn't even in the same league or four leagues below his. The chrome was polished inside. I could see my reflection in. Scotty pushed a button on the touch-screen navigation/DVD/CD/GPS—hell I'm not even sure what all it did—and Kings of Leon began to play

I smiled. "I guess music doesn't differ from angel, Nephilim, to human?"

"Can't beat this," he said, backing up and gunning it down the road.

A few minutes later we pulled into 164th Avenue. Scotty swerved his car into the parking lot and killed the engine. "Let's go, kid."

I followed closely behind him as we went inside. I smelled the best food I've ever smelled.

"This place has the best Philly cheesesteak ever," he told me. "No other place compares. No exceptions. Period."

"I guess I know what I'm getting then."

He turned and looked at me. "You have no choice."

The waiter greeted us. He seemed to know Scotty. He sat us by the window and went to get our drinks.

Scotty took my menu as soon as I opened it and shook his head. He pointed toward himself. "I've got this, Sweetheart."

I held back a smile.

The waiter returned and pulled out his ticket book and pen. "What can I get you two?"

"Two Philly cheesesteaks, fully loaded, with Cajun fries, extra crispy."

The man smiled and took the menu. "That will be out in just a little while."

Scotty nodded and looked back at me. "You're going to love them. I can tell."

"How could you tell what I like?"

"I have that gift. I'm a food teller."

I managed not to laugh but it was hard. "Hmm. Oh really, now, then what is my favorite cereal."

"Frosted Flakes."

"Wrong. Mini Frosted Wheat's."

"Same damn thing, kid. Frosted is frosted."

"So not the same thing but I'll take it. What is my favorite cheese?"

"Gouda."

I managed a surprised face. "That one is right. People, we have us a food teller in our presence."

He stood and pretended to bow. My phone, which I had set on the table, started to vibrate. Mom's name came across the screen.

"Aren't you going to answer that? It is your mother."

I shook my head and pressed ignore. "I'm not allowed to answer."

"Why not?" he asked, leaning against the table.

"Darrton says no one can know where I'm at. They will try to come and get me and make me go home. Then basically

Caden and Warren will come and kill me," I said, twisting my straw around in my cup.

"You weren't lying. You do live in a teenage soap opera." Scotty leaned back and shook his head. "How did you get mixed up with Darrton, anyway?"

"Well, he kind of just showed up in my back yard. He was hiding in a bush."

He chuckled. "Well-hidden, Darrton."

"He was hurt when he fell."

"So, it was just the luck of the draw that your house was the one he landed behind? Well, don't you have the shittiest luck ever?"

"I guess you could say that." I frowned and watched my phone blinking a red light, telling me I had a text. Scotty snatched my phone up and opened the text. "You ever hear of privacy, Scotty? Or do Nephilim not know what that is?"

"Lizzie, please tell me where you are. I'm so confused. I can't remember anything, it's like there are holes in my memory." Scotty cocked an eyebrow. "Who is Trevor?"

I groaned.

"Ah! The boyfriend in the drama."

I shook my head as the waiter brought our cheesesteaks over to us and set them down. "He isn't my boyfriend, at least not any more. I had the biggest effin crush on him ever. We had a fling during the summer and dated for like a week this year."

"So..." Scotty said, squirting ketchup on his fries and drowning it in salt and pepper, "What's the problem, Liz. I'm afraid I don't see it."

"He—he was kind of pushy."

He cocked an eyebrow with a fry hanging out of his mouth. "You mean he wanted you?"

I nodded and took a bite of my cheesesteak. "This is delicious."

"Are you avoiding the subject, Miss. Lawrence?"

I rolled my eyes. "Yeah, I guess he did."

"And you didn't want him?"

I nodded. "I did. At first...I mean...no I didn't I was scared...I wasn't ready and he wouldn't leave me alone about it."

He nodded. "Can't blame a guy for trying."

"Yeah." I laughed. "I can."

He fluttered his eyes in an eye roll. "Where does the 'holes in the memory' thing come in?"

"We can thank Darrton for that. He kind of saw him trying to..."

Scotty choked on his fry. "Good God, and Trevor is still alive?"

"Barely. It wasn't pretty. Darrton was...mad."

"Yeah, I can tell he cares about you. It's not even really in his nature now to love. I'm surprised you got under his skin the way you did. You must be one hell of a kisser, kid."

I blushed. "Shut up."

"Awe, you're blushing, sweets."

I flipped him off.

"Now, that's not ladylike."

I ignored him and took another bite. Suddenly, an eerie feeling started crawling up my back. I glanced around and saw a girl looking at me from the bar. Her eyes were squinted and her dark hair was cut in a short bob, close to her head like Halle Berry's. Her skin was a milk chocolate color. I looked back at my food and tried to eat some more.

"Scotty, the hottie," I heard someone say. The creepy girl was standing next to our table. Her hand on her hip and a sneer was directed in my direction.

"Ariel, how are you, dear." Scotty stood up to greet her but she excused him with a hand wave and took a seat right beside him.

Her hazel eyes narrowed. "Scotty, you're not going to introduce me to your girlfriend?"

"Oh! I'm not his girlfriend."

Scotty rolled his eyes. "Lay off, Ariel. This is Elizabeth Lawrence."

"Your girlfriend?" she asked again.

Scotty sighed and glanced over at Ariel. "Lizzie is not my girlfriend. I think she has enough guy trouble without me. She is one of my dad's friend's daughters. She is staying in town for a little while."

She leaned forward. I coughed. "So, are you Scotty's girlfriend?" I asked.

Scotty leaned back, shook his head, and mouthed, "Hell no."

"No, who wants to know?" she asked.

"Just wondering."

"Hmm."

"Ariel is a Nephil, too, Lizzie."

"Why the hell would you tell her that, Scotty? Maybe I didn't want her to know about me? You being a Nephil, is your business to tell, but me being one is not?" Her eyes darted back to mine. "Are you a Nephil?"

I shook my head. "No, I'm…just human."

"How do you know about Nephilims then?"

"Because of Scotty."

"She knows Darrton," Scotty said, finishing off his food.

She stopped and looked back at me. Her face had changed, it was scared. "Oh, Darrton."

Scotty laughed. "Speaking of Darrton and fiery Horsemen," he said, nodding his head toward the TV hanging in the corner. "Looks like someone has made their way back to America."

The news channel showed a flash of videos and images that were a plague of red. My skin crawled in a slither down my back.

"They're in Rhode Island," Scottie said. "They're making their way across the country." Scotty placed his drink down and reached into his wallet, throwing a fifty on the table. "Let's go. We need to get hidden before Warren and Caden find their way to us and rip us to shreds."

Ariel followed us out to Scotty's car and crawled into the back seat. "Why would they want to find us, Scotty? What did we do to them?"

He sped off, heading home. "They don't want us. They want Lizzie. Darrton refused to kill her and Warren and Caden want her dead because she knows too much. So now they are coming to kill her."

Ariel scoffed. "So this is all her fault? They will come looking for us because of her?"

"No one invited you, Ariel. You didn't have to come. I'm here to protect her while Dad and Darrton go and try to find Ferdia."

"Well, I'm staying."

"No bitching then." Scotty swerved around several cars. "Lizzie, you're tense over there. It's going to be okay."

I cleared my throat. "What exactly can a Nephil do? Do you have, like, powers or strength?"

"We have strength. We fly...ya know, the normal stuff."

"Yeah, normal."

Ariel made her way in between our seats the best she could. "We also have an ability to save one person's life. If they are dying."

Scotty nodded. "Yes, but in return we die. We give our life for the one that we are trying to save."

"That sounds like witchcraft."

Scotty nodded. "It is. Well sort of…when the angels were damned to Hell in the beginning, they weren't good. They were bad. One of the archangels that was damned had fallen in love with a human. When he died, she wanted to save him. She went to a witch and begged to have the power. She gave her life for his. And so on…"

"That's creepy."

Scotty shrugged. "I guess it could come in handy."

That didn't really make me feel good. *Why would we have to worry about that?* God, I hoped that nothing happened that would lead to that.

When we got to Scotty's house, Ariel barged in like she knew her way around. "I'm going to the bathroom."

I waited until she had made it upstairs before I said, "What the hell is wrong with her? Either she is just an utter bitch or she slept with you and you ditched her."

Scotty acted taken back. He placed his hand on his heart and said, "I can't believe you would suggest that I would take advantage of a girl?"

I cocked an eyebrow. "Well, seeing as your father is always drinking…I'm just saying maybe drinking runs in the family and maybe being a drunk lover runs in it, too?"

He laughed and I followed him toward the living room. A flat screen pulled down from the ceiling and Scotty pulled up the Netflix screen. "So, what are we watching today? Any request, ladies?"

Ariel walked in the room and squeezed in between Scotty and me. He pushed his blond hair from his face and rolled his eyes.

"How about *Angels in the Outfield*?" I suggested.

In unison they both looked at me.

"Are you trying to be funny?" Ariel rolled her eyes and kicked off her combat boots, while propping her feet on the table.

Scotty laughed. "*Angels in the Outfield* it is then, since we have no more takers."

We watched *Angels in the Outfield* and Scotty ordered a pizza. I didn't say anything but it always shocked me that angels ate regular food. *I mean come on*? In the stories vampires drink blood, werewolves, eat people and what about fallen angels…to my surprise anything that humans eat. *Whatever.*

Ariel fell asleep on Scotty and he left her there snoring while we went upstairs. "She always does that," Scotty said.

"Does what?" I asked.

"Falls asleep, on purpose." He rolled his eyes and gagged. "She is one of my dad's friend's daughters. Her mother is a fallen as well. I've known her since I was young. She was born in the '60s, and ever since we were kids she has been a bitch. I don't know what it is. She isn't a nice houseguest."

"She wants you, Scotty," I said, smiling and walking into my room. I tried to block out the *Iofiel* that was above the door but seeing it formed a knot in my throat.

Scotty leaned in the doorway and watched me sit down on my bed. "He'll be okay, ya know."

I didn't look up at him; I pressed and drew my fingers along the threads on my bedspread. "Yeah, I know."

"You're scared, I can sense it."

I cocked an eyebrow. "Is that another gift?"

He scoffed and came over and sat beside me. "No, it's a hunch. Because you wouldn't be human if you weren't."

I chocked back a cry. "I am scared. So scared. What if they take my family? What if they take Millie? Or Trevor? It's still not fair to him whether I hate his guts or not. They didn't do anything wrong. They've been dragged into this because of me and…Darrton, he could die. He could die fighting for me."

Scotty stared at me, his dark eyes watching every move. "You left someone out."

I wiped my face. "Who?"

"You. What if something happens to you? Aren't you worried about that?"

"Rather me than them."

He smiled. It was a sympathy smile but he smiled. He stepped forward, sat beside me, wrapped his arms around me, and whispered into my hair. "I won't let anything happen to you. You'll be fine. Darrton and Ian will be back soon and everything will be okay," he promised.

"Don't make promises you can't keep."

He didn't reply. We both knew he couldn't promise that. Scotty got up and went toward the door. He looked back before he left. "Get some rest, Iofiel. You deserve some rest. It's been a long day for you."

I nodded and turned my back, so he couldn't see the tears wanting to escape.

After my shower, I slipped into a pair of Victoria Secret's pink flannel PJs. I sat on my bed with a wet head and looked at my phone. I had 46 missed calls just today and 62 texts. All from my parents, Millie, and Trevor.

I looked through a few and my blood went cold. Underneath was a text from my Mom it said, *Can't find*

Samantha. Please call us, Lizzie. Millie says she talked to you the other day.

I scrolled down. This one was from Millie. *Just heard your sister is missing, please come home. I'm so scared.*

My phone fell from my hands. *What do they mean, missing?* She had to be there. Who would have taken her? Who would have not brought her back after ten minutes of her rattling mouth? My stomach churned. *This is not happening.*

I dialed Darrton's number and cried into my hand.

"Hello!" Darrton said, panic and menace in his voice.

"Darrton, oh my God, they have her!"

"Who, Elizabeth. They have who?"

"Samantha, my sister, they have her I know it."

There was silence on the other end.

"Darrton, please tell me you are coming home. I don't need to be alone right now. I'm freaking out."

"Elizabeth. You have got to listen to me and calm down. We will get her back, okay? They won't kill her. They are only using her to get to you. Please, calm down and breathe. Where is Scotty?"

I sniffled. "Downstairs, I think."

"Stay close to Scotty tonight. They are coming for you, not Scotty. You have to stay close to him. He can protect you better than you can protect yourself."

I didn't answer. I couldn't.

"Elizabeth, I have to go, please listen to me, Iofiel."

I nodded as if he could really hear me. Finally, I mumbled, "Yes. I promise I will listen. I'm going to get him now."

"Elizabeth."

"Yes."

"I'll be back for you soon."

The call ended.

It took me five minutes just to get up from the bed and walk downstairs. Scotty was sitting in his armchair with a beer in his hand, reading the newspaper.

He looked up and his eyes skimmed down me. My face flushed and I wrapped my arms around my stomach. *Damn it, I forgot to put my bra back on.*

He cleared his throat and stood up. "Is everything okay?"

I shook my head and bit my tongue to keep from crying. "No, they have my sister. They took my sister."

He furrowed his brow and ran his fingers through his hair. "How old is she?"

"Twelve."

"Bastards," he mumbled.

"Would it be okay if you slept in a room close to mine tonight?"

Scotty's face softened. "Of course, kid. Let me get ready and I'll be up in there in just a couple of minutes."

"Scotty."

"Hmm?"

"Thank you for this."

He winked. "Anytime, kid."

I turned to go up the stairs but stopped and asked, "Where is Ariel?"

He sighed. "Thank God, she went home."

I smiled and walked up stairs.

About three minutes later, I heard a slight rap on my door. "Come in. It's your house."

Scotty leaned up against the door frame. He had his shirt off and a pair of basketball shorts on. He wasn't big, but he had long, lean muscles in his chest. "Yes, but it would be awfully rude of me not to knock. You are a lady and I am a gentleman and it is late at night. I've got to make my bed for the night."

I blushed. *Is he staying in here?* "You don't have to stay in here. You can stay in another room. I don't want you to be uncomfortable."

He brushed me off. "Wouldn't have it any other way, kid." Scotty put a blanket on the floor and I threw him a pillow from the bed. Once we were settled in, I relaxed. At least this would help a little.

"Scotty."

"Yes."

"Are you scared?"

"About the Horsemen?"

"Mmhmm and what they are doing. Turning all of us against each other?"

"They won't hurt me. They won't hurt a Nephil. They are trying to rid the Earth of humans. We are like them. We have been damned to Earth by God. They won't hurt us. But I'm scared for the outcome of the world. I'm scared I'll wake up one day and not ever see another human again. Or get to fall in love, or have a normal life."

"Do you think they will make it? Do you think they will get the rest of the world?"

He was silent for a while. "They've been doing one hell of a job right now, but I think that if Darrton is careful enough, they can sneak up on them and defeat them. If Ferdia helps, they will have a better chance than without him. If Warren and Caden get to them before Ferdia, their chances are slimmer."

"How do you know their names?"

Scotty was silent for a second and my body quaked. "All fallen angels know who they are."

I sighed in relief. "I hope this all works out okay. I just want my family and friends to be safe. I want Darrton to be safe. I want to be safe."

"Darrton will make sure you're okay. He'll make sure that nothing happens to you or your family. As much as it's a shock to say that he does, I think, he loves you. He's never loved anyone since he died. It's not his nature to love, so I know that he does love you or he wouldn't be fighting so hard to save you. Not that I can blame him. You're pretty awesome, kid."

I smiled up at the ceiling. "I'm glad two people think so."

"Three, Trevor."

"Gag me."

"I'm sure he would."

"Ah! You pervert. That's disgusting."

"Hey, just saying, kid."

"Thanks for coming in here, Scotty. I'm glad I'm not alone."

"No problem. You better get to sleep. I'm an early bird and, plus, Dad and Darrton will most likely make it back home tomorrow. We wouldn't want anything to happen tonight."

That sentence made a chill run over my body. "I hope they're back tomorrow."

"Hey, Lizzie?"

"Hmm," I said into the side of my pillow.

"I'm sorry about your sister. We'll get her back."

"I hope so."

CHAPTER 16

Lizzie

I woke with a start and blinked, trying to focus my vision. I faintly remembered a noise being the reason I awakened. *Maybe a noise down the hallway?* I heard a slight bump again. *I think it's coming from downstairs.* I rubbed my eyes so much I thought that they might pop out from the friction. Once they settled, I looked around the room. Everything appeared normal. I glanced down and noticed that Scotty was asleep. His arm was over his eyes and his mouth was half open.

I smiled. He was adorable. I tried to whisper his name but my throat was scratchy. *I need some water.* I got out of bed and tip-toed out of the room, making sure not to wake Scotty. He never even moved. *Going down stairs for one minute won't hurt.* The hallway was dark and my pulse raced. I bit my lip and slowly walked down the hall.

Sighing, I took the stairs two at a time, trying to be as quiet as I could. I didn't want Scotty to wake up. The kitchen was to the left. I leaped over the last step and tripped over something. "Shit!" When I looked up, I saw a cell phone lying on the bottom step

I felt a stinging on my foot. Bringing it up, I saw a cut on it. There was a flashing light coming from the cell phone. I opened it…and let out a tortured scream.

It's Samantha's phone. She is here. They have her. "Samantha!"

I dropped Sam's phone and ran up the stairs. I could barely see in the darkness but I knew someone was watching me. I could feel their eyes on me, their smiles.

"Scotty!" I screamed and at the same instant, a hand wrapped around my mouth. I didn't even have time to think before I was being dragged toward a bedroom down the hall. I tried to grab the door frame but my fingernails only bent backwards. I let go, unable to bear the pain.

My head was slammed against the wooden floor and I cried out in pain. I tried to regain my vision but my eyes were blurring and there was a ringing sound in my head. I grabbed my head and slipped to the floor.

"Well, aren't you a pretty little thing?"

I squinted trying to see him. I couldn't place his voice, but I knew who it had to be. Either Warren or Caden. "Get up," he said.

I tried to stand up but my legs buckled beneath me. My honey-colored hair fell from my bun to cover my face.

"Get up!" he yelled again.

This time he kicked my side and I felt vomit trying to escape my mouth.

I picked myself up and tried to stand straight. A man with short brown hair and a menacing grin stood in front of me. The perfect smile on his face and his smooth, pore-less skin was something out of a dream, but the devilish red gleam in his eyes could only be something from Hell.

"Now that we are standing—" He smiled while his eyes traveled down my frame and a cold burn traveled the length of my body. "I see why Darrton is so intrigued. You're a pretty mortal." He tickled my chin and I jerked away. "Aw." He shook his head. "Let's not be strangers. I feel we will have to spend a lot of time together, sweetness. Brother."

Watching from the corner of my eye, I saw a man walk out from a corner of the room. The piercing white in his eyes made my body shiver. His smile was not as scary as the other's but I watched closely as he walked. I noticed a bow strapped to his back. He was the one on the motorcycle, at the football game.

The brown-haired one smiled. "This is my brother, Caden, Conquest. Silly me." He slapped his forehead, "I forgot to introduce myself. I'm Warren. And we all know you're Elizabeth. Too bad Darrton isn't here for you now. Isn't it funny how faith works out?"

I didn't know how I managed to force out any words through the tightness of my throat but something inside me made me speak. "What do you want?"

"Oh, dear." Caden smiled and walked closer to me. "What a cliché. What do you want?"

Warren moved closer and a terrible tremble echoed throughout my body. "Dear, we don't want anything but for Darrton to come with us. We are brothers and we intend on keeping our pact. Now, when Darrton comes back, he will come running on his pale horse to your rescue," he spat.

Caden tisked. "The pale horse is not intended to be used for saving lives but for killing. Darrton is stalling our plan. But he has no choice. We won't leave anyone alive if that's what it takes."

"What if I agree to go?"

Caden laughed and it rang in my ears. "You do not have to agree to go. We do what we want."

I cleared my throat and pushed the word past the lump forming in it. "What do I have to do for you to leave Samantha out of this?"

"Now, we're talking." Caden laughed and left the room. He returned a moment later with Samantha in his hands. She was hitting his chest and screaming. When she calmed down, she noticed me and she let out a sob. Caden dropped her to the floor with a thud.

Sam kicked Caden in the shin and crawled towards me. "Lizzie!" she sobbed. He snarled and looked at Warren who glared at him. "Ohmigod! You look horrible," she said, sobbing into my shoulder. "We thought you were dead." She held onto me and wiped her snotty nose on my shirt. Her hair was all over the place, her clothes bloody and torn.

"Have they hurt you?" I asked, examining her.

"Those assholes!" She got up and tried to run toward them, her fist held high, but I caught her. *They must not have harmed her—yet. Since she thinks it's okay to try and fight them.*

"Now, I hope you haven't been teaching her these words. I've never met anyone who I have wanted to slaughter in the first ten minutes, before I met this young lady," Warren said, giving Sam a tightlipped smile.

She gave him the finger. I grabbed her hand and forced her to look at me. Her eyes were dark underneath and she was about to cry. "Sam, stop!"

"You two are stupid assholes!" she yelled.

I grabbed her face. "Stop, Samantha." She tried to interrupt but I squeezed her cheeks. "Samantha, any other time I would let you run your lip, but you have to shut the hell up and listen. You have to do what they say. You have to believe me. Do not hit them again."

She nodded and I sighed as I watched it register in her mind. "Just take me and leave Sam alone. I'll do anything."

Warren stroked his chin and leaned up against the bedpost. "Now, we have to ask a favor from you, Elizabeth."

"Anything," I whispered.

Caden smiled. "We need you to call Darrton. Find out where he is, and then tell him you never want to speak to him again."

My lips betrayed me and I let out a sharp cry. "He won't believe me."

"No, he won't. We do not need him to believe it, and we need him to know that we're here. We need him to come after you. We need him to help us open the gates If he knows we put you up to it, he will know that we're not going to kill you yet. But if he thinks we are making you tell him you never want to talk to him again, he will know that we're going to take you away." Warren smiled. "Do you see what I am saying, doll? We need you to say you're going to leave. Darrton will know we're making you leave and come to your rescue."

The demeaning tone in his voice made me grit my teeth. "And my sister goes free?"

Warren and Caden exchanged glances. "Yes," they said in unison.

"Okay. I–I need my phone. I have to go get it—" I tried to stand up but Warren stopped me with his foot on my shoulder and handed me my phone. I closed my eyes before saying, "Okay."

Dialing Darrton's number, I prayed that he wouldn't answer.

"Hello, Elizabeth. Are you there? Is everything okay?"

"No. Everything is not okay. I—" Warren gritted his teeth and grabbed Samantha around the neck. "I can't see you anymore."

The other end of the line was silent for what seemed like a lifetime. My head was screaming *No! Please! Help!*

"Warren, Caden, I see you've made it."

Warren clapped his hands and Caden laughed. "Good, Brother. You're not losing your touch, just losing your balls."

"Let her go, Warren. She has nothing to do with this."

"What? You don't want me to do this?" Warren grabbed my hair.

I screamed and kicked. "Please, stop! Let me go."

"You heard her, let her go," I heard someone say from the door. It was Scotty. His hair was ruffled and his shorts hung low on his hips. "Let her go, Warren."

A moment of relief brushed my body and I sighed. Warren laughed and dropped me. My knees hit the floor and I crawled over toward the phone and listened to Darrton.

"Well, long time no talk, Brother," Caden said.

A smile spread across Scotty's face. In a moment of silence, I watched Caden take Scotty into a hug. *Oh no.*

A blur of blond hair roamed into my mind. Brother. Not fallen-angel brothers but real brothers. Half-brothers. Caden and Warren had been sent to Heaven long after Ferdia and Darrton. My stomach twisted and I clenched my first. "They're on the same side Darrton," I whispered into the phone.

"Do what they say," he whispered. "I'm on my way."

"Are you alone? Did you find him?"

"We found him, Elizabeth. They have killed him. Now, they have to have a fallen, Nephilim or demon to perform the ritual in place of Ferdia. They must have someone lined up already. Do what they say. I'll be there as fast as I can." The phone went dead.

I pulled Samantha to me. She was shivering and was wrapped as tightly around me as anyone could be.

Scotty turned to look at me. I saw something in his eyes I had never seen before, menace. My mind had stop working for a good minute. Scotty had been playing me the entire time. He showed no signs I could remember that he was bad. *He is with them.* My body was aching from shaking so terribly. *They are going to kill us.* Samantha was clinging to me and a huge pain was hammering down in my chest. *This is all your fault, Elizabeth. My sister is going to die because of me.*

I let her continue to cry on my shoulder while I watched Scotty. His eyes caught mine. There was a dark hint of something lurking in his eyes. *Pure Evil.* When a tear escaped and ran down my face, he squinted. The wrinkles around his eyes showed and there was a deep hidden expression. He was fighting something. There was a tug-of-war in his eyes.

He was the best actor I'd ever seen in my life. "Well, Lizzie, I see you've met my brother, Scotty," Caden said.

It took all my power to make myself speak. *He was lying to me the entire time.* "We've met."

Scotty threw his head back and laughed. "You're so pathetic. You believed every word I said. Oh, the joys of teenage girls. They'll do anything for a boy. Now, are you willing to let Darrton go to save your sister?"

A scream roared in my head. I wanted it to erupt but it wouldn't come out of my mouth. It was too dry and my body was too weak. They were using my sister as bait. I had to choose whether my sister lived or if I'd ever see Darrton again. They needed him for some damn ritual. Darrton had warned me. He told me they would do this. I nodded.

Warren stepped closer to me and said, "You've destroyed our plans. We have to have two Horsemen and Darrton, being Death, is required. The fourth participate doesn't have to be a Horseman. He just has to be supernatural. With Darrton we could have already conquered. We need him to do the ritual! You've ruined him. We could have already ruled everything but no, Darrton had to go and become the gentle knight and try to rescue you." He threw his hands up. "It doesn't look as if he is here to save you now, does it?"

Even though I knew that he was just trying to upset me, it still stung my heart. Darrton had left me here alone with Scotty. Anything could happen—anything was happening.

"I'm the pathetic one, but you're the one who is pathetically trying to take over the world," I said.

Warren smiled and kicked me in the side. Samantha was screaming and my head was spinning.

"I see someone has never been to church?" Warren said. "*'When He opened the fourth seal, I heard the voice of the fourth living creature saying, 'Come and see.' So I looked, and behold, a pale horse. And the name of him who sat on it was Death, and Hades followed with him…'*"

My blood ran cold. *Hades would follow Darrton?* They needed Darrton because the Devil would follow him out…he would kill everyone…we would all die…because the good haven't been sent to Heaven yet…*the Devil would follow Darrton*…I was trying to breathe but it was caught in my throat.

Scotty leaned against the bedpost and took a long look at me. "Are we okay, Lizzie? Are you scared yet?"

Samantha was shivering beside me. Her hands were wrapped around me, and she was sobbing into my shoulder. I didn't answer. I couldn't.

"Well, I guess it's time to go now," Warren said. "We have no need to be here. We have to go meet Darrton so he can try to save his lovely girl."

Caden strolled forward and grabbed Samantha while Warren grabbed me. "Wait, you promised you would leave her. Don't bring her with us. Leave her here. Please, I'll do anything."

Caden looked over at Warren and nodded. "Okay, dear, we will leave her here." Caden dragged Samantha over toward the window and I felt my stomach grow heavy.

"No!" I tried to move but Warren wouldn't let go of me. I watched as she struggled against Caden, as he opened the window. Tears were escaping her face. Her little legs kicked and her eyes begged for me to help.

"Please! Don't!"

Caden tugged on Samantha. I watched as she grabbed a hunk of Caden's hair and pulled. He snarled.

"Let me go, you asshole!" She kicked at Caden as he pulled her toward the window. "You're going to burn in Hell!" she screamed.

I tried to move again but Warren held me tight.

"Let her go, please! Don't do this. I'll do anything. Just let her go!" I screamed. More tears were streaming down my face and my entire body was turning cold.

I watched as he tossed her so effortlessly out the window. I fell. My legs were no longer able to hold me up. I wasn't sure if my heart was even beating. It felt like it would break my ribs from the inside out. My body was shaking in a hard, heavy rhythm.

Caden looked back at me, a smirk on his face. "Now that we have taken care of business here, I think we need to leave."

Warren picked me up, tossed me over his shoulder, and carried me from the room while I kicked and screamed. I did everything I could to try to get free. I hit his back and kicked with all my might but he held onto me with a grip I could have only imagined. Scotty was walking behind us, his face a mask. He wasn't laughing anymore, his green eyes darted toward mine and I could see he was on the fence. He didn't know whether he should run away or fight with them. He might be my only way out of this. He might be my only chance at escaping.

Warren threw me inside a massive black car and I hit my head on the window. I didn't care. It throbbed but I couldn't feel anything past the hurt in my heart. My sister was dead because of Caden. My sister would never turn thirteen, or have a real boyfriend, or go to prom. Her life had been ripped right out from under her. I tried not to cry but I couldn't stop it. The tears stung down my face, and I cringed as Caden slid in next to me.

Caden scowled. "Shut the hell up, I will not listen to that crying the entire way. I refuse."

"I would have thought Darrton would have found a stronger mortal to court," Warren said from the driver's seat. "He seems as if he might be getting weak around the edges."

I bit my lip to stop crying and pressed my forehead to the cold window. I prayed to God that someone would come and save me. I couldn't be with them. I'd rather die of a plague than die with them. I wasn't sure when I fell asleep. I only knew that one minute it was all black. The cold of the window chilled my face and made it numb. I curled into a ball and closed my eyes. I had to get out of here. I had to get away from these monsters.

ꙅꙄꙅ

The car came to a stop and I was flung forward into the seat in front of me.

"Rise and shine, princess," Caden said from beside me. "It's time to meet the day."

The sun was shining down on us, and I knew it was before noon the next day. *How long have we been driving*? *Where the hell are we*?

Warren opened the door from my side and a cool breeze hit my skin. "Get out," he said.

Scurrying to my feet, I glanced around. There was a big body of water, an old warehouse, and a cliff. There was nothing else for miles on either side of us. I tried not to cry. Even if I did escape, I wouldn't make it far. I had nowhere to hide or nowhere to go. Caden kicked me in the back and I fell to my knees. "Get up and keep moving, princess."

The sharp rocks had broken through my pant legs and I felt the blood start to flow. Caden shoved me again. I began to walk toward the warehouse. Warren took the lead. All I could hear were the rocks crunching underneath our feet and the distant waves rolling on the shore below.

The rusted door squeaked as we opened it. Another problem. If I did escape, they could hear me. I tried to memorize any possible way of getting out. My dad, the overprotective father, not only made me carry pepper spray but take a defense class when I was younger. This included ways to escape, things to help you escape, how to always keep in shape to outrun anyone. Unfortunately, none of the things I had learned would help me. I didn't remember learning a way to outrun a fallen angel, Nephil, or a Horseman of The Apocalypse. I didn't recall learning how to kill any of those either. This only made me give into despair a little more.

The inside of the warehouse was bare. There was a room built against a wall off to the side, a couple of tables and a…cage. My body felt sick. I had always believed in God, but I'd never prayed or gone to church like I was supposed to. But in that moment I couldn't think of anyone but God. I prayed that he would get me out of this mess. He would send a meteor and destroy the warehouse. I didn't even care if I was in it.

Caden laughed beside me. "By the look on your face, I think she knows where she is going to be staying."

I gritted my teeth and wrapped my arms around my stomach. Warren grabbed my arm and led me to the cage. He pushed me in and the cold metal settled around me. It was big enough for me to stand up and lay down in, but it was so cold that I thought I might die if the temperature dropped during the night. My legs gave out and I fell to the cold hard cage floor. I shivered and sat down, backing up against the bars. Warren watched me with narrowed eyes, like he was analyzing the situation. He smiled and said, "Take her phone."

Damn! The only hope I had at attempting to stay alive. Not that I know where the hell we are, but maybe the police could trace the call. Maybe Mom and Dad would think to trace it. Maybe they could have located me, in wherever the hell we are. Don't cry in front of them, Lizzie. Don't.

I shook my head. "No."

Warren smiled. "I won't ask you again." He stepped forward and a sick feeling of fear crawled up my body. "Give your phone up."

I didn't move. Warren smiled again and walked toward the cage. He opened the door and ice seemed to crawl through my veins. He grabbed my shirt and pulled me to my feet. I tried to push against him but he reached into my pocket and pulled out my phone. I hit him in the chest but he barely budged. I sank to the ground as he walked out and watched as he slammed my phone onto the concrete and stepped on it.

Another part of me died. *No way of getting it now.* His red eyes seemed to be burning their way into me. It sent a chill through my spine. "Check her hair and pants for any kind of bobby pin, hair clip, pen, I don't care," Warren said, waving his hand and walking toward the room off to the side. I could hear his shoes scrape against the concrete floor. *Bastard.*

Caden flung the cage door open and curled his index finger toward him, wanting me to come. I stayed put. He rolled his eyes, walked in, and gripped my arm so tight I thought it would break. Caden pressed me up against the cage and breathed into my ear. "I have no problem frisking you, love."

I tried not to cry. He ran his hands down the sides of my body, through the length of my hair. I cringed as his fingers ran across my butt and he pressed himself hard up against me. My fingers clung to the bars. A tear escaped. Out of the corner of my eye, Scotty moved. He watched, while his face was hard and cold. I couldn't tell what he was thinking. He never said anything as Caden's hands roamed my body but there was something in his eyes, something almost…civil. I wanted him to speak up, to tell Caden to stop, but he just stood there, hands tucked in his jeans, and his blond hair falling from its upright position, watching his brother touch me.

Caden whispered into my ear, "She's clean." He let his lips roam my skin and I cringed. He turned me toward him. I had never been this close to him. The white in his eyes was one of the most frightening things I had ever seen. The rest of his face was rugged, not like Warren's. His was pretty as a girl. Caden's face was hard. He had a heavyset jawline, a wider nose, and deep -eyes. He had a smile that would make a teenage girl melt. I didn't. Only because I knew he was a monster. I knew what he was doing. His fingers danced along the stretch of my neck and up to cup my face. "It's been so long since I've had a woman."

Oh God.

I swallowed a groan and wrapped my hands behind my back along the bar. *Please put me back in the cage. I'd rather be in my grave.* The smell of his breath was like a mint, but it made my stomach sick. Pressing forward he let his lips rest upon mine. He moved his mouth so soft and then rough against my lips and laughed into my face. "It would be better if you kissed me back."

"Fuck you," I said. I hadn't meant for it to come out, it just did.

Caden laughed at first but then a dark ring flashed in his eyes. His fingers dug into my neck and I felt my legs lift from the ground. "I might take you up on that offer, princess."

With a power I couldn't image he flung me up against the wall.

The room door flew open and Warren stalked out. "Caden, I said search her, not kill her. If she is dead, we won't get Darrton back, damn it. Put her back in the cage and give her some water."

Trying to move, all I could see were red blurs in my vision. Caden cracked his neck and walked toward me. He didn't bother letting me walk. He just dragged me by my arm and flung me into the cage. Tears fell from my eyes. I tried to move my arm but I couldn't. I couldn't do anything but sit there, pathetic and useless, crying like a baby.

Warren went back into the room off to the side and Caden left, leaving me with Scotty.

"Why are you doing this to me?" I asked, barely above a whisper.

Scotty sighed and shrugged his shoulders. "It's all part of the plan."

I tried to keep myself from vomiting. I had believed everything Scotty had said. He had fooled all of us. I'd believed he was there to help me. I'd believed he wanted to help. I'd believed he was still good. I was so wrong. He never looked away from me, his dark emerald eyes watching every move I made.

Caden returned a few minutes later with a glass of water. In any other situation, I would have been happy to have something to drink. But when Caden was the one giving it to me, it only made me sick. Caden walked with the swagger of a millionaire on his yacht toward the cage. A smile evil enough for the Devil himself to wear spread across his face. "Is princess thirsty?"

I didn't answer.

He cocked an eyebrow. With his right hand he held the water above my head. He tilted it over and drenched me with it. He bent down and with his left hand, held my face up to catch the water. "Drink up, sweetness. We have to keep you alive." He stood up and spit in my direction. "Pathetic."

Pathetic. That word roamed around in my head. I was pathetic. I had no courage to stand up and do anything. I had so much fear, I was sure they could feel it radiating off my weak, broken body. I didn't even have the guts to act on being spit on. Without a word, I turned my back to him and brought my knees to my chest.

Caden chuckled and I heard him and Scotty walk out of the room. I was glad to be alone. I was in a cage, but I was sure as hell glad to be alone.

☙☙☙

I wasn't sure if I had fallen asleep or not. I couldn't tell my dreams from real life anymore. It was dark when I reopened my eyes but I could hear someone talking. I closed my eyes again. I didn't want to risk being seen. I didn't want to have to deal with them anymore.

"We have to get him within the next few days. They are getting impatient," Caden said.

Warren hushed him. "I know, Caden, but we can't get them until we have Darrton. He is the key. Everything will fall into place now that Elizabeth is here. Darrton will be here soon."

Scotty laughed. I knew it was him because it was so loud and rugged. "What if he doesn't come? You said it yourself. You aren't supposed to feel love anymore. It's not in your nature. Why is he any different? Why would he, of all of you, fall in love with a mortal?"

Warren sighed. "It's not in our nature. But Darrton was always different. Even after being chosen, for a while he couldn't get over Elizabeth. He was in love with her. He wanted no one but her. When he died and was given the title of Death, it crushed him. It killed Darrton that he couldn't be with Elizabeth anymore. He loved her so much. After some years, he became hostile and closed up. We thought he would never feel it again. We didn't, we don't, but we weren't taken from anyone either. We didn't experience it before to miss it. God knows who can handle what and who can't. He makes no mistakes."

I heard Scotty huff. "Well, where is he? Why is it taking him so long?"

Caden groaned. "He is with our idiotic father. No telling what kind of wild goose chase he has him on for some liquor. He could take a five mile walk and turn it into fifty. Your father is mental."

"He is mental, but he is still my father."

I could hear the sound of dragging metal or something hard on something else. Maybe something being dragged along something else. Then I heard, "He doesn't know, does he, Scotty?"

"I'm sure he does now that Darrton knows."

Warren laughed but it was hard, cold, and dry. "You won't be able to harm your father, will you? I'll have to do it."

There was a long silence. More silence.

"Will you two be able to kill Darrton? He is your brother?"

Caden laughed. "Yes, I will kill that fool. Then I'm going to take that thing over in the cage and have my way with her. Then I'll kill her. I'm sick of seeing her. I'm sick of the fact Darrton is like a lovesick puppy. I want him to get here so we can get rid of her and get this thing together. I'm growing impatient and so are they."

Who the hell are they?

There was a sound like something was pushed up against something hard. "Do not touch the child again until we have Darrton on our side," Warren snarled. "Do you understand that? I couldn't care less what happens to her afterwards. Kill her, I don't give a damn. But if Darrton thinks we will hurt her, he will not help, and then where will we be? Huh? Will we be stuck trying to get through this alone? Is that what you want? To do all the work alone, when it could be done so easily with all of us?"

I heard Caden huff. "No, that's not what I want. I want to hurry the hell up. I'm getting sick of this 'ring around the bush' shit. Now, can we please go? I'm starved and she is asleep."

I didn't hear anything else until the door shut. I opened my eyes and tried to adjust them. When they did, I noticed the bow and arrows that Caden had worn earlier lying on the table.

The bow was black and glistened in the moonlight from the window. There was a book next to it. I couldn't see what it was, but it kind of looked like a Bible.

It only made me cry. At first, I wasn't sure why I was crying, but then it seemed like everything hit me all at once. Samantha being dead, being locked in a cage, having a broken arm, Darrton hundreds of miles away—I thought—not being able to see my parents again, and the Horsemen keeping me hostage. My father had always told me to never feel sorry for myself, to fight back, but now was a time that I really thought I could feel sorry for myself.

Fighting back was always Sam's thing. She didn't have a filter and she didn't care. She was going to say it or bust. I needed her strength to get through this mess. But I convinced myself that I needed to let out all of my pain first. I felt like there was no way I could get out. There was only one hope left. I had to wait it out. The only person that could help me wasn't here at the moment. A team was only as strong as its weakest link. Their weakest link was Scotty. The look in his eyes while I was being taken away was a look of struggle. *He doesn't want to go along with them? Why? It's probably because of his brother.* Scotty would be the only one I could get to. He would be the only one who would be able to help me out.

CHAPTER 17

Darrton

Put the beer down, you foolish, alcoholic asshole," I gritted through my teeth. Ian was sitting on a park bench in Long Beach, California. His eyes were drooping and he was singing some stupid song. I'd heard it before, I was sure Sam, Elizabeth's sister, had been singing it.

"*Baby, baby, baby, oh,*" he sang louder, getting on top of the bench and waving his arms around. "There is no use, Darrton my friend. We've lost her. The demons have her!"

All the people passed us by, whispered, and looked away. My control was weakening by the second and I could see myself tearing Ian to shreds. "It's not too late. We have to go; I am tempted to leave you here."

Ian fell over the bench and bounced back up on his feet. "Might as well. Ferdia is dead, my son is 'gainst me, and I have no hope for the world."

I tried not to kill him, though there wa a red rage growing at the edge of my vision.

Focus. Focus. Control.

Ian stumbled toward the brick wall of the building behind us. "We do not know what's happening to the world. Only so much longer and it will end. Everyone will be in Hell."

I grabbed Ian's shoulders and shook him. "You have to get yourself together. We have to go. I'm going to leave whether you're coming or not."

There was a defeated look in his eyes. He smiled but it was because he was drunk and trying to cover the pain. His child had deceived him. Ferdia was dead. We had found him easily. He was at Ameil's house where we thought he might be. He was there, dead. War and Caden had found him and killed him. I know it was because Ferdia wanted to back out. Being damned to Earth by our Father hurt all of us, but Ferdia took it the hardest. His face, when Father was damning us, was the worst I'd seen. War and Caden knew that he would try to stop them, so they took him out. It made an anger rise in my chest that I couldn't control.

The spit spraying from Ian's signing brought me back. There was a mere inch of hope left in my heart and I pulled it all together. "Ian," I said, slamming him up against the wall. "Listen to me. At this rate I don't give a damn whether you make it or not. But I need your help. I need you to push past Scotty and your Gin and Tonic. I need you to help me. I need you to believe that we can make it. And put down that bloody drink," I screamed, flinging his flask down to the ground.

He frowned as the liquid leaked out of it. "Why, son, did you have to go and do that?"

I hit him. I knew it was wrong and I also knew I didn't give a damn. His jaw cracked and a low chuckle escaped his throat.

His eyes flashed black as a deep roar escaped his lips. He pushed me back. That was all I needed. He followed me toward the nearest vacant alley, and I watched as his black wings broke from his back. A smile crept over my face. This is what I needed. I jumped into the night sky and followed him.

ൈൈ

Lizzie

A steady drizzle of rain fell from the top of the cage onto my forehead and I couldn't care enough to move. It hit the center of my forehead in a steady rhythm. *Drop. Drop. Drop.*

It almost made me smile. It made me feel real. There was an image in my head, telling me I was stuck in a sick dream. I would never get out. The rain made me feel. It was the only feeling I had left. After hours of being stuck in the cage, I couldn't feel my body. There were only two places on my body I even remotely felt anymore. They were the center of my forehead and the soreness in my arm where I had been thrown.

I wasn't sure how many hours had gone by but I knew it had been several. Suddenly, there was a sliding of shoes across the concrete floor. Warren, Scotty, and Caden followed each other. Warren didn't acknowledge I was alive and I let out a sigh of relief. He walked past the table in the center and lifted something from a bag. A scale sat beside the black bow. Caden drew a sword from a holster on his side. It shimmered in the moonlight and I recoiled.

Caden smiled. "Nice to see you again, Elizabeth. Have you missed me?"

I didn't answer.

Warren grunted and disappeared behind the door. "Are you hungry, Elizabeth?"

I looked over and Caden was standing in the cage with me. I brought my knees up to my chest and shook my head. A pain ran through my arm. I closed my eyes and gritted my teeth, trying to ignore it.

"We have to eat, now don't we?" he asked, stepping closer. I closed my eyes and pretended he wasn't there. "What would you like, princess?" Caden bent down to face me. He took his fingers and slid them underneath my chin. His pale white eyes narrowed.

"Caden, we have things to do. Leave the child the hell alone."

Caden stood and gave me a smile. "Scotty, why don't you feed the princess over here? We want her alive."

Caden walked out of the cage and disappeared behind the door. I held back the tears that were trying so desperately to fall.

"Are you hungry?" Scotty asked from outside the cage bars.

I shook my head even though my entire body was shaking from hunger. My head was throbbing from not eating, and my mouth was dry with thirst.

He opened the cage door and leaned up against the frame, crossing his legs at the ankles. "You haven't eaten since yesterday. I know you're hungry."

Clearing my throat I said, "Why are you being nice to me?"

He cocked an eyebrow and shifted his feet, crossing his arms across his chest. "Why am I being nice to you? What do you mean?"

I laughed and sat up, hitting one of my fists against the metal floor. "You've taken me captive, Scotty, and now you're acting like nothing is going on? What the hell is up with you?

I'm so screwed up in the head right now. You're nice to me, then help kidnap me, and then nice to me when no one is around. What's your deal, asshole? Because you're starting to piss me off."

Scotty's face turned serious, his brow furrowed, and he sighed. "I have no choice anymore, Elizabeth. It's not up to me."

Shaking my head, I stood up. "So, let me understand this. You're saying that you had no choice but to help kidnap me and keep me here? What are they doing to you? Please just let me go. I swear I will not tell anyone ever."

He laughed but it was a lost and bitter sound. He turned and wrapped his fingers around the bars of the cage. The cage bars bent. When he turned back around, a deep fire burned in his eyes. "It's not that you would tell. It's that they need you to help keep Darrton in line. He won't help unless he thinks they will hurt you, Lizzie."

I gritted my teeth and ran my fingers through the tangle mess of my hair. "Just help me escape. We can flee and they would never know how I made it out."

His fist slammed on the bars, making the entire cage rattle. It gave me hope. He could break the cage so easily and get me out. "I've taken an oath, Elizabeth. I've made a blood bond. I can't help you. I can't do anything but what they tell me to."

"What kind of bond are you talking about, Scotty?"

His blond hair had stuck to his face from the rain outside and it covered his forehead in a tangled, wet mess. "I've promised myself to…" He trailed off.

"To who?"

"Satan."

A sting of pain shot through my chest and I backed up against the wall. "What do you mean…Satan? Why would you have to do that? Why in the Hell would you even think to do that?"

He opened his mouth to say something and then shut it. "Elizabeth, this is worse than you could ever imagine, I swear to you. There are things that are going to happen that I couldn't even explain if I wanted to. Things are going to cover this earth, to take over this world."

"Tell me, please, Scotty. I have to know."

Looking over his shoulder, he stared back at me. His emerald eyes darkened as he pulled up his shirt up and revealed a deep, dark, engraved sign on his lower side. It looked like it was carved with a knife. It had started to heal. It read: 666.

I let out a cry and closed my eyes tight. "Scotty, get away from me. Get away from me!" I screamed and pushed against him.

The door flung open and Warren walked out. His eyes were dark and his fist clenched. "I will not say it again. Leave the child alone. She needs to be safe. Give her something to eat and leave her the hell alone. If one finger is put on her again, I will kill each and every one of you myself. We can't get Darrton if the girl is dead. Do I make myself seamlessly clear?"

Scotty nodded but didn't look him in the eye.

Warren turned on his heel and strode back into the room off to the side.

Scotty walked over and pulled out a cheeseburger from a sack that they had brought in then set it inside the cage door. I eyed the cheeseburger as he went back toward the table. When he returned, he was holding a drink and pushing a straw into it. He placed it beside the burger. "Eat something, Lizzie. You will feel better. Don't worry. Just eat and get some sleep."

I mumbled a laugh. "Don't worry…"

Scotty walked toward the door that Caden and Warren had disappeared into and looked back at me. He attempted a smile but it was forced. "Elizabeth, I'm sorry I can't help. This is out of my hands."

✌✑✌✑

The burger sat there for hours. I was too scared to let my stomach process anything. The smell made me sick. Everything in the last twenty four hours was making me sick. The carving in his side roamed around in my head. He had the mark of the beast. That wasn't supposed to have happened yet. There was a screaming inside of my head, a heat burning into my heart. A dagger cutting into my flesh. Everything was wrong. Everything was happening that was never supposed to happen.

Scotty, Caden, or Warren never came back out of the room they had disappeared into. They stayed locked in that room, whatever it was. I wasn't sure if I even wanted to know what it was. *What could they be doing in there*? One thing was for sure, I knew it wasn't anything good.

I drifted in and out of consciousness. When I finally re-opened my eyes for good, I could see a faint light in the distance. I wasn't sure what had awakened me. It might have been the cold metal floor that had been my bed, or the fact that there were two of the three Horsemen left in the other room, plotting to kill the world. Although that didn't feel right, it was something different that woke me up. I narrowed my eyes and saw a weak light outside of the window in the far right corner of the warehouse. The window was at least twenty feet off the ground, so I didn't really know anyone that could have reached that. The light went off.

Someone was out there. I didn't know who could be worse than the three guys in the next room, but I prayed it was someone to help me. *Maybe it's Darrton or Ian.*

The window creaked. I stepped forward in the cage, looking as far up as I could through the bars Scotty had broken. All I could see were shadows in the darkness. I could see a dark shadow. It jumped from the window and landed gracefully on the floor. My heart skipped a few beats and I gripped the cage bars.

"Darrton?" I whispered into the dark.

"Shut up," someone said. It was a girl. *Who the hell is that?*

"Who are you?" I asked again, narrowing my eyes, trying to get an outline of the person walking toward me.

"I said shut the hell up." The voice was closer now. The girl stepped out of the shadow and I noticed the nice chocolate color of her skin and bright eyes. Ariel.

A hopeful scream was begging to get out of my throat. "Oh my God," I said.

She threaded her fingers through mine around the bars. "If you want out of here, shut up and do exactly what I say. Am I clear?"

I nodded.

She gave me a quick smile. "Now, don't say anything else."

My body began to shake as she gripped the bars and bent them backwards. She never once even glanced over her shoulder. But I sure as hell did. The door never opened, never budged. The bars bent back like Twizzlers in her firm grip.

"Would you like to stay in there?" she asked, hand on her hip.

I slipped through the bars and felt a weight lift off my shoulders. I knew she didn't like me, like at all, but I hugged her, anyway.

"Thank you so much," I said.

"Thank yous later, okay? We have to get out of here before the assholes realize you're out. Be quiet and don't say another word, damn it."

We tip-toed across the empty floor and made it to the door. It squeaked as we opened it, loudly. We both stopped. I'd forgotten about it. I was so excited about being set free that I forgot about the squeak. There was movement behind the door they had gone in. I clenched my fist, gritted my teeth, and pretended to be invisible. The door flung open. The silence weighed heavily in the air. Scotty.

Ariel took a deep breath as she saw him walk toward us, his blonde hair now washed and combed back. He looked like an angel. He furrowed his brow and set his jaw. "What are you doing, Ariel? You can't take her."

She was breathing heavily and her eyes were hard, and cold. "I can and I will. You've changed, Scotty. What the hell happened to you? You've sided with the enemy and after I thought you were someone else. Screw you and your kiss-ass attitude. You would have never done this before. What has gotten into you?"

He reached for my arm but she stood in front of me. She was about six inches shorter than Scotty but she looked like she could stand her ground in a fight. "I can't let you take her, Ariel. I've taken an oath."

She spat, "You've taken an oath and now you've lost your spine. Never thought that would ever have happened to you."

Scotty's eyes narrowed. He stepped forward. "Give her back and I won't say anything to them about you even being here. They will kill you and not think twice about it. This isn't play fighting with friends, Ariel, this is real shit. This is real. You don't understand. They will kill you, me, and then Lizzie. They have plans and they don't like people getting in the way of those plans."

She shook her head. "No you don't understand, Scotty. I would be just as much of a coward as you if I didn't stand up for Lizzie. She has done nothing to deserve any of this. I would hate myself forever if I let anything happen to her, even though I've cared about you for God knows how long. Just given the fact that you took the oath proves to me that you aren't who I thought you were. Just because Caden did something, doesn't mean that you had to. You've proved to everyone that you're too scared to do anything but what Caden tells you to do."

Scotty reached forward with a pleading look on his face and placed his hand on her forearm. Ariel pulled away. I could tell she liked him. I could tell she wanted him to hold her, but she pulled her arm away and pushed him. He flew back and stumbled to the ground.

"Bye, Scotty, hope you've found what you've always wanted, to be pushed around and used. Too bad I won't see you on the other side."

With that, she grabbed me around the waist and we ran. Well…more like she carried me and we ran. Her wings spread and ripped her shirt from her body. It was kind of weird being carried by such a small person, but her strength was very great for her size. She didn't speak to me, didn't look at me. She just flew. I had no earthly idea where we were going. I just hung onto her and let her do her thing. She probably still disliked me. It took a lot for her to swallow her pride and help me. But it was the right thing to do. She really was an angel. She did the right thing no matter that it broke her heart.

When we slowed down, I started to look around and see if it was any place familiar. We were in the middle of the woods. A big emerald cluster of trees surrounded us. It was definitely not located up town, but I didn't even know where the hell the warehouse was, anyway. The last place I had been, where I knew where I was, was in Vancouver. She landed and her wings disappeared back into her bare back.

She began to walk, leaving me behind.

"Are you going to talk to me?" I asked, running alongside of her just to keep up. For a small person she certainly took some massive steps.

She huffed. "What do you want me to say?"

I ran in front of her and stopped. Glancing around, I noticed we were in the shadowy part of a clearing in a forest. In the distance I could see a little white building. "I wanted to say, thank you. You will never know how much I appreciate you for this."

She wouldn't look me in the eye. "It was the right thing to do."

I nodded. "They will probably come after us, you know."

"Yeah, I know, and if you don't mind—" She gestured to her bare stomach. "I would like to go get some clothes."

I nodded and followed behind her. "I'm sorry for whatever I did to upset you when we first met. I never meant to make you mad."

She was shaking her head and mumbling underneath her breath for the longest time. "It's not your fault. I just…I don't like people being around Scotty."

I cocked an eyebrow as we made it to the old church. It was a Baptist church and it looked almost vacant. "You like him, huh?" Not that I didn't already know this, but it seemed kind of rude to admit I had assumed it after she just saved my life.

"I used to like him. I don't anymore. He isn't who I thought he was." She turned around and looked at me when we made it to the stairs of the old white wooden church. "Why am I telling you this? You're as bad as your sister."

Sister? I slowed to a stop. "You knew my sister, how?"

She turned toward me, her hazel eyes shimmering. "I know your sister, because I saved her."

A loud thumping was in my chest. "You mean when Caden threw her out the window?"

Twisting the door knob, she walked into the church. "Yeah, I was there. I had a bad feeling about leaving you two alone together. I knew Scotty. Anyway, I figured I would stick around and see if I was needed." She rolled her eyes. "And you can see that I was needed. When I saw him throw her, I caught her and brought her back here. I knew there was no way I could fight all of them to save you. So I followed their scent and waited until I thought it was safe." She shrugged and stopped on the left side of a pew. Pulling down the attic string, she moved back, so the ladder could come down, and motioned for me to go up.

I climbed up the ladder slowly, cautious as to what might be up there. It smelled like old boxes and old books. To my surprise it was really well lit up there. I could hear the faint sound of a TV and I knew it was Samantha.

"Samantha?" I yelled, reaching the top step.

She was sitting on a few boxes, her hand in a chip bag. I noticed she had brushed her hair since the last time I saw her. "Lizzie?" she asked, dropping the chips and running toward me.

Embracing her, I felt something for Sam that I had never felt before. Relief when I saw her. Normally I couldn't stand to be around her, but then her little arms wrapped around me, and her sobbing into my shirt was the best sound I had ever heard.

"I was so scared you didn't make it, Sam."

She laughed without humor. "I thought I was going to die." She sniffled, pulling back and wiping her snotty nose on her hand. "I'm so glad that you're okay, too. What is going on, Lizzie? That girl over there won't tell me anything," she complained.

Ariel was pulling a shirt over her head. "This girl's name is Ariel and I told you to ask your sister. I'm not your history teacher. Nor did I take you to take care of you." She turned to me. "I have no idea how you have lived with her this long."

I smiled. *Finally, someone feels my pain.*

Sam stuck her tongue out and went back over to her spot. "Lizzie, I want to know what's going on, now. You've got messed up in some whacked up shiznit, sister."

I nodded and walked toward her. "Samantha, do you know anything about what is going on?"

Her little fingers twirled around one another and she shrugged. "They have wings," she whispered.

I nodded. "Do you know why they have wings?"

Tears were welling up in her eyes. "I think they're bad angels. But that can't be it, can it?" Sam glanced up at me, a worry line on her forehead. "There aren't supposed to be bad angels, Lizzie. Angels are supposed to be good, aren't they?"

Ariel come over and sat down beside me, her hands intertwined between her knees. Her face was calm, elegant, and serene. She was beautiful when she wasn't sneering. "There is a lot that I think neither one of you knows. There is so much going on that it scares me. I can take care of myself, but I'm afraid I can't take care of you both."

Samantha wiped her face. "Why is this happening? Does this have to do with all those people killing each other?"

I nodded. "Samantha, do you remember when Trevor told you that we'd run into our cousin at The Picnic Basket?"

"Yeah, Mom says you're crazy. We don't have a cousin named Darrton."

Ariel snorted. "I see the lies haven't changed over the years. The lies never get old. Cousins? Really?" She laughed and I groaned.

Samantha waved her hand in front of my face. "Hello, sooo, this Darrton isn't really our cousin?"

Ariel sat back. "Well, I guess he could be. If you trace your ancestors back to the 1800s, you might be able to find out."

Samantha grimaced. "Ewe! He is like a thousand, gross, Lizzie!"

"Samantha, it isn't that easy. He doesn't look that old...he is like..."

She gasped. "A vampire?"

Shaking my head, I held it in my hands. "No, he is a Horseman, Samantha."

Her face went calm. There was no emotion.

Ariel nudged me and cocked an eyebrow. "Is she okay?"

I leaned forward and shook Samantha's knee. "Sam, are you okay? Did you hear me?"

Her eyes crinkled and she smiled. She began to giggle behind her hands. Ariel looked at me and shook her head, her eyes huge. Samantha began to laugh again, falling over herself.

Irritated, I stood up. "Samantha, this is serious. Darrton is *Death* of the Four Horsemen."

This only made her laugh harder. Grabbing her shoulders, I made her look at me. "Samantha, this is serious, this is not a game. They are going to kill the world!" I screamed.

She recoiled and looked up at me. Her eyes were wet and her face smooth. She didn't have any make-up on and she looked much younger than usual. "They plan on killing us, don't they?"

"I won't let them hurt us, Samantha. Darrton will come back and he will protect us."

"Wait! He isn't here right now?"

"No, he went to go find Ferdia, the third Horseman. Listen, Samantha, War and Conquest are the other two Horsemen. They are taking The Apocalypse into their own hands."

Ariel snorted.

Annoyed, I turned around to face her. "And what the hell is so funny?"

She got up, walked toward the window, and looked out. "Taking over the world would take more than just Caden and Warren. It will take more. They plan on having more. There is more to all of this than what even you can think to know, Lizzie."

I placed my hand over my chest. "Well, would you care to enlighten me? Because I would love to know what the hell is going on."

Ariel pressed her forehead against the cold window and blew a blanket of fog onto the cold glass. "They can't do this alone. They have to get Darrton in the circle before it can happen."

I nodded. "I know that much. So, why is Darrton so important?" I asked, sitting down beside Samantha. She had begun to shake. I tried to steady her with my hand but it only made her worse. Samantha was beginning to realize this was all real. I could feel her shivering. She knew.

"After Darrton, who is Death, Satan will follow, that is what they are missing. They need help from the underworld for it to happen. They need Darrton, to call on Him. If they have you, they think Darrton will do anything to keep you alive. They think that he will call upon Satan to keep you from dying."

Samantha shivered and let out a silent cry. "Why is this happening?" She stood up and kicked the boxes she had been sitting on. "I want to go home, and I want to go home, right freaking now."

Ariel rolled her eyes and ran her fingers through her short hair. "Listen, kid, sure I could take you home but your parents wouldn't be able to help you at all. They would die and so would you."

"Ariel, don't you have any compassion at all?"

She shrugged. "It's the truth. Sometimes it hurts."

Samantha turned her back and began sulking into her hands. "Sam, listen there isn't much time to be crying right now."

She jerked her head toward me and narrowed her eyes. "This is all your freaking fault, Lizzie. You're the one that started hanging around that crazy Derrick guy."

"It's Darrton."

"I don't care!" she screamed. "We are going to die, Lizzie. Have you not figured that out yet? I'm only twelve and I freaking see it!" Samantha stood up and crossed her arms. "I think I would like to go die in my room. If they come for me, I would like to be listening to Bieber in my bed and eating cookies and cream fudge from The Picnic Basket."

Ariel laughed and took off her shoes. "Well, I'm not going out there to take you, hon. You better get to walking."

I glared at Ariel. "Samantha isn't going anywhere. She is staying here with me."

"I don't want to freaking be here with Ms. Hateful Ass and Ms. I Make Friends With Monsters!"

"Do you think I want to be here, Sam? Don't you think I want to be home with Millie, going to school? I'd rather people throw popcorn at me at school. Throw me into the freaking trash! I don't give a damn. I would like to be anywhere else but here! I can't help it. Darrton fell into our yard and I can't help that I care about him!"

Ariel was shaking her head and continued to take off her socks.

"Is that funny to you, Ariel? Because I think it's funny that you love Scotty. After he has completely ignored you."

Ariel was in my face before I could regret what I had said. Her eyes boiled over and a growl escaped her throat. "I've loved Scotty for years. I wish he had given me any kind of attention, but at least I have to guts to walk away from him when I know he is bad. At least I didn't continue to love him after I knew he signed with the Devil."

"Whoa, hold up. First, I couldn't get away from Darrton. He threatened to kill me. Second, how do you know he signed? I thought he had to obey Warren and Caden."

She seemed to be mellowing out a little. "Yeah, they all signed with the Devil. That's the sign of the beast. I saw him show it to you. Warren and Caden are in charge so he has to do what they say. Caden and Warren get their orders from Satan. They have all taken an oath. There is no stopping it now. That is one tattoo that can't be taken off."

"I don't understand why he would do this," I said.

She nodded. "I'm not sure why he signed, if they threatened him or what, but something happened. He wasn't always like that."

"So what does that deal include? I mean, what is his part of the bargain?"

Shrugging, she stepped back from me. "It could be a bunch of things. But all the deals end with their souls being his."

"His as in the Satan's?"

"As in Satan's."

Bile began to come up my throat. "Darrton is stuck in his own personal Hell and he can't get out?"

"No. Would you try and break that deal?"

I shook my head. "Why haven't I seen the sign of the beast on Darrton then?"

She shrugged. "Have you looked?"

I shook my head. "No."

Sam hadn't said anything since we'd started talking about that. She stood by the window. Her long curled hair was lying almost flat and a tear trickled down her naturally blushed cheek.

"Everything will be okay, Samantha."

She didn't even look at me. "I sure as hell hope so." She walked past us and started down the steps. "Going to take a shower."

"There is a shower here?"

Samantha nodded. "Yes, it's open and in the pastor's study."

"Let me come with you!" I said, protectively.

"I can take my own freaking bath!" she yelled down the hall.

Ariel sighed. "They can't get in here, Lizzie."

"Why not?"

"It's holy ground. They can't."

Relief flooded me. "But wait, how are you in here?"

"Nephil, remember?"

"Yes, I remember." Taking a seat I tried to clear my mind, but all I could see were their faces, so close to mine, so menacingly beautiful. There was something happening soon. I could feel it in my bones. Darrton had to be here. He had to come.

Ariel stood up. "Heads up." She threw something my way. I barely caught it. A long silver sword was held in my good hand. "What is this?"

"A sword."

I rolled my eyes. "I know that. But why did you give this to me?"

"In case we have to fight." She cocked an eyebrow. "Unless you would like me to give that to Samantha?"

I shook my head. "I didn't even know they could be killed."

Ariel nodded slowly, running her finger along the sharp edge of her own sword. "You can't just stab them. That won't do."

"Then how?" I put the sword down. It felt heavy and unfamiliar in my hands.

"You have to cut off their wings."

I sucked in a deep breath of chilled air. "Wings?"

She nodded. "It's pretty simple, the things growing out of our backs."

"Are you ever nice?"

"Rarely."

"Is it easy? Darrton wouldn't let me touch his. I tried once but he stopped me."

She smiled. "Our wings are sensitive. It's the one place that you can feel how we feel. It's the one place where we keep our secrets. It's where we can face Death."

That sent shivers down my spine. "So I could kill an angel or horsemen? All I have to do is cut their wings off? That's it?"

She nodded. "The wings are easy to cut through. You could pull the wings out, too, but I doubt you would want to do that. That is the cruelest way to kill them. It is also harder to keep the angel still to pull the wings out. Either way, it's going to work. Either way, it's going to kill them. But it's just cruel to do it that way." Ariel threw the sword up and caught it. "That is how they were killed when damned to Hell at the beginning. Lucifer would pull their wings out, nice and slow, letting the other angels that wanted to go back to Heaven, feel every single inch of the pain. That's why we normally don't do it that way. We normally just cut them off. I've never killed an angel, but we all know how angels are killed. We all have to know."

My body felt frozen in place. "Pulled their wings off?" I whispered. "Like a butterfly?"

Ariel glanced down at the necklace that I was gripping. "Just like a butterfly. That's how he would do it, but maybe you should practice." She snapped her fingers. "Today. Come on, put your sword up."

I dug the toe of my Converse into the wooden attic floor. "I'd rather not. I took marital art protection classes when I was younger, but they don't seem to be coming in handy here."

Ariel placed her hand on her hip and rolled her eyes. "Well, I'm sure your instructor didn't think you would be battling fallen angels either, now did he?"

"Probably not."

"Okay, then. You're getting a lesson in killing angels from me." She pointed toward herself as if she were the greatest gift on Earth. "Okay, put up your sword. For me, the easiest way to hold it is on my shoulder. You might have to use both arms to give it a good swing. Don't miss."

I placed the blade an inch from my shoulder.

"Good. Now you want to get on the side of the angel, okay? When you swing it, you want it to go a straight line, parallel to the middle of the back. It needs to hit right where the wing connects to the shoulder."

Bracing myself, I took a practice swing. Ariel shook her head. "That was horrible. Give me a grunt with it."

"I'm not grunting."

"Come on, grunt."

Shaking my head, I said, "No, not going to do it."

"Here watch me." She swung the blade and grunted as she did it.

I laughed and dropped the tip of my sword to the floor. "I'm glad you enjoyed that, but I'm not doing it."

"Okay, well at least give me a semi-good swing. Your swings are girly."

"I am a girl."

"But you don't want to swing like one, especially when our lives are at stake."

Sighing, I brought the blade back up to my shoulder. I swung with everything I had, trying to make a straight line. "Is that better?"

Ariel shrugged. "I guess that will have to do. Maybe when your adrenaline kicks in you'll do better."

"You just said it was better?"

"Better, but not as good as it needs to be."

Ariel took my sword and placed it to the side with hers.

"Ariel, do you think that we could walk out of this fight alive? I mean, what are our chances?"

"Slim."

"You're not scared of slim being our chance at winning?"

"I've been around a long time. I'm not scared of dying, especially since it's the right thing to do."

"Ariel."

"Hmm."

"Thank you for saving me and my sister. I will never be able to repay you for this."

"You don't have to. Just kill a fallen angel for me. That will make us even."

I nodded. "I'll give it the best I got."

Ariel smiled and looked down at the swords in the corner. "I'm scared that our best might not be good enough."

☾☽☾☽

Dawn broke and I was up to watch it. I couldn't sleep, thinking about what was going on not too far from us. Just thinking about Darrton and realizing he had no choice but to call Satan. Or Scotty, giving his soul up when I knew he still had good in him. Mom and Dad wouldn't get to tell us goodbye. The reality was, Samantha and I probably wouldn't make it out of this alive.

It's only a matter of time.

Warren, Caden, and Scotty will find us eventually.

The sun made its appearance over the trees in the distance. It would have been a pretty sight any other day, but not today. I had a gut-wrenching feeling that this would be our last day to see the sun.

CHAPTER 18

Darrton

Ian's house was empty. There were chairs knocked over, sheets torn, and no one in sight.

Ian had been more serious in the last hour than I had seen him in the entire time I'd known him. He shook his head and stroked his chin as he walked through the messy, cluttered house. "Well, at least we know it was them."

My patience was running thin. I kicked the staircase and noticed a cell phone laying on the bottom step. I picked it up. It was pink and had some sort of jewels glued on it.

"Whose phone is that?" Ian asked from behind me.

"Shit."

Ian cocked an eyebrow. "Well."

"It's Samantha's, Elizabeth's little sister. They have her with them."

Ian spat. "Bastards. I wish I could stick my boot up their asses. What do we do now? We don't know where to go?"

Following the trash and broken furniture up the stairs, I stopped at an extra bedroom. This must be where they had kept her. I closed my eyes and I could watch as Warren grabbed

Elizabeth's honey-colored hair. It made my stomach heave. In the middle of the bed, surrounded by ripped bed sheets and mess was, a single piece of paper. *They'll never be safe, Brother. Meet us at the warehouse. You'll be able to find us.*

The paper dissolved as I crumbled it up in my hand. "We have to go. They have her by the lake. I swear if she is hurt—"

Ian stopped me with his hand on my arm. "They haven't hurt her, Darrton. They won't. They will keep her alive until you make the oath and then they will kill her. We have to get to her without them knowing."

Nodding I sighed into my hands. "I know. I just pray they haven't hurt Sam. I pray that we can get to her before they kill her. After I do the deed, she may as well be dead anyway. Everyone will die then. They will kill everyone, take on the Earth."

"For someone so strong, you are awfully whiney sometimes."

"Whiney?" I said through my teeth. "The only girl I have loved in years is about to die, you ass. It has been ages since I've felt anything for anyone. All my emotions have been hidden for decades and now they are here. I can't let them leave me again."

Ian rolled his eyes. "Drama queen. We will get to her in time, Darrton. Quit complaining. Spread your wings and fly, brother."

We had barely made it out of the door before my wings burst from my back. There was no time to waste. We had to go save Elizabeth. Without her I would be nothing.

$$\mathcal{C}\mathcal{S}\mathcal{C}\mathcal{S}$$

"There it is," Ian said, pointing nonchalantly and taking another drag off of his cigarette. "That's the only warehouse within twenty miles from here. It has to be it."

I sniffed the air and could smell the raw earthy scent. "Yeah, they're here, all right."

"Well?" Ian gestured for us to go. "Shall we?"

Grunting, I turned to him. "You still think that it's a good idea just to walk up to them and say release her?"

Ian shrugged, dropped his cigarette into the fresh dirt, and stepped on it. "Do you have a better idea, partner?"

"Well, I think it's a hell of a lot better than yours."

Ian laughed, throwing his head back in his overly dramatic way. "Well, let's have it, Wilson. Give me the plan and I am your solider."

"It's not really a plan—"

"Ah! As I thought."

"Shut the hell up and follow me," I mumbled, starting toward the warehouse. *They have to be inside.* Ian had said this was the only warehouse close by the water. It was eerily silent but I could feel in my bones that someone was here. Ian stepped toward the door and I pulled him back.

"Dag gum, partner. Don't give your only solider a heart attack before the battle."

"We need to look inside first."

Letting my wings break free, I coasted up to look in the window. It was almost bare, except for a table, a door, and a...cage. Rage engulfed me. I knew she had to...*she isn't here?*

The door burst open. Warren pushed Scotty out, with Caden following behind "You've let her escape, you son of a bitch! You were supposed to watch her!"

Scotty staggered up. "Why is it my fault? I have no idea what happened to her?"

He laughed. "I can't go away for two fucking minutes without you two messing everything up!"

"I wasn't in charge of her, he was," Caden sneered, pointing toward Scotty.

"Don't play it like you weren't as enthralled as Scotty was," Warren yelled. "You were the one with your hands all over her, you horny bastard!"

Red hot rage flooded me and I reached for the window. Ian flung me to the ground and held me there. "Don't get your panties in a wad, Darrton. We have to listen to what they are 'bout to do. Stay here. I'll go see." Ian glided up and floated there for what seemed like forever.

He was touching her? A sick twisted rage bubbled in my stomach. *I can't believe I've been so imprudent.* A Horsemen...*Death of the Horsemen.* How stupid I was to involve a human girl. Such a fragile being. I let my head fall back against the hard brick of the building and waited for Ian.

So stupid. So freaking stu—Something tickled me. Opening my eyes, I saw a butterfly resting on my nose. I pulled it off. It fluttered in my hand, it's wing spreading out then back in. *Elizabeth.*

"Aw, a butterfly."

I gritted my teeth and rolled my eyes. The butterfly flew away. "So, what's going on?" I asked, standing up and preparing myself.

"They are going to a church."

"But they can't get in. Why would they do such a stupid thing?"

Ian smiled. "They think that is where whoever is hiding Lizzie put her, because that is where they can't go."

"Hiding Lizzie? Where is she? Who could have her?"

Ian shrugged. "Now that, my friend, is the mystery of the hour. They think you were the one to kidnap her and are hiding her in a church nearby."

Who could have her? It's not Scotty, or her parents. Trevor isn't smart enough to try and Millie would probably be too heartbroken to move.

Ian placed his hand on my shoulder. "Well, my friend, I think we need to duck and cover so we can follow them. Don't you think?"

Pulling myself back to earth, I nodded. "The roof," I said, pointing.

We jumped, lifted ourselves up, and rested on the roof. There was movement inside. They were rummaging around. "I wonder what they have in that room," Ian said.

"Probably the things for the ceremony."

"Ceremony…as in the calling?"

I nodded. "As in the calling."

"They need you for that, don't they, son?"

"They won't get me for it. I've changed my plans and my ways. I won't do it. I won't call Satan."

"You will if Lizzie's life depends on it, will you not?"

I didn't answer. I couldn't. I knew deep down if she were about to be killed, I would put my own soul down for the entire Earth. But calling, now seemed utterly wrong. I couldn't dream of calling the things to Earth that I would tremble to encounter myself. *I can't hurt those innocent people like this. Not yet. Lizzie was right. It's not time.*

"You don't have to do it. Let's just pray it won't come down to that," Ian said.

I laughed. "You know, this is the first time I've seen you as you, not fallen over drunk."

Ian's smile crept up his face. "Hey now, would you like me to take out my flask? It's in my pocket."

"I never thought it would be anywhere else." Sitting down, I tried to position myself where I could keep an eye on the ground by the door. "Ian, speaking of doing things we don't want to, do you think that you could hurt Scotty? He is your flesh and blood."

Ian seemed not to move for a long moment. "I don't see myself doing it, because I try not to think about it. But I feel if it comes down to it and the circumstances are bad enough, I would have to. He has given himself up. He doesn't seem like my son anymore."

"He is your son. He has just taken an oath he will never be able to break. He is bound to someone else for eternity. It's a terrible thing, and I wish it had never happened, but it did and I'm sorry."

"It's not your fault, Darrton. Yes, you made a bargain with your brothers to do what you were born to do. You've signed with the devil. It was wrong at the time, but you were born to do it. But you've changed. They haven't. You've changed your life and ways but they won't. They will never change their ways and we both know it. We both also know that they will not hesitate to kill us. I know they will. We have to guard each other's back when the time comes. We have to make sure we both stay alive, because without the other, there will be three against one."

I placed my hand on his shoulder. "I know. I have your back, Brother."

Ian smiled and shook his head. "I have yours."

Thirty minutes passed before the floor squeaked below us and the door flew open. "Come the hell on, Scotty. We don't have all day."

Caden laughed. "Well, we actually have eternity, Warren. We don't have to do it today."

Warren snarled. "You two don't understand the consequences of this mission do you? We have taken an oath. We have to do this, you fools! There is no turning back even if we wanted. We have to carry out the duties we were given."

There was silence for a moment before Caden sighed. "We understand, Warren."

"Good, now let's go. We have a Ms. Elizabeth to find. Darrton has to have her and we have to be careful. Let me do the talking and no one moves until you are commanded to. Scotty, can you handle this?" Warren asked in a slick voice.

"Of course," Scotty said.

"So, if you need to kill your father, will you do it?" Caden asked.

I could just see a grin on his face and his cocked eyebrow.

Warren snarled, "Stop instigating, Caden. Do you think you can kill Darrton?"

"What a dumb question. Of course, I can. I've always liked him the least."

I snorted. *Likewise.*

Gravel shuffled below their feet. Warren's whispers were in a sinister voice. "Scotty, do you think that you can kill Ian if needed?"

Silence.

Ian didn't move beside me. He only stood still, as if hearing the answer would release him from his trance.

"Yes."

Ian stiffened even more.

"Well then, let's go, Brothers."

They were off in a lightning-fast move.

"Are you okay?" I asked Ian.

He nodded. "He isn't my boy anymore. He really has given his soul up. He can't get out of it."

I nodded. "He is your boy. He just got into something he can't get out of. I'm sorry. I'm sorry this is all happening."

Ian stood, dusted off his pants, and smiled. It was forced but it was an attempt. "Well then, I think we have a lady to save, Darrton. After you…"

It sickened me to see Ian and Scotty this way. It sickened me to see my brothers and me the same way. But this couldn't happen. *I can't let them hurt her.*

I nodded. "Let's follow them."

We flew for what seemed like an hour. We tried to stay far enough behind them, so that they would never suspect any followers.

When we stopped it was midafternoon and the sun was shining brightly down on us.

We stopped at the edge of the woods. From there, we watched them as they dropped down into the clearing ahead of us. There was a little white church sitting calmly in the center. The outside was wooden and it seemed like it had been built years before.

"You think they are here?" Caden asked.

Scotty nodded. "Yes, this is the closest one from the warehouse."

"Well, why don't you go look?" Warren asked.

Scotty glanced at Warren and then Caden. I wondered if he knew they were throwing him underneath the bus. By the way he set jaw I would say that he probably did know. *He is their only way in. He needs to be taken out.* I took a sideways glance at Ian. He crouched beside me, eyes focused on Scotty. *I can't kill Scotty. I would never forgive myself.*

I watched Scotty walked up the stairs and opened the door. Scotty could go in because he was Nephilim. God banned the Horsemen from being allowed in churches when they were damned.

He went inside slowly and we all waited hesitantly for him to come back out. Five minutes later he returned. "No one is in here. Maybe they aren't at a church or this church at least."

Warren clenched his fist. "Where the hell would they be then? They've left no clues at all!"

My body automatically relaxed. *She isn't here.*

Ian laughed lightly beside me. "She isn't here, Darrton. That's a freakin' relief."

I nodded. I took another look at the church and my body froze. In the window of the attic I saw her. She saw me. Her face was so smooth and calm, glancing down at me. Her hair was combed to the side and her hand was on the window. Her eyes burned at me. She smiled and my stomach felt sick. I motioned for her to get down but it was too late. Warren saw her.

Then I heard Warren laugh. "I see we have missed the attic, Scotty." Warren pointed up to the window. "They're in there. Upstairs."

Caden laughed. "Go get her, Scotty. I can't stand to be away from her much longer." He was smiling a conniving smile. "I know she misses me."

Warren snorted and barred his teeth at Scotty. "Go get the girl, Scotty.

Scotty disappeared into the darkness of the church.

CHAPTER 19

Lizzie

"D arrton?" I whispered, not sure if I even said it. His eyes were focused on mine. The pale blue forced an energy through me that ran down to the tips of my toes. He motioned for me to get down, hide, and that's when I noticed the others. Scotty was walking toward the church. Warren and Caden stood back, waiting for Scotty to do their bidding.

I gasped, taking in a large chilled breath, and turned around. "They're here, Ariel, what do we do?" I screeched.

Her face remained calm. Her smooth milk chocolate skin looked more radiant than I remembered. She picked up the sword from the edge of the room and tossed it to me. "This is where we defend ourselves. Remember what I told you?"

The sword seemed to be weighing me down. Its sharp edges were like spikes from Hell. "Go for the wings, the part where they connect to the back," I said. My mouth was dry and a pain started to throb deep down in my chest. "I'm not sure if I can do this."

Ariel cocked an eyebrow and placed the sword in a scabbard at her side. "Too late, kid. We have no choice. Get your ass up and be serious. Our lives are at stake here. It's two against three, and you're just human."

"Darrton is here and Ian," I said, gripping the sword and wondering how close Scotty was to opening the stairs to the attic.

"What! Where? You should have told me already."

"They just got here. They are hiding in the woods," I said, watching Samantha who was uncharacteristically quiet. I began to click my tongue automatically and realized I was doing it. But I was too afraid to stop.

Ariel nodded. "That's promising, hiding in the woods when we need help," she grumbled.

There was a creak from downstairs. "AH! God, he's close," I said, holding my sword in front of me.

Ariel gripped my shoulders and hit her flat palm to my forehead. "Calm down! Listen, this is what we are going to do. When Scotty opens the attic door, I'm going to jump down, okay?" She waited until I nodded before she continued. "I'm going to need you to take care of Samantha. You two will need to jump down, fly down, crawl down, I don't give a damn how, but get the hell out of this attic. Being trapped will only make it easier to be caught. Then get to Darrton and Ian, somehow. Sneak past those bastards outside. Just get to them. Do you understand?"

I swallowed the lump forming in my throat. The noise from below us meant we only had a few seconds. "Yes, I understand."

"Okay." She let go of my shoulder. "Get your asses over there behind the wall. We are going to do this. Lizzie, be careful, okay?"

Tears were forming in my eyes. I wasn't sure if it was because I knew I could die in two minutes, that Samantha could die, that Ariel was risking her life for my sister and me, or because Darrton was just right there and I couldn't get to him. "Ariel," I choked out, "Thank you for this."

She pulled her sword out as the door in the bottom of the floor fell open. "Thank me after you're safe, okay?"

I cringed. The top of Scotty's head appeared up the steps. Ariel gave me one last look. It seemed like she was hurt. She had to try and kill Scotty. The pain showed in her eyes, but she knew *what* was right. She knew they needed to be killed. She launched from her spot and screamed as she went.

There was a lot of bumping and hysterical noises coming from them as they tumbled down the attic steps.

Squeezing Sam's hand, I pulled her along. She hadn't said a word, but by the grip of her fingers, I knew she was scared. How could she not be? We hurried down the stairs and saw a few overturned pews, church hymns, and bibles strewn all over the place. I didn't want to know where they had gone but by the mess and the noise coming from the front, it sounded like they were in the lobby. *It sounds like thunder.*

I tugged Samantha along toward the back. I couldn't let Scotty get her and bring her to them. I had no idea where I was going. It was my first time in the little church. Most of the doors led to small Sunday school rooms or bathrooms.

"I'm scared," Samantha whispered. "Please, get us out of here."

"I'm trying, Sam, give me a minute." I opened another door and it creaked. It led outside. I stopped. "Okay, Samantha, this is what we are going to do. I'm going to go find Darrton. I want you to run into the woods and hide. We will come find you when everything is over."

"No!" she screamed, hanging onto me. "You can't leave me; I don't want to go out by myself, please!"

I tore her from my clothes. "Samantha, this isn't a game. I need you to understand that. This is do or die. Please." I hugged her tight. "Go Samantha."

She wiped her small hands over her reddened cheeks, wiping away the tears that were streaming down. "Promise you will come get me?"

I smiled. "I wouldn't leave you out there. Now go before they bring their fight back here."

She nodded. Taking one baby step at a time, she walked out of the door down the steps, and then broke into a run toward the woods. She disappeared into the emerald shadows and didn't look back.

The weight of the world lifted off my shoulder. *As long as she is okay.* Then a heavy pressure slammed down on my chest. "I have to find Darrton," I whispered to myself. The air was calm and it set off an eerie wave of emotion. There wasn't anything that seemed out of the ordinary except the erratic sound of Scotty and Ariel fighting in the church. *I hope she is okay.*

Creeping along the outside of the church, I held my breath. I peered around the corner and no one was there. *Where are they?*

Rounding the corner, I made it to the front of the church where they had been standing. Darrton wasn't where he had been ten minutes before. There was banging from the inside of the church and I wondered what shape they were in. I jerked around when I heard crunching in the leaves behind me. My breath caught in my throat.

"Darrton." I was shaking as I watched him walk toward me.

He put a finger to his lips and shook his head. I knew in my heart it was the wrong moment to be turned on but I couldn't help it. His shirt was off. Sweat poured off of his chest. He looked as if he had just run a marathon. The V he had was poking out of the top of the jeans that sat low on his slender hips. His dark hair was tied at the nape of his neck and his jaw was set. The black edges of his wings were glowing in the sunlight. He was only a few yards away from me. My foot took a step without me even thinking about it. He shook his head again. His eyes were everywhere, looking for them.

When he stopped, he sighed. He motioned with his index finger for me to come toward him. A blaze set off inside me. I ran to him, reaching up to wrap my arms around him, when something gripped my hair tight pulling me back.

"Well, sorry to break up the reunion but I'd much rather you'd be with me," Caden whispered. His chest was against my back, his lips touching my ear. I tried to scream but it caught in my throat. A sick feeling snaked its way through me. My sword dropped to the ground. I closed my eyes at the pain in my arm.

Darrton stopped in his tracks. His pale blue eyes caught fire. "Caden, nice to see you again, Brother."

"Yes, very nice," he said, gripping my ass in his hand.

I tried to push him away but he only drew me closer.

"Damn it, Caden, stop teasing Darrton," Warren said, rounding the corner, dusting off his hands. He smiled, his red eyes glaring at me. The slender point of his nose gave him a feminine look. When he smiled, it made him look devious. "Well, nice to see you again, Elizabeth. I see you got away from us here recently."

I didn't answer. I couldn't. I was too afraid to move, too afraid to even think. I just wanted Darrton to come and rescue me. I wanted this to all be a dream.

Warren looked at Darrton and smiled. "Nice to see you, Brother. I hope you're ready to perform the ritual. I'm growing tired and so is He."

He as in Satan? I shivered.

Darrton laughed but it was without humor. He ran his fingers down the length of his face. "Warren, I'm not going to perform the ritual. I've told you both that I have changed my plans," he said, glancing at me.

Warren rubbed his hands together. "As I've told you, Darrton, you've made a deal and you can't go back. I am going to forgive you for not killing Elizabeth when we told you to. Now look what you have done. Involved her sister, too."

Bile tried to come up my throat. "Where is she?" I whispered.

Caden rubbed his hand across my stomach. "Some place safe, sweetheart. She is doing just fine."

Darrton clenched his fist and stepped toward me again.

"Don't take another step toward her, Darrton. It is nothing for us to snap her neck. We don't want that now, do we?"

He didn't answer. He kept his eyes on me, his face hopeless.

"Now, if you come with us over toward the clearing, we will start this process. I'm getting antsy," Warren said.

"I told you I'm not doing it," Darrton replied.

Warren jerked his head back. I could see the anger building in his face. "Okay, then. If that's what you want." He motioned to Caden.

Caden grabbed my arm, the one that was already hurt and pulled it behind my back, it felt like it might pull from the socket. I screamed and my legs gave out from underneath me.

"Stop," Darrton said. "Okay, I'll do it."

"No! Darrton, don't. Just let them kill me. Please think about what you're doing. This will destroy our world," I said through the pain working overtime in my arm.

"Shut up, princess. He might be able to spare your life."

"I have no other choice, Elizabeth. I can't let them kill you. I would never forgive myself."

Warren smiled and began walking toward the back of the church. Caden tried to make me walk but I couldn't move. My arm was throbbing. Caden picked me up and tossed me over his shoulder. His blond hair was pushed upright and I tried to fight the urge to pull it.

"Darrton! Help me! Please, stop. Let me go, Caden. Put me down! Please!"

"Be calm, Elizabeth. I won't let them hurt you," I heard Darrton say.

I bit my tongue to keep from screaming. I wanted to punch Caden in the back. I wanted him not to touch me at all. I wanted to jump down and run to Darrton.

Darrton was behind us. I wanted to lift my head and look at him but my arm was hurting too much to put anymore strain on it. I wondered if Ariel was all right. She and Scotty had left a long time ago. *And where is Ian?*

I closed my eyes and stopped listening to anything around me. I just let Caden carry me wincing from his big footsteps. When we stopped, I lifted my head and noticed we were in a clearing. There was a circle of rocks and in the center were the things I had seen at the warehouse.

Caden dropped me and sat me down. He pressed his face close to mine and inhaled. "Hmm, you smell pretty, baby girl."

I looked the other way but he grabbed my chin and forced my face to his. His lips were chapped and rough against my lips. "Caden, damn it. Leave the girl alone!" Warren shouted.

Tears filled my eyes when I noticed Darrton standing next to Warren. His face was a mixture of emotion. I wiped my lips and curled up into a ball. "Go get them, Caden," Warren said.

Caden left. Warren placed the Bible in the middle, a scale, sword, and lastly Caden's bow around the Bible. Darrton never looked at any of it. He stared at me, his blue eyes sliding over me. "I'm sorry," he said to me.

"Ah! Brother, don't be sorry for her. You're sparing her life."

"For what? For her to die afterward by the plagues, by the demons you're letting out."

This sent a shiver down to the tips of my toes. They are letting out demons. *This can't happen. This will kill everyone. The entire world will die.*

"Correction, we're letting out," Warren said.

Caden returned a moment later. Scotty was behind him, blood gushing from his face. There was a cut oozing blood down the length of his jaw. When he looked at me, I saw Scotty, the one I knew when I first met him. There was anger and fright in his eyes and then disappointment. He knew he had no choice anymore. Behind was Samantha. I stood up, holding my arm. Caden shook his head. "Sit down, princess. I'll bring the little bitch to you."

I opened my mouth to say something. Darrton shook his head no. Caden pushed Samantha into me and she fell at my side. "I'm sorry, I tried to run but he caught me, Lizzie. He caught me."

I watched Caden walk away from us and disappear behind a tree.

I grabbed her and rocked her slowly in my arms. "It's okay, it's fine. None of this is your fault. It's mine."

When I looked back, I noticed Caden coming from behind a large tree with something in his hands...or someone...Ariel.

"No," I whispered, shaking my head and holding Samantha tighter.

Scotty wouldn't look at Ariel. He kept his eyes glued to the ground.

Warren clapped his hands. "Well, we have a sacrifice. That is great. We don't have to kill one of the girls."

That was his plan all along?

"Hold her while I get in position," Caden said to Scotty. Scotty didn't move. He sat there, ignoring Caden as if he hadn't said anything. "Hold her!" he screamed this time, making the hair on the back of my neck stand up.

He shoved her into Scotty's hands. Her body was limp, bruised, and cut. A tear fell down my face. *She died trying to save us.* The thought of them giving an angel's dead body to Satan, repulsed me. I figured they would resurrect her and use her powers for evil. She would have never been involved, if not for me. She would have lived without even knowing what had happened. *This is all my fault.*

"Places," Warren said, as he pulled out a short blade and cut his wrist. "Now it's time to give up blood for our master."

"Close your eyes," I whispered to Samantha. "Don't look unless I say it's okay." Sam hid her head against my shoulder and began to shake.

I watched as they each cut a slit in their wrists and let one drop of blood drop on the Bible in the middle. *This is happening.*

"Now, Scotty, place the sacrifice on the ground. We are giving her soul to him." Warren's red eyes were glazed over.

Scotty slowly bent down. And from beside me, out of the bushes, I saw something fly. It was silver and small. It hit Scotty in the head with such force he collapsed.

"Who is that?" Warren screamed.

Scotty was lying on top of Ariel and on the ground beside him was a flask. Scotty didn't move. *Maybe he is just knocked out*? I turned my attention back to the flask. *A flask*? *Ian.* I almost smiled at the fact that he would waste a good flask, hitting someone. I was utterly surprised. But I couldn't stop looking over at Scotty. Ian had killed his son? I bit back a cry. *Scotty was being forced.* He was good.

"Well hello, my darlin's. It's nice to see ya 'gain, Caden. Son, I seen you've taken the wrong route. 'Two roads diverged in a yellow wood.' I always liked that Frost guy. Do you wish you'd taken a different route, partner?"

Caden snarled and I quit smiling. It was menacing.

"Oh, hello, Lizzie?" Ian said and waved nonchalantly.

"Hey," I whispered.

Warren laughed but it was harsh and evil. "So, you think you can come over here and stop us, right? Do you really think that I won't kill you?"

Ian cocked an eyebrow. "Well, I believe if you would kill your own brother, you would certainly kill me. But I've killed Scotty, my own flesh and blood. Who seems worse to you, scout?" he said, smiling and slicking his hair back out of his face.

"I killed my brother because he was foolish, just like this one." He pointed toward Darrton. "Both of you falling in love with mortals! Idiots. We can rule everything. Start a race, have the world to ourselves, the list is endless, and you both decide to fall in love with mortals."

Darrton stepped back from Warren and looked at both of them.

"You're not backing out of this, Darrton, or the girl gets it," Warren said. "I swear I'll kill her in front of both of you."

Darrton shook his head. "You've got it wrong, Warren. I am backing out on this and you won't even try to take her." Darrton's movement was so quick that I thought I was dreaming it at first.

He picked up the sword lying a few feet away from the circle and swung it. He missed by a mere inch. Warren slammed Darrton up against the tree and grabbed his throat.

"You might want to run now, Lizzie. We will find you," Ian said from beside me. He dusted off his hands and balled up his fist. Caden walked toward him. Ian cocked an eyebrow and stepped toward Caden. Ian had already killed one of his sons. I hated that he would have to kill another.

I grabbed Samantha and began to run. We ran toward the tree line and stopped behind a great oak. Warren was on his back with Darrton's blade at his throat. But right when the blade would get close, Warren would kick Darrton off.

"They're going to kill each other!" Samantha screamed.

"Shhh, let's hope only two end up dead today," I mumbled. The ground shook when Caden picked up Ian and slammed him down on his back. His dark wings fluttered as Caden grabbed them. *Oh no. Cut off the wings and you can kill them.*

Without thinking about it, I ran toward them. My hair was blowing back in the cool breeze and my eyes were on Ian's sword, laying off to the side. I had no idea what I was doing, but the adrenaline was rushing through my veins too fast for me to care. Ian's sword was heavy in my hand, and it took every ounce of my power to swing it. I lifted it over my head and swept it down through the place where Caden's wings met his back. He stopped. Blood poured down his body.

When he raised his head, the white in his eyes had turned green. *What*? His body shrank and his wings disappeared. It took me a second before I realized I was seeing a glimpse of what he'd looked like before he was a Horseman. A human. He let out a scream and fell to his knees. His hands hit the ground and he began to fade before my eyes.

Then he was gone.

Darrton and Warren had stopped what they were doing and froze. There wasn't a trace of Caden left. I imagined how stupid I must have looked—a sword in my hand that I could hardly hold, and tears in my eyes. Ian couldn't move. He was unconscious.

Warren let out a scream, ripped his sword back, and swung it at Darrton. It hit his wing. Darrton fell to the ground and hunched over on his knees. "Stay back, Lizzie, I'm fine," he mumbled through intakes of breath.

My lips began to tremble. I was trying hard to make sense of everything roaming around in my head.

Warren looked over at me. "I see you have ruined everything, you little bitch. Do you understand that we can't do this without at least two horsemen and two creatures from Heaven or Hell?"

I didn't answer. I was too shocked to say anything. Blood was dripping from Darrton's wing. I wanted to run and help him. Warren laughed and was on the verge of being hysterical. "I have an offer for you, Elizabeth. I'll make you a deal."

"No!" Darrton screamed. "Don't do it, Lizzie. Don't listen to a thing he says."

Warren kicked Darrton in his side. "Silence. This is your fault. If you would have just done as I said, she wouldn't be in danger right now."

Darrton spit out blood. "No, she would have been dead."

"I'll give you a choice, Elizabeth. You make a deal with me now. Your two choices are, you let Darrton die here, or you make a blood oath to me and Darrton lives."

"No, please, Lizzie," Darrton whispered. "Don't do it."

Warren smiled. Taking his blade, he stuck it at the edge of Darrton's wings. Darrton screamed and clawed at the earth below him. "Don't, Elizabeth! He'll own you! Please, do not do this." He struggled to get up, but Warren pressed the blade harder into Darrton's wing.

A lump was forming in my throat, and I couldn't feel my entire body. It took every ounce of my strength to keep my feet underneath me. *I have to do this.* Through my watering eyes I glanced at Darrton. "I'm sorry."

Darrton shook his head and slammed his fist into the ground, while Warren pressed the blade harder into him.

"Okay," I whispered.

"No, no, no, no, Elizabeth," Darrton whispered into the dirt. "Don't do this to her. Warren, don't." He tried to push up off of the ground but Warren pressed the blade into his wings harder, making Darrton scream. Warren kicked him again, harder. Darrton tried to move but fell back to the ground.

Warren smiled and walked toward me. I watched in pure fear as he lifted the blade and slit his other wrist. "Hold out your hand, Elizabeth."

I dropped my sword and stepped closer. I put my hand out and it began to shake.

"Bend you elbow," he ordered. He bent his own elbow and slid the blade across my wrist. It stung and I let out a moan.

Warren intertwined our fingers together as the blood dripped down my wrist to the crease of my bent elbow. "Repeat after me," he said. "I, Elizabeth Lawrence."

I opened my dry mouth and forced the words out. "I Elizabeth Lawrence."

"Do solemnly swear, to do Warren Barnes's bidding for the rest of my natural life," he said with a nasty smile.

"Due solemnly swear, to do Warren Barnes's bidding for the rest of my natural life," I repeated.

Warren smiled and released my hand. Knowing that his blood was mixed with mine, made my skin crawl. "Now, Elizabeth. This isn't the end of anything for us. It's the beginning." He smiled and wiped off his bloody wrist.

Ian grunted as he rose from the ground and shook his head, as if trying to clear his vision. When his eyes saw my bleeding wrist and Warren's, he closed his eyes and shook his head. "I think it's time for you to go now, Warren. I see you have fucked up everythin'."

"Nothing but the best for my master," Warren said. "This isn't over, princess. Darrton will end up calling on him. When we're ready again, I'll be back." He turned to leave and Ian grabbed me. "Oh and, Elizabeth, I will be calling. You'll know when, and you will come. Because you have to."

Warren disappeared into the forest but I knew he would be back soon. And when he did return, I would have to do whatever he said. There was nothing left for him to do until he found some others to help. Then it would be my turn to do what he said forever.

Ian tried to comfort me but I shoved him away and ran toward Darrton. He pushed himself up to his knees, and I fell down to the ground with him. He stroked my chin, my face, my neck. He was touching me so tenderly.

"Iofiel, I can't believe you just agreed to that," he said, pressing our foreheads together.

"I had to. I couldn't let him kill you. I would never have forgiven myself for it," I mumbled through my sobs.

Darrton pressed his lips to mine, and I felt myself automatically relax. His hands were so rough on my back, I thought he was trying to make us one. He ruffled his fingers through my hair and pressed his tongue into my mouth. "I can't be away from you again, Elizabeth. We have to stay together. I won't let them hurt you ever again. Is your arm okay?"

I was still light headed and was trying to wipe the smile off of my face. At any other moment, I could afford to smile but not then. "I thought it was broken at first but it's okay, just hurts."

"We'll get it looked at," he said, glancing back over my shoulder.

"I feel like I should cover Samantha's eyes over here." Ian pointed toward my little sister who was standing there wide eyed. "Well, hell I might need to cover my own."

I blushed. I stood, helping Darrton up. He had a limp and a bad cut but other than that, everything was fine. "Samantha." I cleared my throat. "This is Darrton."

She opened her mouth in awe. "Our cousin?"

Ian snorted. "It could happen, I mean back down the line he could have been—"

"No, I'm not your cousin. I'm in love with your sister."

My heart stopped beating for a clear two seconds. *Did he say love?* My cheeks were heating up and his hand on my lower back wasn't helping the blushing situation.

Samantha rolled her eyes. "Well, the Darrton that loves my sister, could you please take me home?"

Wow, two seconds after the drama and she is already being a diva again.

Ian laughed. "That is a lovely idea. I would love to go home. Even though my home is trashed."

Darrton smiled and kissed my forehead. "I think it's a great idea, too. We need to get you both home before your parents have any more time to freak out." He glanced back over his shoulder at the bodies. "We'll come back and lay both of them to rest."

"What will we tell them?" I asked, clicking my tongue but stopping when Darrton's lips pulled up into a smile.

"That you don't remember anything," Darrton said. "You either, Samantha."

She nodded. "I don't care what we say, but I just want to go the hell home." She sighed and ran her fingers through her now nappy hair. "Eww! I need to take another bath. Let's go."

"Yes, let's go home," I said.

Ian smiled. "Hop on, sister friend," Ian said holding his arms out to Samantha.

She snarled. "Not this again. Please hold me tighter than Ariel did. She almost dropped me. I'm grateful she caught me but that flight to the church was rough."

Ian smiled and tipped an imaginary hat. "You have my word, dear lady."

She looked back over her shoulder and gave me one last look. She held on to Ian as he lifted off the ground and headed toward our house.

"Um, Darrton," I said before he lifted us up.

"Yes, Elizabeth."

"Back there when you said you...you said that you..."

"Loved you?" he asked, his lips parting and making my body melt on the inside.

I nodded. "Ummhmm. Were you serious?"

He smiled and kissed my lips. "I am always serious, Iofiel."

"I love you, too, Darrton."

His mouth pulled up at the corner and my heart fluttered. His fingers traced my jawline and he kissed my forehead. "That's great to hear you say. Now, let's go home, Iofiel."

CHAPTER 20

Lizzie

Darrton and Ian dropped us off at the curb. Samantha wasted no time running toward our house.

Ian smiled and nodded. "I'll see you soon, Lizzie."

I watched as he ran down the road and disappeared.

"Everything will be okay, Elizabeth."

I nodded. "Where are you going? You're not leaving, are you?"

"I'll be back when everyone goes to sleep. Now go, before your parents come looking for you." Darrton kissed my forehead and disappeared down the road.

Samantha was knocking on our door when I rounded the corner. "Mom! Dad! Please! Open the door!"

The door opened. Mom flung herself out and onto Samantha. She looked up and began to cry when she saw me walking toward her. She ran to me, without any hesitation, and grabbed me. "Oh. My. God. I thought you two were never coming home!" she cried into my hair.

Dad was hugging Samantha by the door and I watched as his eyes studied me closely. He didn't smile. A look of confusion crossed his face. He was starting to get a little stubble on his chin and his eyes were tired.

"Come inside. We have to call the police. We have to tell them what happened."

"I don't' know what happened," I stated. We had made it to the front steps. Samantha looked up at me. Her face was serious.

"Me, either," she said. "We just woke up down the road in the ditch." She lied so perfectly.

I nodded and felt a tear slide down my face.

My dad coughed and asked, "You two don't remember anything that happened? Nothing?"

I watched Dad's gaze travel down our bodies, examining our cuts and bruises. His eyes met mine. He didn't believe us.

"Tommy, leave them alone, they just got home. I'm going to go cook you guys something, and, Tommy, you call the cops and tell them they are okay. Tell them we will have the interviews tomorrow after they've rested."

Mom led us into the house but Dad stayed back, eyeing me closely. *What did he know?*

Surprisingly, Mom cooked us pizzas. This was normally not on her menu, ever. Samantha ate six slices of pizza by herself. After dinner, I told them I wanted to shower and get cleaned up. I was tired and I wanted to go to bed. They didn't argue. I think they were scared, too. They just wanted us to be okay. Mom kissed my forehead and Dad watched me closely, only saying goodnight before I disappeared up the stairs.

After scrubbing the blood, dirt, and grime off of my bruised body, I walked back into my room. Since my other PJs were trashed and bloody, I put on a pair of blue ones. When I opened the door Dad was sitting on my bed. His hands rested between his knees and his brow was furrowed.

"Oh! Hey, Dad, is everything all right?"

He smiled. "I should be asking you the same thing, Lizzie. You were the one who was kidnapped."

"Um, I think everything is fine. I mean I told you we didn't remember anything. So, I really don't know if I'm fine. I'm not hurt. My arm is a little sore, that's all."

Dad shook his head and stood up. He pulled a huge black feather from his jacket pocket. I stood up straighter. A warm rush of nerves covered my body. "What's that?" I asked.

He shrugged and placed it on the bed then dug his fingers into his pockets. "I don't know. You tell me. It's rather big for a bird, isn't it?"

I pulled at my long-sleeved shirt sleeve. "Uh, yeah, it's really big and weird. Where did you get it?"

"Your tree house. I found it when we were looking for you two."

"Hmm. Never saw it before. Maybe you should take it to the lab and see if you can figure something out," I said, walking past him and sliding under my covers.

He nodded his head and rocked back and forth on his heels. "Maybe I will. I guess I'm going to go to sleep. Get some rest, hon." He started to walk out and stopped. "If you think of anything or know something, you will tell me, right?"

I nodded and pulled the covers up. "Yes, I promise to tell you, Dad."

He gave me a look of disappointment and nodded. "Okay, then. Goodnight, Elizabeth."

After he left, I felt frozen in my bed. It should have felt warm and inviting but it wasn't. It seemed cold, frigid, and like a…lie. *He knows something is up. Why would a feather, even a really weird feather, make him think that?*

I never fell asleep. I was too anxious for Darrton to sneak in. When I heard him tap on the window, I tiptoed over and unlocked the latch. He wasn't in the tree. He had floated up. As soon as his feet hit the floor, he grabbed me up. His lips found mine and he pressed us together. "God. There for a little while I thought that I might not get to do this again," he whispered against my lips.

I giggled and he laid me down on the bed. He pulled us together, spooning underneath the covers. "Elizabeth, I'm so sorry all of this has happened."

"What will happen next?"

He didn't answer for a while. "Warren will lay low. He can't risk us finding him and destroying him."

"After that?" I asked, turning to face him.

His face was calm and beautiful. "He will try and find other fallen angels or demons to help complete the ritual with him."

"Then?"

"He will do it again and he will try and get me to call Satan to finish the procedure and then they will take over the world."

I nodded. "What will he do with me?" I asked, almost shaking with fear.

He grabbed the sides of my face and kissed my forehead. "I won't let him hurt you, your family, or anyone. I swear. Ian is going to move down here and we are going to stay close together to deal with any bad situations that may occur."

I nodded. "But what will he make me do?"

"Anything he wants, Elizabeth. Anything he needs done, you will have to do it. You are bound to him."

I felt sick. *But if it means Darrton is alive, then it's worth it.* "How am I bound to him? In what kind of way?"

His fingers trailed down my side and back to cup my butt. "Not in this kind of way," he whispered into my ear, letting his lips barely graze my lobe. "It's a different kind of way. A business way. You do what he says and he leaves us alone, basically."

I tried not to cry but the tears fell anyway.

"Shhh, don't cry, Elizabeth. We will make sure everyone is safe."

"It's not just that. My dad knows."

"Knows what?"

"He brought your feather in, said he found it in our tree house, and asked if I had ever seen it before. He is acting suspicious." I pulled the feather out from underneath my pillow and showed it to him.

He froze. "You have to keep playing dumb, Elizabeth."

"I know, but I don't want to get him involved. I want him safe."

Darrton pulled me closer to him. "I swear to you, I will keep all of us safe. No one else is getting hurt. Now, go to sleep. You need rest, Iofiel."

I nodded and cuddled up against his strong chest. While he breathed soft and pure at a steady rate, I smiled. I knew everything could get bad again soon, but life was so right just then. I prayed Darrton could keep us all safe and Warren wouldn't want anything for a really long time.

About the Author

From a small town in Arkansas, Brittany Booker always wanted to do bigger things with her life. A senior at the University of Arkansas at Monticello, she graduates in May of 2013 with a major in English and a minor in journalism. She plans to go back and get her MA after getting on her feet with her book and literary career. She is the co-founder and literary agent at The Booker Albert Literary Agency, where she represents a few amazing authors.

When she isn't reading manuscripts, writing YA or reading queries, she likes to spend time with her family, her boyfriend, and her Chihuahua, Zeus.